IT WAS PAST MIDNIGHT.

THE PARKING LOT WAS EMPTY.

EXCEPT FOR CANDY...AND THE HOOD.

Candy jerked her head around and peered out the back window of the car. At first she couldn't make out who it was. Then she caught the silhouette of a hood.

Candy went rigid. The man quickly stalked toward her door. A thundering jolt of panic shot through her. He grabbed the outside door handle, but it would not move. He pulled and tugged at the door, but it held. The car began to rock from side to side.

He lowered his face and let the hood come within inches of the window. Candy could see two glazed, violent eyes piercing at her. Her hand moved to the ignition. "Please start," she sobbed, pumping the throttle, "oh God, please start!"

AVON
PUBLISHERS OF BARD, CAMELOT, DISCUS AND FLARE BOOKS

THE HOOD is an original publication of Avon Books. This work has never before appeared in book form.

AVON BOOKS
A division of
The Hearst Corporation
1790 Broadway
New York, New York 10019

Published by arrangement with the author
Library of Congress Catalog Card Number: 83-91195
ISBN: 0-380-86009-0

First Avon Printing, January, 1984

AVON TRADEMARK REG. U. S. PAT. OFF. AND IN OTHER COUNTRIES, MARCA REGISTRADA, HECHO EN U. S. A.

Printed in the U. S. A.

WFH 10 9 8 7 6 5 4 3 2 1

This novel is dedicated to
The Cherokee Trail Experience

For their patience and encouragement

Joan
Janet
Dan

Part One

Chapter One

Evelyn Maruchi walked briskly into the employees' lounge to pick up her lightweight windbreaker. She was short like her mother and possessed a wide, beaming smile, which showed off her year-old braces. Being a salesclerk was a new experience for her, but after two weeks of training she was beginning to feel more relaxed behind the cash register and dealing with the public. She worked with people who liked her and trusted her judgment, and that helped her self-confidence, so important to a sixteen-year-old. She strode out of the lounge toward the group standing near the door.

Carol, her supervisor, waited until all the women had arrived. "Okay"—she waved her arms and snapped her fingers to quiet the chatting voices—"it's been a long night for all of us, but before you go, I want to thank all of you for helping out with the extra work. You make my job a lot easier and I appreciate that."

She put her hands on her hips and stood straight. A tired smile came to her lips, but there was still a sparkle in her eyes. Tilting her head, she moved her gaze around the gathering. "Now, are we missing anybody? Supposed to be eight of us." With her eyes moving to each person, she counted out seven, plus herself. "Now, does everybody have a ride home?" Like a teacher before dismissing the class, she once again passed her attention over the group, then unlocked the glass door and gave it a shove. The women strode out into the wide shoppers' walkway, talking lightly as they passed a bookstore, and ambled into the dimly lit north side parking lot.

No one noticed the silver sedan roll to a stop at the edge of the lot fifty yards away. Its headlights were out, its engine clicked off.

"Now, Evelyn, all you have to do is say the word and I'll give you a ride. It was my fault that we had to stay late." Carol wrapped her arm around Evelyn's shoulder and gave her a serious look.

"No, honest, Carol. Thanks, but my boyfriend George said he'd pick me up. He'll be here in a minute. Go on. I'll be all right. Don't worry about me. I'll be just fine."

Carol's expression changed to a motherly smile. "I know you will. It's just... well... I don't want anything to happen, and... I'll stay if you like. We can sit in my car."

"Listen, Carol. I'm a big girl now. You don't have to wait. Go on. I'll be fine, honest. Go ahead."

"Well... if you're sure." Carol slipped behind the wheel and started the engine. "I'll see you tomorrow then. We start at two, remember." Her smile widened, and she gave a cheery wave as she drove away.

Evelyn stood by herself for a minute and watched the taillights of Carol's car disappear. She carried her windbreaker loosely crumpled up in her hand as she walked under an overhanging light, then into the darkness toward a bus stop. A warm summer breeze swept across the parking lot.

The engine of the sedan came alive, and the car began to roll slowly across the deserted lot.

I wish George would hurry up, Evelyn thought. He'd have to change his habits and be more prompt in the future. When she got to the bench, she peered up and down the dark, lonely street for the third time. Still there was nothing. In hopeful anxiety she sat on the wooden bench to wait. *It sure gets dark out here,* she thought. *The city ought to fix the streetlight. Where is George?*

The silver car drifted slowly and silently across the parking lot.

Evelyn glanced down at her watch but couldn't see the dial. She couldn't keep her mind off the darkness. How isolated she felt. How vulnerable. She tried to force the upsetting thoughts away. She remembered the surprise birthday party for her father two weeks ago. The good time—lights and laughter.

The sedan idled closer, then abruptly came to a stop a hundred feet directly behind the bus stop. When its lights snapped on, the beam shot straight across the asphalt and flashed onto the back of the wooden bench.

Evelyn jerked her head around toward the lights. Who was it? George? No, he wouldn't come from that direction. Her body stiffened and she felt cold.

The car moved again. This time it rolled straight toward the bus stop before stopping twenty feet behind Evelyn. Its lights were flicked to high beam.

"What's going on?" Evelyn said, shading her eyes. "George . . . ? That you . . . ?"

Several seconds went by before the car moved again. When it did, it swung left and eased away, its engine making a soft muffled sound.

Evelyn sat rigid in the darkness, letting only her head move as she watched intently while the car crept across the parking lot and out a nearby driveway. Its front end veered right, and again the headlights glared at her. Its engine grew loud as the car rolled up to the curb and stopped in front of the bus stop. Then the engine clicked off and an ominous silence settled around Evelyn's frightened body. She froze to the bench. Her eyes were transfixed in a searching stare at the car's window. Who was it? What did he want?

Suddenly the passenger-side window cracked open and slowly began to roll down. It was too dark to see the driver.

"Need a ride?"

It was a man's voice. He seemed friendly but... She sat braced, her hands gripped tightly around the wooden board running underneath her legs. *Calm down,* she told herself. "No, thank you." Her mouth was dry, her voice strained. She cleared her throat with an anxious cough. "My boyfriend will be along in a minute."

The engine gave off a low humming sound as it started again. Evelyn could smell the faint hint of exhaust fumes as the man put the car in gear.

"I hope he gets here soon. It could be dangerous for a good-looking cunt like you to be out on a lonely street like this." The window rolled up and the car drove away.

Evelyn felt her heart pounding wildly. Chills raced over her body. She tried to follow the car with her eyes, but her head would not move. *Calm down,* she thought to herself. *He's gone now. George will be here in a minute.*

A car turned onto the street from the other direction. With considerable effort Evelyn released her grip from the bench and managed to stand. She prayed it was George. She stared hopefully at the lights as they approached. *Oh, God, please make it him.* She leaned out over the curb and peered intently toward the car, trying to see what kind it was as it came close, then drove by. The car was an older-model station wagon. It continued to the next intersection and turned left.

Her fears immediately returned. She looked both ways along the street, but it was empty. Clasping her hands together nervously, she sighed heavily and returned to the bench.

Suddenly she felt a hard tap on her shoulder. She jumped and twisted around. Through the darkness she could see the white outline of what appeared to be a hood. Three black holes penetrated its white surface.

Panic, fear, helplessness struck her all at once. She froze.

"I told you it was dangerous for a good-looking cunt like you to be out in the dark by yourself."

Evelyn desperately tried to open her mouth to scream, but her jaw would not budge.

The hooded man moved rapidly. He stepped to the front of the bench, grabbed Evelyn by the head, and pulled her face to the zipper of his pants.

"This is for you, cunt."

Evelyn felt her nose smash against the cold hardness. Her fright bore down on her with such intensity that her mind was blown into a state of unreality. A nightmare. *Mommy will come soon. Daddy will smile and keep me warm. Someone will help me wake up.*

Evelyn's mind whipped back to reality. She didn't hear the words, but she caught the man's demanding tone.

His grip was tight, his fingers clamping against the back of her head. Suddenly, his hands let go of her head and he grabbed her around the shoulders. Evelyn was yanked from the bench and held helplessly off the ground. Her eyes bulged wide in terror as she stared at the two round eye slits.

The man's large eyes glistened back at her. They were strong, violent eyes. "You want to kiss me, cunt? Is that what you want?"

Evelyn could only stare into the dark holes cut in the white hood. Suddenly, the man cocked his head and moved toward her lips as if he were going to kiss her. She came to her senses, jerked back, and twisted.

"That wasn't nice, cunt." The man threw her to the bench, her body landing hard against the wood. "That wasn't nice at all."

Quickly he slid his arms under her and hoisted her up. He carried her across the lonely street to an area hidden behind a small commercial building and surrounded by shrubs.

Evelyn began to realize what was happening. Not knowing what she was saying, she started to plead with the hooded stranger. "Oh, God! Please. Please don't. Please! I won't tell anyone. Please don't hurt me."

The man stopped for a second at the edge of the shrubbery. He didn't say anything and appeared to hesitate.

Maybe he's not such a bad guy after all. Maybe it's a dream. He'll let me go now. Everything will be all right.

Without a word, the hooded man flung her into the bushes. Evelyn landed on her back. She could feel her elbow crack a twig and crash into the soft dirt. *Oh, no, not me, this couldn't be happening to me,* she kept thinking.

The man took a quick step toward her. His right hand lurched out and grabbed her face. "If I hear another word, cunt, I'll break your jaw."

"I won't say a word. I promise. Don't hurt me, please. I won't scream," Evelyn sobbed.

The man attacked her in swift, unrelenting movements. He tore at her clothes. She tried to hang on to them, but she was completely overpowered. Buttons, zipper, elastic ripped quickly, leaving red marks on her skin.

Her mind reeled in frenzy: *This can't happen to me. It's not supposed to . . . Daddy!*

The man's leathery hands moved over her body, exploring her breasts, then his fingers jabbed at her pubic hair. "There's a good cunt. Stripped and ready for a man's cock."

The hooded man plunged into her.

Evelyn felt a sharp pain, then the trickle of blood as her chastity was crushed within her.

"That's a good cunt. Right where you belong. Lying in the dirt getting your pussy fucked."

The actual rape lasted only a moment. To Evelyn, it seemed like a lifetime. When it was over, the man stood up and moved with deliberate speed. "Tell your boyfriend you've been fucked by the mightiest. And the first time, too. You won't forget this time. Ever." He nudged her leg with the point of his boot. "Now you're a slut!"

Evelyn lay motionless and numb. The words pounded into her head and she couldn't block them out. Tears quickly formed in the corners of her eyes.

The dark holes of the hood stared down at her for a long while. Then suddenly the man whipped his head around as if he had seen something across the street in the parking lot. Without another word he was gone.

Evelyn could hear the thumping of his heels as they struck the pavement on the street, then the parking lot. His car door opened and closed with sharp cracks. The car started and she could hear it pull out of the parking lot.

Chapter Two

Molosky swung the police cruiser into the east side parking lot. He let the engine idle as it carried him over the white-striped asphalt. It had been a busy night for the department. The calls for service had come in batches. Nothing of major consequence, but a lot of minor disturbances and even more traffic accidents. *Everything seems to happen at once,* he thought, and guided the blue and white cruiser around the shopping mall onto the back parking lot on the north side. Easing to a stop near a bookstore at the end of a row of small retail stores, Molosky turned his radio up and stepped from the car, leaving the door open. In the distance, he casually observed the lights of a car come on as it eased out of the lot toward Forest Avenue. Probably a pair of lovers, he thought.

As was his custom, he began to stretch. First a couple of toe touches, then one or two knee bends, then a short walk and some window shopping. It only took five minutes, at the most ten, but Molosky needed to get out of his police car and be alone.

He approached the bookstore and as he stood in front

of the window eyeing the colorfully displayed books, he caught a reflection of himself in the glass. He had put on just five pounds since the day he got out of boot camp weighing one hundred eighty-five. In his police combat boots he was just short of six foot three. His body was narrow but showed well-developed contours of limber muscle around his shoulders and upper arms and especially in his legs. His neck was long and sturdy, his face angular with clean firm lines. His hair was medium length, jet black, parted neatly on the left side. He had a large masculine nose and a rather solemn looking brow. His eyes were a clear, handsome brown, large, deep-set, and very expressive.

"Sixty-one fifty-one," the Channel Two operator called.

Molosky strolled past the bookstore window, ears alert to the radio call. He could hear Bert Yarnell answer.

"Sixty-one fifty-one," the operator said in a monotone drawl. "Four-fifteen, disturbance at First and San Salvador. Reporting party inside a bar, stated a man and a woman were yelling at each other on the sidewalk. Crowd starting to gather. Be advised you're the only one in service."

Yarnell acknowledged the call. Sergeant Molosky walked back to his car and slid in behind the wheel. "Control Two, Sixty-five hundred, I'll respond on that call with Fifty-one." He swung out of the parking lot on the Forest Avenue side and turned east.

By the time Molosky arrived at the scene, he could see that Bert Yarnell was getting the situation under control. His giant arms were directing unneeded people away from the area. The small crowd reluctantly moved back. Molosky stepped from his car and approached. "What's going on, Bert?" he asked.

"I'm not quite sure, Ray." Yarnell spoke in deep, resonating tones. "As far as I can tell, the older man over there was apparently out for his late evening walk and got stopped and hassled by Candy. She's in the bookstore huffin' and puffin'. She'll come out roaring in a sec."

Molosky eyed the old man standing near the curb. It

was Marvin Ashwood, the educated hobo. Ashwood had been wandering the streets of District Five for as long as Molosky could remember. Sometimes he would disappear for weeks or even months at a time, then like a missing thread from society's fabric he would appear to be interwoven into the texture. Molosky would spot him trooping down the sidewalk in the middle of a rainstorm or sitting on a park bench chatting in the afternoon sun.

Molosky had heard occasional rumors that at the downtown Rescue Mission Ashwood was one of the most respected men. No one seemed to know much about his background, only that he enjoyed helping out with whatever needed doing. It was said that he counseled the men and held group therapy sessions with them occasionally. For some reason the old man did not take to policemen; maybe he had a reputation to protect.

Ashwood stood with a stoop, hands in his pockets. When his eyes focused on Molosky, they were the sad eyes of a man who had just lost a chance to make a friend. "Sergeant, I've seen you around before, haven't I?

"Yes, for many years we've been pounding these streets," he continued in a tired voice. "I don't know what went wrong tonight. I was just out for a walk, heading for my other hangout over near the college; serve good coffee there. Most times I don't make comments to the street girls. Usually just say a silent prayer for them. I feel for them, feel sorry; they're so lost, all of them. I've never really been able to reach them." He slid his hand out of his pocket, drew it to the back of his neck, and scratched enthusiastically. "Can't say that I've given it my best effort, but...I'm not the Almighty; have to leave some of the work for other people. Money and the greed for it have taken over them. In a lot of ways economics and man's spirituality are wedded together." His glance left Molosky and followed a path to the front of the bookstore. "This one I called a slave, and I shouldn't have said that. It wasn't called for. When I tried to apologize, things just got worse."

Candy stood leaning against the doorframe of the well-lit bookstore. Her eyes shot toward Molosky, then shifted abruptly to Ashwood. Molosky gave a sidelong glance to Yarnell, then turned his attention to the prostitute. Suddenly, she stalked away, pretending not to see him. She moved with animal grace straight for the old man. "It's my body and I'll use it anyway I want to," she yelled.

Molosky stepped forward and blocked her path. She tried to step around him, but he took hold of her arm with a firm grip. She tensed and tried to pull away, but the grip held. She looked up at him with disgust.

"Hey, Molosky, why don't you tell that old bastard over there that that's what I do for a living?" Her eyes were busy, accusing. They darted to the bigger policeman standing to the side, then fiercely came back to the old man. "That's right, I fuck for a living. And if you want a piece, it's gonna cost you. Slave, ha! Men are the fucking slaves."

Molosky struggled to guide the prostitute to the passenger's side of his patrol car. "You have two choices, Candy." He spoke in a firm whisper, putting his face close to hers. "One is to calm down and you can ride with me in the front seat. Or you can keep up the jabber and I'll put you in the back cage."

"Big fuckin' choice," she muttered. "And take your hands off the merchandise." Molosky released his hold and the prostitute opened the front door and slid inside.

Molosky quickly moved to the driver's side. Yarnell had moved closer to the old man. "Bert, the old man really doesn't have a case to press. If you can handle things here, I'll take the girl over to the donut shop on Santa Clara and drop her off. Meet you in a couple behind the bank on Market."

"Okay, Ray, see you there," Yarnell said.

Molosky paused before getting into the car. "I'll see you around, old timer."

"I'll be here," came the reply.

Molosky slid in behind the wheel and accelerated toward Santa Clara Street. Candy looked straight ahead, stewing. He knew better than to begin a friendly conversation.

He turned onto Santa Clara Street, pulled to the curb in front of the donut shop, reached across, and opened the door.

Candy stepped out without hesitating. "Thanks a lot for the ride, Molosky. Just keep that old asshole out of my way." She slammed the door.

Molosky swung around the block and within minutes was in the bank parking lot talking with Bert Yarnell.

Chapter Three

Molosky was awakened early the next afternoon by his cat, Noah. The cat always sneaked into his room soon after the radio alarm clicked on to KCBS, the twenty-four-hour news station out of San Fransisco. After entering the room, Noah flirted around the bed until he found a suitable place to hop aboard. Once on the bed he made his way to the pillow, where he sat comfortably; then he gently rubbed the side of his head against Molosky's. Molosky didn't open his eyes, but only rotated his head away.

Not quite awake yet, he fluffed the pillow behind him and sat up. As he did, Noah sprang away to the foot of the bed. "Come over here, cat. You don't have to run away. Come back here and let me pet you." Noah sat near his foot for a minute, then sauntered over and nestled onto his lap. Molosky stroked his rusty brown coat until he felt ready to move about.

Morning coffee came next; Molosky liked to brew his own. He found his way to the kitchen and set up the percolator for two cups. While on that side of the house he walked into the living room, where he selected three records to play. Over the years he had become a lover of classical music. Today he decided on the vibrant violin of Itzhak Perlman.

When he was younger, Molosky had never enjoyed orchestral music. He was one of rock and roll's biggest fans. But tragedy changed that more than seventeen years ago, when he was twenty-six.

At the time he had been married to the former Clara Halstead, a beautiful girl, with long, flowing strawberry-blond hair and wide, happy blue eyes. Clara was a carefree, full-of-fun girl who loved to dance to the hard beat of Chuck Berry or the tempting voice of Elvis Presley. Molosky did not take to the garbled and blaring voices quite so easily. He would complain that he couldn't understand the words, and when he could understand them, they didn't make any sense.

Nonetheless, Clara Halstead and Raymond Molosky spent much of their senior year in high school either holding hands and walking or holding hands on the dance floor. Those were the good days. Swaying easily in each other's arms, smiling honestly, loving with an innocent touch and a warm embrace.

Marriage came soon after their graduation. It was a big wedding. Families and friends joined in the celebration. A grand reception was held in the church: music and dancing, kisses accompanying warm embraces, love in the air long into the night.

Their union was a strong one because their love for each other ran deep. It had roots which went back to childhood, to the poor east side neighborhood where they grew up, to their families and friends, to the thousand more subtle but nonetheless meaningful feelings of life—its gifts, its sadnesses, its laughter. Their love for each other was as durable as it was passionate.

These were lean years, but they were also years full of warm and wonderful beginnings. Molosky worked as a carpenter for a time, until he received his appointment to the police department. Clara worked as a secretary for an insurance company. Soon they became parents of an infant boy. They named him Nicholas Paul after both their grandfathers.

Molosky had only spotty recollections of his son's first years. Mostly it was changing diapers and middle-of-the-night feedings. However, he had vivid memories of Clara. Before the baby was born she was so light and easygoing. But after she had given birth she became more serene, more mature, complete. Her personality blossomed with a rich fullness Molosky had never seen. The child in her had grown up. For Molosky, watching her was an awakening experience. The way she cared for the child was part of it; but in general her manner was more confident and natural, her voice more subdued and thoughtful, her smile still playful but softer and more relaxed. And the way she carried herself: less girl in her movements, more poise and womanly grace. She had become even more beautiful to him.

The strength with which Molosky loved her, and the budding relationship he was fostering with his first born made it even harder for him to accept their death.

It happened one hot summer afternoon while she was out doing the weekly shopping. She had taken Nicholas with her and was pushing him in his stroller across the street in the crosswalk. Suddenly a speeding car came out of nowhere. Clara spotted it, but it was too late. The car pulverized her body, hurling her into the side of a curb some seventy-five feet away. The baby stood even less of a chance of surviving. He was squashed beyond recognition by the car's front and rear tires.

It was a hit and run. The killer never stopped, never slowed his pace. The car vanished as fast as it had appeared. The only lead the traffic investigators could come up with was that the car was a white, four-door sedan. The incident so startled the witnesses, that none attempted to take down the license number.

Molosky suffered for a long time after that. First he went into disbelieving shock and refused to admit what had happened. Then, after several weeks, a deeper and more profound sadness crept into his soul. Days seemed to go on without end. He went through life as if he were in a vacant pit, a pit full of emptiness and death. He thought he would never climb out.

Fortunately for him, he was taken in by his pregnant sister Phyllis and her husband Joe. But even with that he was only able to hang on by the thinnest of threads. Most of his time was spent in bars, wallowing in the past. Whiskey seemed to help ease the pain temporarily, but only when he was wiped out unconscious did it stop completely. After a time the bodies of easy women also seemed to help him forget, but after awhile he became sick with guilt. To stand himself Molosky stayed numb with booze, and fought the feeling of guilt with dogged determination. Gradually he let himself slide, hoping that sometime he would hit bottom.

His sister, an outspoken woman three years his senior, could take Molosky's wallowing in self-pity only so long. She had watched him sink for seemingly endless nights and helped him keep his balance through dozens of groggy days. *She* was not willing to let him hit bottom.

One evening after Molosky had eaten dinner with them and was about to go out for the evening, she decided that she would no longer stand for his behavior. As he reached for the door to leave, she came up behind him holding his suitcase. What she had to say to him was direct and meant to shock. She told him that if he wanted to live his life in the slums then he was not welcome in her home. She thrust the suitcase into his arms and demanded that he make up his mind that night, then and there.

At first Molosky thought she was kidding; he cracked a boyish smile and gave a halfhearted chuckle. But Phyllis didn't laugh. She stood, feet spread apart, arms folded across her chest, a look of serious intent on her face. Her lips were tightly drawn, her eyes narrowed. She meant what she had said.

Molosky did not go out that night. Instead, he stayed and talked. The three of them stayed up for several hours discussing their feelings—about each other, about the suffering of the past and the promise of the future. By dawn,

Ray Molosky had decided to begin to rebuild his life and set his priorities in order.

Life took another turn for Molosky—a struggling, uphill turn for sure, but still a good one.

It was during this sudden but needed restructuring of his life that Molosky consciously and sometimes unconsciously moved aside many of the burdens in his life. Rock and roll music was one of the influences that he threw out first. It wasn't that he didn't enjoy its vibrations, or that he wouldn't someday want to return to its emotional allure; but, for him, at that time, the music seemed to be holding him back from growing and maturing. He threw away all his rock and roll records and albums and enrolled in a night class in music appreciation.

The television set went next. For entertainment he turned to books, concerts, and plays. To keep abreast of the news he turned to the radio and the local newspaper. The whiskey bottle followed the television set. He stopped drinking hard liquor and in its place found an occasional glass of wine at dinner more to his liking. He also enjoyed a good beer, but usually only after a long run.

It was before one of his workouts one day that he received a phone call from Joe. His voice was hoarse but happy and excited. He was calling from Good Samaritan Hospital. Phyllis had just given birth to a baby girl. She was two weeks early, but both were fine. Instead of running that day, Molosky picked up some flowers and drove to the hospital.

Later that evening he held his niece in his arms—tiny and beautiful. She was named Evelyn Marie Maruchi.

Molosky, his sister, and her husband became very close over the years and it was not uncommon to see them together almost everywhere—at the movies, on the beach, picnicking at the park. When Evelyn was old enough, Molosky would take her to see a good play and occasionally to a concert.

After listening to Perlman for a few moments, Molosky went on with his daily routine. Still dressed in his pajamas, he shaved and fixed himself a light breakfast of one poached egg on toast and a glass of orange juice. After that he had his second cup of coffee and browsed through the paper, with Noah perched on the arm of the chair.

Molosky enjoyed the first soothing hour before he started to work. It was his quiet time—a time to reflect, a time to gather his energies. Then he got dressed in his running clothes, a pair of blue shorts and a red and white striped T-shirt. The drive to the park came next for one solid hour of exercise.

He could feel the currents of heat blow against his back as he stepped from his '74 Ford. He locked the door and stood for a moment, enjoying the natural beauty of Vasona Park.

He surveyed his lakeside track. The asphalt path sloped gently downward under the eucalyptus trees, then came closer to the water's edge. On one side of the path were the trees, the sculptured shrubs, and the blankets of grass; on the other, the water—clear, cool, stored rainwater. Then the path disappeared over a small wooden bridge.

Molosky's eyes strayed across the lake to the path again. It twisted through the western parking lot, looped around the boat docks, and stretched toward his only resting place at the three-mile mark.

With his hands on his hips he walked toward his starting point. Once there, he did a few more toe-touches, then looked across to the three-mile rest stop, trying to decide how far he should run.

For him, this was a crucial decision because it was final. When Molosky decided to do something, it usually got done. If he decided to run six miles and his body tired after four, then his reserve strength and his willpower carried him through. He did not give up easily. He decided on a five-mile run and trotted across the asphalt toward the shade of the eucalyptus.

Molosky's running patterns became like the man himself. At forty-three, his mature legs carried his youthful torso with a matter-of-fact rhythm. His steps moved with a fluid smoothness. His stride was not ostentatious, nor was it timid. It was steady and precise—powerful. He did not have the prance of youth, but what he lacked in speed and flair he made up for with his seemingly limitless endurance.

By the time he reached the three-mile mark, the sun was beginning to deplete his strength. Droplets of perspiration formed on his brow, and his T-shirt was soaked with sweat. He walked as he always did at his midway break, hands on hips, head slightly bent from fatigue. After a thirty-second rest, he was ready to continue. His lungs pumped even gusts of air as he slowly accelerated.

He completed his five-mile tour around Lake Vasona twenty seconds shy of forty minutes. His feet were swollen from the friction generated inside his running shoes, and his body pumped out heat like a radiator. He trekked forward to find the nearest shade. Within a minute his heart rate had descended to a hundred-ten, and within two his breathing was nearly normal. The cooling down period lasted a short five minutes. Molosky glanced at his watch. Two thirty. He started his car and steered toward the Lark Avenue exit.

Chapter Four

He took the highway, and ten minutes later he steered into a space designated for police personnel only.

"Ray, you been out running in this heat?" Sergeant Darrell Wells shook his head as he opened his briefcase and stuffed in the latest edition of the *Wall Street Journal*. He slicked his hair back with his palms, put on his glasses, reached into his locker, took out his hat, and closed the door. "Listen, will ya! Take it from a guy who's been around. It's too damned hot out there to be running around for pleasure. You must have a screw loose somewhere. It's too fuckin' hot to be workin'."

Molosky grabbed a bar of soap from his locker and started for the shower. "That's 'cause you ain't me. And you're right. It is too damned hot out there to be working. You going to be in District Three tonight?"

Wells started for the door. "Shit, I don't know. I can't keep track any more. They keep switchin' me back to One. I suppose. I don't know."

Molosky stepped into the shower and turned on the water. He relished the warm water sprinkling over his skin. When he was through, he toweled and walked back to his locker to dress.

His dressing ritual followed. From jockey shorts to his blue uniform pants, each item came out of his locker in order. After the pants, he strapped on his chest protector. The two-and-a-half-pound bullet-proof vest was his on-duty life insurance policy. It gave his heart and lungs protection from knives, bullets, and other objects which people occasionally propelled at policemen.

He covered the vest with his shirt, then polished his black military combat boots, laced them, snapped on his gun belt, and walked to the mirror. It was here that Molosky pinned on the star, his badge of authority, which separated him from the rest of society and gave him special responsibilities.

The Police Administration Building, known simply by its initials as P.A.B., was a three-story cement blob with squared shoulders and darkened windows. Its bare, dreary exterior was a constant reminder that society's neglected and disturbed were dealt with there. The structure was not warm and welcoming like the other civic buildings; rather, its rough concrete bulkiness was more like a prison than an honorable institution to protect the weak. P.A.B. was cool to the touch and cold to the soul.

Molosky entered through the wire-meshed glass doors that led to the underground first floor. His eyes swept down the hallway, and he saw Captain Frank Harkness and Lieutenant Bob Lesley in conversation. He headed for the coffee room and got himself some canned orange juice from the vending machine before he went to the watch commander's office and went over the watch list. After making some minor changes, he walked to the sergeant's office to check his basket for messages. There he found a telephone note. It simply read: "Urgent. Phone your sister. She's called three times this afternoon." The initials scribbled on the bottom were unreadable. Molosky crumpled the paper and tossed it into the wastepaper basket. He checked his watch. No time to call. He marched out of the office and down the hall to the assembly room.

The room was noisy, with seventy-some policemen getting ready for the night shift. Molosky wondered what Phyllis wanted that was so urgent. He stepped up to the lectern and concentrated on the task before him. He called the officers to order. Lieutenant Lesley entered through the main door, followed by Captain Harkness. The room grew quiet.

Lesley walked up to Molosky to make a last-minute check of the watch list. He was a short man, overweight, with thinning blond wavy hair. "How does it look?"

"Not too bad for a Friday night," Molosky said.

Lieutenant Lesley put his hand through his hair and eyed the paper full of names. "Good, Sergeant. Let's start."

Molosky nodded and called the roll, ending with his own men—Yarnell, Stinson, Steirs, Neal, Scott, Holloway, and Lavine. When the list was complete, he handed it to one of the officers sitting in the front row and asked him to make twenty copies for distribution.

"Couple of other things," Molosky said as he flipped through the various papers attached to another metal clipboard. "First, a lily-white lily-waver. Occurred yesterday at Town and Country parking lot. About eighteen-thirty hours. Suspect: a white adult male five eight, one-fifty, brown and blond. Age, twenty-five to thirty. Vehicle." Molosky paused to let those who were writing catch up. "Vehicle is a light over dark green, full-sized American car. Last seen westbound on Stevens Creek."

"Got a weapon on that heavy caper?" someone asked.

"About as big as yours, Carter," said another.

"She couldn't see the fucking thing if it was yours, Thompson," retorted Carter Duran.

"Why don't you both shut up? Neither of you birds has enough to wave," called a voice from the back.

"You tell 'em, big Bert."

"Right on," said Willie Stinson.

Molosky looked over to the side of the room. There he caught the piercing glare of Captain Harkness standing alongside the bulletin board. His feet were spread apart and his arms were folded atop his barrel chest. His stern eyes shot through Molosky, telling of his disapproval.

Molosky's face went blank and he winced inwardly. His voice became impatient. "All right, guys, let's knock off the levity." The room became quiet. He looked toward Captain Harkness and received a nod of approval.

Molosky settled down, then continued, "Thought I'd remind you guys that the annual barbecue for the Benevolent Association is being put on tomorrow night. I know you all like steaks, and I'm positive you all drink beer. And I'm pretty sure most of you will accept all this, seein' how it's free. You've been puttin' in your dues all year and here's your chance to get back some of your money. The captain has granted as much time off as he could, and the Reserves will be here to help out, so I expect a good turnout. No wives or girl friends, members only. So just bring your beautiful bodies." He paused and looked toward the back of the room. "That includes yours, too, Bert," he said, grinning at Bert Yarnell, the biggest man in the room.

"Any questions? Okay, let's get 'em."

"Excuse me, Sarge," a voice said hesitantly. "Got a minute?"

Molosky turned to see Alan Lavine, the junior man on his team. "Sure, come on down to the sergeant's office. Whatcha got?"

"The Hood struck again last night, Sarge. This time at the bus stop over on Redwood."

"Again, huh? Any luck?" Molosky asked, half joking. He remembered that he had been in that area some time the night before.

"Sorry, Sarge, not this time. No chance. Thought you'd like to see the latest report. Didn't finish it until six thirty this morning. I seem to be getting my share of overtime lately. Victim waited till she got home and took a shower. Her mother was the one to call."

Molosky sat down behind the brown oversized business desk, and Lavine sat across from him.

"We've got to catch this damn pervert, Sarge. He ain't

gonna stop. He ain't goin' away till we put him in the joint."

"This creep has no pattern. He's all over. Strikes any time, day or night. How many does this make?" Molosky asked.

Lavine thought for a minute. "I think this is number five. All of 'em in our district. . . . Let's see. The first one occurred at the apartment complexes off Twenty-fourth, then there was the twelve-year-old at the bus depot." Lavine scratched the side of his head. "The old lady over on The Alameda, the school teacher on William Street, and this one on Redwood." He opened his clipboard and pulled out the fifth crime report and handed it to Molosky.

"Type of Crime: Forcible Rape," the title of the report read simply. Molosky scanned the top portion of the fact sheet to get the essential information. His mind wandered briefly. He thought of Phyllis and wondered what was so urgent. His face showed a distressed concern as he read the time the crime had taken place.

He had been *there. Right there.* Stretching and relaxing near the bookstore. The crime had occurred a few yards from where he'd been, and he hadn't seen it.

He scanned the page to the place where the name of the victim was neatly printed. Molosky stared at the name in shocked astonishment. His face became strained. His eyes bulged wide and disbelieving. His stomach tightened into a knot. He let his gaze move to the next line to check the address.

It was Evelyn, his niece. His eyes watered and he blinked several times trying to hold back the tears. He swallowed hard, then drew in a long sorrowful breath. He let the report drop to the desktop. His head sank down to his waiting hands and he gently massaged his face, trying desperately not to cry.

"What's wrong, Sarge?" Lavine asked.

Molosky gave a deep sigh without showing his face, then slowly lifted his head. A teardrop squeezed its way out of the corner of his eye and down onto his left cheek. He brushed it away with the side of his finger. "I'll be all right." His voice was choked. "It's just—it's just that the victim is my niece." He stared blankly at Lavine. "Kind of took me by surprise, that's all." He wiped under his eye again, then lifted the report and stared at it. "Can I keep this?" he asked, not hearing his own words.

"Sure, Ray," Lavine answered awkwardly. "Listen, I didn't know that you were the girl's uncle. They never said anything." He twitched in his seat nervously, then stood. "I think the whole family was humiliated by what happened. They didn't want to let on that you were the uncle. They were nice people. I liked them." There was a long descending pause. Molosky kept his head bent, eyes in an awkward stare, fixed on the report. Lavine fumbled with his clipboard. "Listen, Ray. I've got to get out to the beat. If there's anything I can do..."

Molosky shook his head mechanically. "Thanks. But I'll manage. I'll catch you later."

After Lavine had left, Molosky sat transfixed for nearly an hour. What was he going to say to Phyllis? That he was sorry? That it shouldn't have happened, but that it happens every— But it was too late for that. The damage had already been done. *The system catches animals too late. Maybe if I caught him, I could shoot him. That would solve the problem. Or would it? Why did the fucking pervert have to pick on my family? I'll kill the bastard!*

These personal clashes filled Molosky's head. Sorrow and anger. Bitterness and frustration. Confusion and vengeance. He was caught in a situation he had never dreamed he would have to deal with. And he had to do something about it. But what?

First, he had to call his sister. Reluctantly he leaned forward and picked up the phone and dialed.

"Hello." It was Phyllis.

Molosky cleared his throat before responding. "Sis. It's me."

There was a brief silence. "Ray, I've been trying to get you all day. Where have you been? I tried your home. No answer. I called the Department and you weren't there. Where have you been?"

"Calm down, Sis, please. I pull the plug on the phone when I'm sleeping, that's all. I forgot to put it back in when I got up. I'm sorry. I didn't mean to miss your calls."

"I'm sorry, too. I didn't mean to blow up at you." Her pace slowed, but Molosky could read her disturbance between the lines. "Everyone has the right to sleep, I guess." There was another tense pause, longer this time. "Ray? Are you there?" Her voice nearly cracked. "Ray?"

"I'm right here, Sis. I just heard what happened." Molosky's voice started to falter. He coughed nervously. "I don't know what to say. It was difficult just to dial the phone, let alone tell you how I feel. How is Evelyn?"

"Well, you're supposed to be the policeman." Her inflection changed again, this time to a frustrated anger. "You're always bragging to us what a good police force San Jose's supposed to have. You can't even protect your own niece?"

The pause again. This time more abrupt. Molosky wondered what she would say next. He decided to interrupt before she said something that she would regret. "Use me as a scapegoat if you want. You can blame the whole world if you want to, but that's not going to change what happened. I love all of you. You know that."

This time he sensed a guarded relief through the silence.

"I'm sorry, Ray. I shouldn't have said that." She gave off a disgusted sigh. "It's just that we're all so upset around here. At first we all cried. Then we all tried to pretend that nothing had happened. That didn't last very long. Before you knew it, we were all mad. First at what happened. Then at each other. Then at the whole lousy world. At one point I almost broke out in laughter. I thought it was all a big joke. Now I'm just numb. Stunned by the whole thing. I don't know what to do."

Her voice sounded more normal now. Molosky leaned back in his chair and relaxed. "I don't know either. Maybe the best thing to do is not to do anything. At least for a while. As long as we stick together, everything will turn out for the better."

"Well. We'll see. If we can hold on, we'll make it," she said, her tone steadier. "Joe couldn't take it. He gave up about noon. Left the house. Must have smoked five packs of cigarettes. He left the house and went for a long walk. Heard from him an hour ago. He was somewhere on the other side of town. Said he could make it home in a couple of hours, if he's lucky. If he gets tired, he'll catch a cab or something."

"He's gonna die of high blood pressure one of these days."

"Yeah, I know. That's what I keep telling him. But what are you gonna do? We're all gonna die someday."

Molosky let her words settle for a moment. He wanted to ask about Evelyn, but found it strangely awkward putting the right words together. "Umm..."

"Don't be shy, Ray. I know what you want to say. So say it. Don't be afraid. You don't have to be ashamed."

Molosky loved his sister for her many good qualities. She managed to be so straightforward about things, while at the same time remaining sincere and sensitive. She possessed that nearly perfect balance between strength and vulnerability. Outwardly she handled herself as a solid, secure individual carrying out her responsibilities and obligations with a kind of rugged perseverance. But Molosky knew that sometimes she was shy and delicate on the inside, that she needed support, attention, and love more than most people.

He slowly straightened up in his seat and rubbed his forehead. "Well, I just wanted to know how Evelyn is doing. Is she holding up all right?"

"As far as I can tell. Physically anyway. There are still a lot of things going on inside her that haven't come out yet. It'll take time. I was thinking of a trip. Maybe back East to see Aunt Mary. Might do us some good. I don't know. Everything is so up in the air."

"Yeah, I know what you mean. Is there anything I can do? Can I talk to her?"

"You could if she were awake. Finally got her down

just after four. Poor thing. Hadn't slept all day or night. She'll be all right. Sleep will do her good."

"Well, tell her I called. I'll drop by tomorrow afternoon."

"Okay. I'll tell her. Listen, I'm glad you called. I needed to hear your voice."

"I wish this had never happened. We're just gonna have to do our best. I'll see you tomorrow."

Chapter Five

The shade of the late afternoon added to Sergeant Molosky's sense of foreboding. The shadows seemed strangely twisted somehow, and the normally welcome cool breeze carried with it a chilly omen. From Central Supply he checked out a twelve-gauge shotgun, rested it on his shoulder, and made his way across the wide parking lot through the maze of parked police vehicles.

As he walked he thought about the phone conversation he had just had with his sister. He knew that her strength would endure. She would pass it to Evelyn, and Evelyn would not sink to self-denigration. And Joe. Well, he had his own way of coping. Maybe a visit with Aunt Mary would help the situation.

Molosky walked into the police garage. On the far side, standing near the gas pumps, he briefly got a look at the attendant, Frank Franklin, as he stepped into the parts room located next to the pumps. Molosky let his eyes stare absently over the blue and white police cars. He was looking for car number 306, but his concentration strayed and he walked past it.

Franklin stepped back out into the main area and started walking toward the car he was servicing.

"Hey, Frank," Molosky yelled, his voice resonating between the hollow concrete walls. "Where's three-oh-six? You guys playing musical chairs with the cars again?"

Franklin's face broke into a half grin and he started to walk toward Molosky. "You blind or something, Sergeant? You know I always got your car on the line." Suddenly he stopped and pointed to the car Molosky had just walked past. "Right there!" He shook his head. "You need glasses. Thick ones."

Molosky tilted his head back and eyed the car. "I'm sorry, Frank," he apologized and cracked an embarrassed smile. "I'm not with it today."

"Don't go bein' sorry now. It's too late for that. You just remember, ol' Frank Franklin Junior always takes good care of the swing-shift troopers."

Molosky acknowledged this, cocking his head to the side in an awkward flinch, then he got into the car and eased out of the garage on the east side. He had known Frank for years. He shouldn't have sounded off at him like that. He steered the car to the rear of the locker room in the adjacent building.

He entered the locker room and quickly returned to the car with his flashlight and briefcase. *They're turning policemen into bureaucrats,* he thought as he flicked open the case full of report forms. He took out four shotgun rounds from the back, loaded the twelve-gauge, and secured it inside the police car. He walked around to the rear of the car, popped the trunk lid open and saw two boxes of flares, sufficient for emergencies. He shut the lid and checked the tires.

Behind the wheel again, he fastened his safety belt, then swung out into the streets. He picked up the microphone and placed himself in service. The radio traffic was slow. He hoped it would stay that way.

Steering south on Second Street, he tried to recall the days when San Jose wasn't so crowded. Years ago, Second Street had been a wide two-way street where kids played football and baseball. Now it had three lanes one-way and there was too much traffic for kids to play.

Molosky wondered what had caused such haphazard growth. Only yesterday, San Jose was a mere pueblo. Now nearly six hundred thousand people lived and wandered through its streets. It seemed to him that growth had been the city's number one industry since the early 1950s; its number one industry and its number one problem. The city fathers had been pressured by the bulging population to make inept and often costly decisions. Allowing greed to determine the future course of the city, they bowed to the all-powerful land speculators and the huge housing-tract developers. Carving up the once fertile farm acreage and dooming it to rows of look-alike houses, the modern carpetbaggers poured into the city, exploiting their constitutional right to build.

Suddenly images of his niece being attacked returned. Frightening images of the man who wore the hood. Molosky steered the car off Second Street and slowly drifted toward Redwood Avenue to examine the crime scene. He knew it was to be a fruitless effort, but he had to go through the motions.

The police cruiser rolled to a stop several feet in front of the bus stop. Molosky looked at the wooden bench, then turned his head and eyed the small business building across the street. It was a trim-looking building, low roof line, manicured shrubs running around the side toward the back. The building contained three businesses—a shoe repair shop, a real estate office, and an insurance agency.

He let his eyes stray back to the bus stop, then he pulled to the curb and got out. He made his way to the bench, sat down and tried to put himself in Evelyn's place. Looking behind the bench he saw that the north side parking lot was busy with moving cars. He could see the sign for the bookstore in the distance. He remembered stepping from the patrol car and seeing a pair of headlights come on, then slowly move out and turn onto Forest Avenue westbound. *That must have been him,* he thought. *I was no more than fifty yards away.*

Molosky got up and walked across the street to the small business building. Keeping his eyes moving about the well-kept shrubs, he searched for any possible clue. Slowly he walked down the driveway to the back.

There was nothing. Only the dirt and the neat bushes. At the back of the building was a small parking lot, large enough for no more than a dozen cars. Molosky turned the corner and walked only a few steps into the parking lot. There was nothing. Just as he had figured. No physical evidence.

As he turned to walk back along the driveway, the back door to the real estate office opened and a man stepped out—well-dressed, broad-shouldered. Molosky watched the man as he started across the parking lot toward a late-model car parked in the corner.

The man did not see Molosky at first, but after only a few steps he appeared to hesitate, as if he had forgotten something. He turned back toward the door, and as he did he spotted Molosky. An anxious expression shot over the man's face. The expression turned cloudy, then questioning. Finally, as the man walked up to Molosky, the expression cleared into a friendly smile.

"Officer, I didn't see you there. You startled me. Is there something I can do for you? I'm Owen Sheldon, of Platinum Real Estate. Something I can help you with?"

Molosky smiled back pleasantly. "I'm sorry. Didn't mean to startle you. I was just back here looking for evidence. But I don't think I'm going to be very successful."

"Well...ah...what kind of evidence? Maybe I can help." The man shaded his eyes, but the smile persisted. It was a pleasant enough smile, but Molosky got the feeling that there was more to it. The man's face seemed to give off strange signals.

"Anything, really. Anything would help. It was a rape case. Happened last night. I thought I might find something."

"Right here? That's hard to believe. How awful."

The man was quick with his response. The words seemed correct, but somehow Molosky thought that the man wasn't all that concerned. Maybe the man was in a hurry. Or just maybe *he* was too emotionally involved and was reading him all wrong. "Yeah, it was pretty awful," he replied trying to be polite. "I'll be on my way now. I know you must be a busy man."

The man let his hand drop. There was no smile, just a hard, blank expression. "I wish I could help, Officer. If I see any strange-looking characters hanging around, I'll be sure to call."

"Thank you. We'd appreciate that."

The man nodded, turned, and walked toward the back door.

Chapter Six

Molosky's mind remained focused on what had happened to his niece. He swung the patrol car into the corner parking place across the street from his favorite restaurant and requested Code Seven.

"Stand by," the operator barked. "All units. All units in District Five. Just received a silent holdup alarm at Papa Joe's Liquor Store, Ninth and Santa Clara."

All thoughts of his niece, of rape, of the hooded rapist were swept aside. Molosky was less than a half mile from the liquor store. He powered the blue and white cruiser across San Carlos Street and steered around slower traffic. Behind the wheel he moved in quick, controlled movements. He had done this a hundred times. While he steered with his left hand, his right lashed out and grabbed the microphone. He clicked himself on the air as he braked and moved between two slower moving cars. "Sixty-five hundred. I'll respond on that. Have Fifty-eight come in from the east and Fifty-four cover the north."

"Ten-four, Sixty-five hundred.

"Sixty-one fifty-eight copy," Willie Stinson answered. "That's my beat, so I'll be responding to the scene."

"Sixty-one fifty-two copy. Responding," Gilbert Steirs answered.

It took Molosky slightly less than thirty seconds to make the three-block run to Santa Clara Street. "Just nine easy ones now," he said to himself as he braked and dropped the transmission into low gear, then punched it eastbound on Santa Clara Street.

"Sixty-five hundred and all units responding on the holdup alarm. Witness across the street states possible shots fired."

"Control, Sixty-five hundred. If you still have that witness on the line, get a description of the suspect, then start an ambulance." Molosky's words came out with rapid-fire authority. He steered over the double yellow lines, running oncoming traffic off the road. He weaved back into his lane and around slower cars.

"Units on the holdup," the operator barked. "Suspect described as a white male, yellow shirt, blond hair, just left eastbound on Santa Clara driving a maroon-colored motorcycle."

Eastbound, Molosky thought. *He should be in front of me somewhere.* His eyes darted back and forth, scanning the traffic ahead.

Suddenly, he spotted the yellow shirt of the robber as he sped through traffic. "Suspect in sight, eastbound Santa Clara at Tenth," he radioed and wrapped the microphone around the inside rearview mirror, letting it hang as he prepared to pursue.

"Restricted traffic on Channel Two," the operator responded, allowing Molosky to be the only one to use the frequency.

"He's really flying at Fifteenth," Molosky shouted as he accelerated to seventy miles per hour.

The yellow shirt of the robber filled with air and puffed out like an overstuffed bag. He had no helmet over his sandy blond hair. He looked like he knew how to ride the bike. Suddenly, his brake light came on; he quickly angled to the right and zipped around the corner at Seventeenth Street.

Molosky was too close to his rear to make the turn. He jammed on the brakes and was immediately drawn into a drifting four-wheel lock skid. The rear of the police cruiser began to come around on him. He immediately let off the brakes and counter-steered. But it was too late. The car went out of control and spun a hundred and eighty degrees and began to roll backwards. Without hesitation, Molosky soft-pedaled the brake, then jammed the accelerator. The engine sputtered. "Don't die on me now!" he said in exasperation.

The powerful engine took hold and the back tires squealed on the pavement. Molosky turned the corner and raced southbound on Seventeenth.

The motorcycle had almost a block on him. "South on Seventeenth," he called into the dangling microphone.

The robber made another right turn at the next intersection. He sped around the corner and disappeared from sight.

Molosky touched the brake pedal lightly, then made a hard right. His car skidded across the pavement and nearly slammed into a parked car. "Back toward town on San Fernando," he yelled. He could see the motorcycle two blocks in front of him. He flipped on the siren, hoping anyone on the cross streets would hear him. He pushed the car to eighty-five, faster than he should in a residential area, but he had no choice.

"Approaching Tenth Street," Molosky shouted over the blaring noise.

The robber scooted around the corner, banking the bike expertly to the left. In the middle of the turn, he whirled his head around to check his position. His jaw dropped, his eyes popped open wide. The police car was nearly on top of him.

At Tenth Street Molosky dropped the car into low gear, then braked easily trying to avoid a slide. He controlled the car around the corner, tires squealing, but not losing traction. He pushed his foot to the floor.

"South on Tenth," he called into the microphone as he sped through traffic, swinging in and out of lanes like an overzealous rookie.

The robber drove through the red light at Tenth and San Carlos without slowing.

Molosky slowed for the same light. He knew he could not go through it at the same pace. He was sworn to protect the public. His car eased to thirty miles an hour and the light flicked to green twenty feet from San Carlos Street. He quickly swung around two idle cars and hurriedly tried to regain lost ground. The cycle now was one and a half blocks ahead of him, approaching the Interstate 280 overpass.

The maroon bike veered to the right and scrambled up the on-ramp.

"He's heading north toward San Francisco on 280," Molosky yelled as he prepared to turn onto the on-ramp. "Notify the highway patrol."

Easy does it, Molosky thought, trying to slow his adrenaline.

"Ten-four, Sixty-five hundred," the radio operator acknowledged.

The six-lane freeway was not as crowded as Molosky had expected. Commuter traffic had dissipated and there was a lull in the evening shopping crowd. The robber drove the bike through a small group of cars and edged over to the far left lane.

Molosky floored the accelerator until the police car reached ninety-five miles per hour. "Got any District Two units near the highway?" He shouted over the roar of the engine and the squeal of the siren.

"Stand by, Sixty-five hundred," the operator said.

With that, Molosky reached down and flipped the siren switch off. "That thing will drive me crazy," he said to himself. The roar of the engine without the siren was like heaven. Sirens only intensified an already tense situation.

"Sixty-one twenty-one, I'm at Lawrence and two eighty," Officer Dwight Savia answered.

"Good," said Molosky. "I'm about two hundred yards in

back of this guy and he's really moving. Set up a roadblock down below at the Lawrence Expressway exit."

"Ten-four, Sixty-five hundred," responded Savia.

Molosky was only guessing that the robber would exit onto the expressway, but he knew that the highway patrol would soon be with him, so he wanted to cover the main exits leading back to the city streets.

The bike weaved in and out of traffic. Molosky stayed as close as he could, picking his lanes, remaining steady on the accelerator. At one point, he saw the man look back again. His face showed extreme tension—deep lines across the brow, tight jaw, eyes in a stiff glare. Molosky knew he had him rattled. All he had to do now was to let him make the first mistake.

Suddenly, the cycle made a desperate swerve and jerked between two large trucks, cleared the back bumper of a convertible, and bounced over a marker curb and onto the Lawrence Expressway off-ramp.

Molosky quickly downshifted, braked, and steered around the rear of the convertible. He came within inches of a concrete ramp divider, punched the accelerator, and started down the long descending exit ramp.

"Here he comes," Molosky shouted into the radio.

Dwight Savia positioned his police car, blocking the exit ramp at the lower end. He quickly dismounted with shotgun in hand and ran toward a concrete pillar to take cover.

Molosky eased off the throttle. He kept his eyes on the back of the robber, his shirt no longer puffy, but now flapping in the wind. He slowed the patrol car, wondering what the robber would do to get around the blockade.

Suddenly, there was the yelping sound of skid as the robber's tires gripped the pavement. Then smoke. Burning rubber. Molosky saw the man losing control. His rear wheel snapped to the left and the bike began to slide sideways. The robber hit the black pavement in a near prone position, forcing his contorted body to roll end over end. The motorcycle continued straight ahead, sliding underneath the parked police car and jamming into the undercarriage.

Molosky stopped his car fifteen feet from where the man

lay trying to get to his feet. Like a panther after its prey, Molosky leaped out of the car and charged. Jamming his polished black boot into the man's shoulder, he hoisted his six-inch revolver and put it to his head.

"One move, and you're dead."

Chapter Seven

Before Molosky departed from the exit ramp, he checked with Savia to insure that everything was progressing smoothly. The robber's gun had been retrieved from the bushes where it had landed. A tow truck had been called and would soon have the wrecked police car and the maroon motorcycle cleared from the roadway. The perpetrator himself had been taken to the hospital by a pair of homicide detectives. Apparently the store owner was dead.

"Yarnell should be here in a sec," he told Savia from behind the wheel of his patrol car. "He'll give you a lift to the garage. If you guys need me I'll be at the detective bureau report-writing. Probably take me awhile. Catch you guys later. Good job."

Molosky was feeling wired, tired, and hungry by the time he got to the police building. He picked up a cold sandwich from a vending machine, then marched to the Homicide Unit and withdrew to the lieutenant's office to write his portion of the report. Letting the door close, he sat at the desk and rubbed his eyes while he pondered the evening's events. He wished for the peace and serenity of

Lake Vasona, the quiet of its gently rolling hills and the life that hummed along the water. A place where he controlled his life. Where life's dramas didn't burden him. He reflected for a while, then shook his head and began to write the crime report.

An hour later a knock on the door distracted him from his thoughts. Putting his pen down he stood, and opened the door. It was the square-jawed, stockily built Henry Fowler, a reporter from the local newspaper. "Hank, come in."

"How goes it, Ray?" Fowler had a friendly smile. His words flowed in a mild-mannered professional tone. "I was looking for the lieutenant, but I think you probably have more details. You got time for a few quick questions?"

Molosky leaned back behind the desk. "Sure, but there's not that much to it. I spotted the guy, chased him down, and caught him. The dicks are over at the hospital. They'd probably have more for you."

Fowler sat in front of the desk and slipped out a notepad from his breast pocket. He sighed heavily, and seemed to be staring through Molosky.

"This is personally a sad story for me to write, Ray. I grew up on Seventh Street, right down from the school. I used to work for Joe Hendrixson—stocking shelves and cleaning up around the place. Know all his sons. Went to school with the oldest." Fowler crossed his legs and drew in a deep breath, held it for a second, then blew it out slowly. "Worked for Joe my senior year in high school, and every summer after that until I got my B.A. Always treated me fair. Liked him a lot."

Molosky listened from behind the desk. A dull, aching exhaustion seized his muscles. He had had enough for one day. He realized that he could not keep his strength up much longer without breaking down. He needed something to eat and a long, long sleep. He let his eyes follow a path to the bulletin board directly in back of Fowler to the black embossed words: "Local—Most Wanted." Under that there were three headings, each in smaller black letters. They read: Rape, Robbery, Homicide. Under the title Rape was an eight-by-twelve sheet of paper. At the top in bold letters it said The Hood, and below there was a black and white drawing outlining the features of the hooded disguise.

Molosky felt a sudden nausea. His stomach turned over; he tried to swallow but his throat was caked from dryness. He was incapable of speech; his whole system seemed to cave in. He sucked in two long, tight breaths, then stood awkwardly and hesitated clumsily. He coughed roughly and swallowed hard. Pictures of Evelyn being raped streamed through his mind. He had to excuse himself.

"Listen Hank"—his voice was a nasal whisper—"ahhh...I'm not feeling up to an interview right now. Maybe you should talk to the detectives. They'll be here shortly. They can fill you in. I've got to go now. Excuse me." With that, Molosky opened the door and hurriedly departed.

Henry Fowler sat with a wide, questioning stare. He thought for a minute, then realized that there must be something very powerful going on inside the policeman. He had never seen him act like that before. Slowly, he scratched his chin and decided to let well enough alone.

Chapter Eight

Instead of regaining his composure, Molosky left the police building immediately and made quickly for the locker room, where he hastily threw off his uniform, jumped into his sweat clothes, and marched to his car. Once behind the wheel he sat for a moment wondering what to do, where to go.

Acting on impulse, he drove to a nearby liquor store and purchased a fifth of Jack Daniels. Not wanting to go home, he steered to the only place he could find solitude and collect his thoughts—Vasona Park. As he drove, his mind was not on the traffic. He stared blankly at the road, driving by instinct and habit. He turned off Highway 17 and found University Avenue. Molosky had never been to the park before in the middle of the night when it was closed. The road and the landscape seemed different; there were no cars along the road, no people walking.

A high protective fence ran along the park's western border. He drove alongside the fence for several hundred feet to a low place, parked, and got out. Vaulting the low metal automobile barricade, he slipped down the steep dirt embankment onto his running path. With one hand he clutched the bottle of whiskey wrapped in a brown paper bag, with the other he brushed the dirt off his clean blue sweat suit. Then he stumbled through the dark until he reached a wooden bench near the water.

This place can kill you at night, he thought. With his free hand he felt the outline of the back of the bench, made his way to the front and sat down. The twisting and breaking of the seal on the bottle crackled into the stillness around the sleeping lake. He took two quick gulps and felt the whiskey begin to soothe his weary nerves and calm his troubled head. He thought he should sit in the park more often and let the warm night air surround him with peace and quiet.

Slowly the weakness he had abandoned many years ago crept back. There was a certain pleasure, a certain physical comfort that the whiskey offered. It was like the return of an old friend he had missed and secretly yearned for through the years.

He sat for a long while sipping small but steady gulps. His eyes were fixed in a distant gaze, and every once in a while his face would break into a wolfish grin.

The good times. Being young and reckless. The Marines. Stationed aboard the USS *Bremerton,* a heavy cruiser and flagship for Task Force 77 in the Pacific. Being part of Underwater Demolition Team 12, Repulse Bay, Hong Kong. The brawl at the Silver Dollar bar, a sleazy hangout for whores and G.I.'s located at the far end of a pier. The fight had lasted only ten minutes, and being outnumbered, his team took a severe beating from the forty or so paratroopers.

It felt good getting drunk again. Under the influence was the only way to live, he thought. A carefree stupor. Every night, all night. Seven days a week. Let the *good times roll.*

The fun times rolled through Molosky's memory. However, the drunker he got, the more cracks developed in his shell of good thoughts. Slowly at first, but then more disturbingly, thoughts of his wife and her early death, then of his favorite little girl, Evelyn, crept into his mind. He tried to stop the sad and tragic thoughts from interrupting the good times, but his resistance was low. These were the people he cared most for in his life, the people he loved. He just couldn't toss them out of his mind in a drunken whim.

So the good time thoughts passed and harsher images invaded his mind. Frightful pictures of a man wearing a white hood came to the front of his brain. He tried to imagine the man. A towering savage, long powerful arms, drum-tight skin, wild and terrifying. And under the hood a twisted, jagged face alive with violence.

The images of the hooded man creeping through the dark became so powerful in Molosky's head that they scared even him. He sat up straight and remained motionless for a moment. His breathing became light as he listened for strange sounds. But there was only the cool resting quiet of the lake.

He took another swig. Then suddenly, acting on impulse, he leaped off the bench and whirled himself around. "You can't fool me, you hooded pervert." His face had a wild look on it, his eyes fierce and probing through the darkness. He waved his arms in front of him, holding the whiskey bottle by its throat.

"I know you're out there somewhere. Show yourself! Show me your eyes! Show me your fucking hood and I'll blow it off your fucking shoulders." He held his right arm out straight, the whiskey splashing on his wrist. "Pow! There's one right between the eyes. Pow! There's another. Pow, pow! You filthy scumbag bastard. I ought to blow your balls off."

With those words Molosky's anger and frustration had been shouted out. As quickly as the words came, they were gone. He slowly let his arms come to his sides, then turned around and faced the water. He felt stupid. *What good does it do to yell at the night? What a fucking fool you are, Molosky—a drunken fool.*

Slowly the darkness and the silence of the water began to get to Molosky. He suddenly had the urge to leave. Not wanting to litter the park, he stuffed the brown bag in his pocket, capped the whiskey bottle and clung to it by the neck. The embankment was only thirty feet high and looked simple enough to climb. He hoisted his running shoes onto the steep dirt hillside, grasped for solid footing, but slipped. The dirt was crusty and sooty and wouldn't take his weight.

"I got down here," he said to himself, his lips feeling numb, his tongue thick. "Now I've got to climb out somehow."

Stepping back a dozen paces, he tightened his teeth together and charged. His footing did not hold but his tenacity did. As the dirt slipped under him, his legs moved quicker. Moving and churning, they slowly pushed him toward the top and the light. He slipped again, but this time he did not falter. Grasping and groping with his hands, he pushed upward, then plowed over the top and rolled onto the lonely street.

Huffing and sweating, he felt like he had just completed his last mile. He let his arm droop across his eyes so that he blocked out the brightness of the street light. He lay there on the asphalt roadway wondering what his forty-three years had taught him. Was he to end up a common drunk sleeping in gutters? He hobbled to his feet and slowly made his way to his car.

Once inside he found his keys still in the ignition. He laughed out loud to himself. "I must have been really strung out to do that." He started the car and quickly cranked the wheel to the left and raced the engine. The car squealed out from the curb. "Slow down," he told himself. "What's the rush?" He giggled, then licked his lips.

Across the street he noticed a Shell station and at the corner of the garage portion of the building he spotted a telephone booth. *What a fantastic idea,* he thought, and accelerated through the intersection, over the driveway, coming to a stop alongside the booth. Clicking off the engine, he stepped from the car and fished in his sweatshirt pocket for a dime.

"Hello?" The voice sounded sleepy.

Molosky smiled and thought himself silly for being

drunk and calling a girl from a gas station phone booth. But what the hell, you only live once.

"Hello?" The voice repeated.

"It's me, Colleen. Ray Molosky. Did I wake you?" A stupid question.

There was a pause. Molosky could hear what sounded like someone moving the phone. "You there, Colleen?"

"I've only been asleep an hour. I usually don't get phone calls at this hour." She yawned loudly. "Are you home?"

"I wish I was home. Boy, do I. No, I'm in a phone booth somewhere." He started to laugh. "I'm in a phone booth somewhere. Somewhere on the earth, I guess." More laughter. "On the west side of the earth, somewhere. Hell, I don't know where I am. Near Vasona some place. I guess. I hope, anyway. It's good to hear your voice."

There was silence, a long tolerant silence. "Hear my voice. You're the one that's doing all the talking. And laughing. And drinking."

"Oh my goodness! How could you tell? You must have smelled it on my breath." More laughter. "That's pretty good. You must have smelled it on my breath. Not bad, hey?"

"I don't mean to interrupt your fun and games, or anything like that. If you want to continue talking to yourself, that's fine with me. But is there some particular reason why you called me at this hour?"

"Well, I don't know, Colleen. It's just been kind of a rotten bad day, and I just thought... ahh... Hell! I don't know what I was thinking. I shouldn't have called. I'm sorry."

"Sounds gloomy. You want to get it off your chest?"

Molosky leaned against the inside glass of the booth and switched the receiver to his left hand. He sighed deeply. "I don't know what I'm doing all this laughin' for. It's just... just... ahh... Evelyn. Evelyn got attacked. Evelyn got... Evelyn was raped. Last night. I was on duty, and I was within a stone's throw of her when it happened. I wish the world would stop so I could catch the next one." There was a painful pause. Molosky wondered if he had done the right thing. Quickly, he decided that he shouldn't have burdened her. "Colleen? Colleen, are you still there?"

"Yes. Numb. But still here."

"Colleen, I'm sorry. I shouldn't have called. Goddamn! How could I be so dumb? I'm sorry."

There was silence on the wire. Molosky felt like hanging up and starting over.

"Now at least I know why you've been drinking. It's just that you shocked me. Is she all right? Is there anything I can do?"

Molosky drew in a long breath. She wasn't mad, or at least she didn't sound mad. She understood. "I don't know. I don't think so. Phyllis has things under control. I don't know. I hope she does anyway. 'Cause I sure don't. What a rotten world we live in."

"How long have you been a policeman? Long enough to know that the world isn't made of peaches and cream and apple pie."

"Yeah. Long enough to know, I guess. But not like this. I didn't think it was like this. I never thought the perverts would attack like this. So close. You know what I mean?"

"Listen, Ray." Her voice had a sting to it. "The knot in my stomach hasn't gone away yet. I'm still in shock. Don't forget, you've known about this for a while now. I was just awakened from a sound sleep. I'm not sure what I'm supposed to be reacting to. You? Or Evelyn? Or the crime of rape? I can't put them all together and come up with an easy explanation, you know. Not in the space of three minutes. It can't be done. I feel sick."

Molosky knew that he shouldn't have called. Not in the middle of the night. Not drunk. Not to tell her this. "Colleen. I'll try and act sober. I called because I guess I was angry and upset. I acted on impulse. I shouldn't have. Can we talk sometime, when I'm not under the weather? And, you know..."

"Ray, I'm glad you called. Do you want to come over and we can talk?"

Molosky slid his free hand into his sweat shirt pocket. If he went over there he would just make a bigger fool of himself. He'd probably end up telling her that he loved her. "Thanks for the offer, Colleen. I'd like to, but I don't think I should. Not in my condition. But I'd like to see you sometime."

"Will you call me tomorrow?"

"Sure. I might have a hangover, but I'll call."

Chapter Nine

Molosky awoke early the next afternoon to the soft voice of a newscaster announcing that the San Francisco homicide rate was up eleven percent from the year before and that rapes had increased fifteen percent. The number of arrests had dropped in both categories.

Only half awake, he turned over, hoping the bad news would go away. When he did, the sheets crackled in his ear and he felt tender all over. His head felt like spongy mush. He lay still and tried not to be awake. But he wasn't going to have the luxury of sleeping any longer. Soon he felt the purring rub of his faithful cat.

It was extremely difficult at first, but he managed to sit up and plant his feet on the floor. There he sat for a moment, head bent, arms draped across his knees. When he felt ready, he stood and peeled off his sweat suit and found his way to the shower. He must have been really out of it last night, he thought, to fall asleep in his running gear. The warm water poured over him, and he stood silently, grimly taking his medicine. He hated hangovers, and even more, he hated himself for being so weak and falling into the bottle again. As he turned off the water and reached for a towel he swore off whiskey; he would not let it rule his life again.

He felt better after breakfast and coffee, so he decided that after he had finished his second cup he would wash the kitchen floor before starting on the backyard. Later, he would go over to see Evelyn.

As he turned down the tree-lined street where Phyllis and her family lived, Molosky's thoughts turned to Evelyn. Suddenly, he felt an almost overwhelming urge to turn the car around and postpone their meeting. What was he going to say to her? So far in the last two days, every time he opened his mouth the words fumbled from his lips and he ended up apologizing. He didn't think he could face Evelyn. But what was he going to do? He couldn't just run away, even though he felt like it.

Easing the sedan to the curb in front of the house, he spotted Phyllis coming out of the front door carrying what looked like a picnic basket, and she had a towel thrown over her shoulder. She looked toward him and gave a short wave.

Molosky stepped from his car and called to her. "Hi, Sis. How is it going?"

Phyllis continued toward her car, which was parked in the driveway. She had a certain soundness about her. Her short body was trim and fit. She wore a plain housedress and flats.

"I'm glad you stopped by. Joe and I are taking Evelyn to the beach. We thought it would do us all good to get away for a while."

"Sis." Molosky walked across the lawn closer to her. "Ahh . . . I don't know what to say. I mean to Evelyn. Where do I start?"

"Well, welcome to the club." She opened the trunk of her car and put the basket and towel inside, then shut it and turned toward him. "There's nothing anybody can say at this point. We've got feelers out for some professional help, if it comes to that. Maybe you can check one of them out for us. But the best thing you can do, Ray, is be here. You don't have to say a lot of words. Just being here shows you care. And that's all that's really needed."

Molosky rubbed his eyes. He wasn't completely over his hangover yet.

"Come on in and say hello. We're going to be leaving in a couple of minutes." She walked past him with a gleam in her eye. "You want to come with us?"

"Can't today, Sis. But thanks anyway."

Phyllis reached the door and turned around. "Well, are you going to stand there or are you going to come in and say hello?"

When Molosky entered the house there was no one in the living room. Phyllis walked into the kitchen. "They're probably still out in the backyard. They both decided that the lawn needed doing, so they went at it. Been out there for the longest time." She stopped near the kitchen window. "Evelyn," she called, "your uncle is here. You guys are going to have to finish up. We should be going pretty soon."

"We're all done, Mom." The back door opened and Evelyn stepped in. "Dad's putting away the mower; he'll be in in a sec."

Suddenly, she looked toward Molosky. The bright smile she had for her mother slowly wilted from her lips. He could see her shy eyes turn down. Her hands came together in front of her. She was waiting for him to say something. There was sudden silence in the room.

"Come here, honey, and give me a hug." Molosky extended his arms to welcome her.

Evelyn let her eyes drift to him. A blushing smile came to her lips. "Oh. I'm glad you came over, Uncle Ray." She ran across the room and wrapped her arms around his neck.

Molosky sucked in a deep emotional breath. He couldn't speak. All he wanted was to hold on to her for a long time. *Everything will be okay,* he thought. *Don't worry, child, somehow things will work out. I'll protect you.*

"I'm glad I came over too, honey. I haven't seen you in

nearly a week. Your mother tells me you're going to the beach. Sounds like fun." He released his grip from around her. "Now there's a good girl. Hey, you're going to be taller than me if you keep growing."

The back door opened again and Joe walked through carrying a pair of hand clippers. He was a thin man with a narrow face and big ears. "Well, let's all pray that she doesn't get that tall. Or she might turn out to be that ugly, too." He glanced at Molosky from the corner of his eye.

Molosky grinned. "Good to see you too, Joe. I see you haven't lost your sense of humor."

Joe turned to Phyllis. "Phil, I'm ready to go, as is. Why don't you and Evelyn get what you have to get, and let's get going."

"Good idea," Phyllis said. "Come on, Ev. Let's get to gettin'. Your father's got the bug."

Evelyn didn't look at either of them. Instead she took hold of Molosky's hand and squeezed. "Thanks for stopping by, Uncle Ray. It means a lot to me."

"You mean a lot to me, too, honey. You all do. Except your father." Molosky shot Joe a compressed, sly smile.

When the two women had left the room, Joe followed Molosky to the front door. "Not bad, for a cop." Joe tilted his head and pulled on his ear. "I'm glad you stopped by, Ray. I think it helped Evelyn quite a bit. Appreciate it."

"Sis said something about professional help. You guys got anybody particular in mind? She said she might want me to check out one of them."

Joe gave a sarcastic laugh. "What she meant was, that *you* needed one. She was just trying to be polite to you, that's all."

He smiled playfully and tapped his lower jaw with his fingertips. "She mentioned some guy over at the university. Teaches some kind of class over there. I don't know what it's all about. Supposed to be good. I don't know. I don't trust those people over there though. What the hell do they know? Half of them are Communists, if you ask me. The other half are queer. Don't get me started or I'll go on for hours."

"What's the guy's name? Maybe I can help."

"Evans, I think she said it was. Hugo Evans, that's it. Supposed to be a professor over there somewhere. Check him out and see what side of the coin he's on. Probably a little of both."

Molosky shook his head and grinned. "Yeah. Probably. I'll catch you guys later. Have fun at the beach."

Molosky drove around for a while. His mood became reflective. Evelyn seemed all right, from the outside, anyway. He wished he could have said more to her. As he was driving he found himself near his favorite bookstore, located in the city of Campbell a short distance from his house. Whenever he had free time and wanted to be by himself, he would generally drift in there and browse for books.

As he walked through the doorway of the rather spacious shop, he could see many people milling about, looking and thumbing through the displayed books. They were quiet and nondistracting. Molosky browsed for a short time before he found a book that looked interesting. After buying it, he walked to the back of the store, where there were tables set out for people to sit and read and drink espresso coffee. He found an empty table and relaxed in its wooden chair.

"If it isn't the mad phone caller!"

Molosky looked up from the book. A wide smile came across his face. A warm responsive gleam showed in his eyes. He stood and pulled out a chair. "Colleen, what a pleasant surprise. Sit down. Can I get you a cup of coffee?"

Colleen Brennan smiled back at him and nodded. "What are you doing here, Ray? Policemen aren't supposed to read books."

"Let me get you a cup. I'll be back in a minute." He went to get another cup.

When he returned, he found her thumbing through his book. "Ray Molosky, I always knew there was something special about you." She put the book down and let her eyes move to meet his. "*Siddhartha* is a very wise book. I've read it three times."

"I was in sort of a philosophical mood, and I saw this book."

"Tell me, were you in a philosophical mood last night when you rang?" She smiled teasingly.

Molosky smiled back, slightly embarrassed. "No. As a matter of fact, last night I was just plain drunk. The roof caved in; I got drunk, and now everything is back to normal." He held out his hand and tipped it from side to side. "More or less, that is."

"You're okay then? Except for a hangover and maybe an upset stomach?"

"Yeah, I'm okay. I don't do that much anymore. It was kind of fun while it lasted. The aftereffects are nothing to brag about. But I paid my dues. Promised myself when I woke up that I wouldn't do that again."

"Good. Then I won't kid you about it anymore. Okay?"

"Fine by me."

A short silence fell. Colleen lifted the cup to her lips and let her glance move over his face. "How long has it been, Ray?"

Molosky looked at her. "Three months, maybe four. I've missed you. How did you do at school?"

"Not bad for a college returnee. Beats waiting tables full-time. Final grades won't be mailed until next week sometime, but I did just fine. At least that's what my teachers said. They want me to apply for the Master's program at Berkeley. I haven't made up my mind about that yet, but if everything works out, I'll at least apply." She sat back in the chair and relaxed. She wore no makeup. Her eyes were a sensitive pale blue. Her body was slender, small-breasted, and athletic.

"Are you sure you're okay, Ray? I mean about Evelyn and what happened to her?"

Molosky rubbed his chin and turned his eyes away briefly. "To tell you the truth, I'm not exactly okay. The guy who did it is still out there somewhere. He wears a hood. Nobody knows what he looks like. So, that part isn't okay. And then there's the fact that the pervert only strikes in my district. He's attacked several times so far. All where I work. All in District Five. And that's not okay. In fact, that's the part that's really starting to bother me."

"Maybe he lives in your district. Or works there or something?"

"Yeah, that could be it. I've thought about that too. But it would be impossible to check out every man who worked, played, lived in, or was simply passing through the district. Trouble is, there are no patterns. No times of days, no particular area of the district, no certain type of victim—age, color, that sort of thing. No nothing. Just the hood. The white hood."

Colleen fingered her cup as she listened. "Have you talked to Evelyn yet? Is she going to be all right?"

"Thanks to Phyllis. I don't know what we would have done without her. She's shook up. I can tell. But she'll make it fine. Phyllis is a tower of strength." Molosky paused. "We're all concerned for Evelyn. She looks good on the outside. But it's too early to assess the internal damage. We'll see. We'll all stay close and pitch in when we're needed."

"You know I'm available if you need me. I don't know what I could do. But I'd like to help."

"That can be a family decision. I just wanted to tell you that, if the need is there, you can count on me."

"Have you ever heard of a guy named Hugo Evans? He's supposed to be a professor at the university. Teaches some kind of class over here."

"What's he supposed to do?"

"I don't know. Phyllis mentioned him. I don't know where she found him. One of her friends or something. Supposed to be an expert of some kind. Nobody's told me what he's supposed to be an expert at. Sex or rape or something along those lines. They're thinking of sending Evelyn to him if they feel the need some time down the road. Tell you what. I'll make an appointment, one of these weeks, and you can come with me. We can both size him up. How about that?"

Colleen sat up in her chair and glanced at her watch. "That's fine with me. We can compare notes." She put her hand on top of his. "I have to run, Ray."

"You don't have to go so soon, do you? You just got here. Please stay. I haven't seen you in so long; it feels good being with you again."

"I know. It feels good for me, too. But I got a summer job as a waitress at the Hyatt. I start in twenty-five minutes." She stood up tall and smiling. "You know, you could call me sometime, and we could go out on a real date, instead of to some professor's office." Her eyes glistened.

Molosky's eyes brightened and a happy smile came across his face. "You're on."

Chapter Ten

Of the three social events—the retirement dinner in March, the Christmas dance, and the Benevolent Association's barbecue in June—Molosky enjoyed the barbecue the most. Perhaps it was the atmosphere of friendly informality. Or, maybe it was because only police personnel attended. No outsiders to play up to or dress up for. No strangers to lie to. Only brother and sister officers.

It was quarter to seven by the time Molosky pulled into the parking lot at Alpine Park and found a spot in the far corner from the entrance. He felt relaxed as he walked across the dirt lot to the wooden entrance gate. As he pushed through the gate, he could hear the low roar of several hundred voices rising from the picnic tables.

"Over here, Molosky," called Ken Fisher. "Got to check in before you can eat."

"Fisher, how's the ten-speed department these days?"

"Hey. It's busy busy, Ray. Over five hundred bikes taken last month."

Molosky let his eyes play over the large group, mostly men. "How many people are here?"

"About four hundred and some, I reckon," Fisher answered.

Molosky wandered through the crowd toward the barbecue pits, waving and greeting brother officers as he went. Bert Yarnell stood behind the barbecue grill dressed in a red and white checked apron.

Molosky greeted him. "You look tired, Bert. What's wrong?"

"I am tired, Ray. I've been cooking for three hours now. We had to get here early. You know, to set up everything. Charlie Garrett was supposed to relieve me for a spell; that was an hour ago. You seen him around?"

"Just got here a minute ago. I haven't seen him. I'll send him over if I do." Molosky gestured toward the steaks. "Give me one of those medium-well ones, will you?"

Yarnell looked over the twenty or so steaks cooking on the grill. Forking and flipping a half dozen of them, he finally decided on the proper one for Molosky. "Here you go, Ray. Best one on the grill. You oughta try the garlic bread. Baked most of it myself, and I don't mind braggin', it's the best."

"I'll take two, then. Where are the guys sittin'?"

"I think I saw Neal and Scotty with some of the other guys over on the right, toward the back some place."

"Come on back and sit a spell when you get a break," Molosky said, and started to walk away.

"Hey, Ray." Molosky turned around to look at Yarnell again. "Look at who just walked through the gate." Molosky peered toward the entrance and spotted Charlie Garrett. "I'll grab a plate and see you and the guys in a minute."

Molosky nodded and headed through the crowd to get a Coke. Beer didn't sound like a good idea yet. From there, he balanced his way back to where Yarnell had directed him.

"You boys mind if I sit down?" He stepped over the bench and nestled in among the policemen.

"Sure, Sarge, just sit any place," John Neal spoke up.

"Sure, go ahead, sit down, Ray," Scotty chorused. "We're not particular who we're seen with in public."

"Over here, Bert." Stinson waved Bert Yarnell over to the vacant space next to him. "Been saving this place for you for an hour. Where've you been?"

Yarnell placed a large glass of beer on the table, then sat down and squared his dinner plate in front of him. "Garrett. Hour and a half late. I swear he ain't been on time in ten years. Shows up and tells me to hurry back 'cause he's got a date."

"He's a fucking prick," Stinson jumped in.

"Yeah, a real asshole," John Neal agreed.

For the next half hour Molosky sat with the group of officers. He listened to their stories, chatted some, and laughed lightly. Yarnell was the first to leave. He had to get back to the barbecue pits and tend to his steaks and garlic bread.

After he left, the stories and jokes seemed to take a sharp turn down. Molosky felt very sensitive about hearing words like "fuck," and "fuck her," and "cunt," and "snatch." He remained pleasant and smiled at the end of each quip and short macho story, but over a period of time, he began to feel sick. He found it hard to reconcile the jokes and obscene language with the thoughts of Evelyn and what had happened to her.

Not wanting to be pleasant and smile anymore, Molosky sat expressionless until he had finished his Coke. Then he politely nodded, excused himself, and wandered away. For the next hour, he meandered from table to table, visiting and chatting and putting on a smile.

It was early, not quite eleven thirty, when Molosky spotted Bert Yarnell, who was still at work behind the grill. Most of the policemen and women had left by then, leaving only a few hangers-on knotted in small groups throughout the grounds. Molosky thought he would keep Bert company.

Yarnell was a big man, six feet five, square-shouldered, husky, with a leather-tan face. His hair was auburn, parted neatly. His cheekbones were spread wide. He wore a thick, bushy mustache curled at the ends. With a smile, his face was kind and gentle; without one, it was sturdy and compassionate. Molosky liked Bert Yarnell. He was a good and decent man.

"You going to stay here all night?" Molosky asked.

Yarnell looked up and smiled warmly. In the artificial light the lines across his brow appeared more pronounced. "What do you say, Ray?" He picked up two cartons of leftover rolls and carried them into a small room toward the back. "I'll be just a couple minutes more. I don't mind, really. I think everyone enjoyed themselves. Pretty good turnout this year."

"Not bad at all. One of these days we're going to have to change the location. If the Department keeps growing like it has."

Yarnell picked up another carton and started for the back. His voice was deep and clear. "It's the city, Ray. As long as people keep pouring in here we're going to grow. Been that way since I was a kid."

Molosky leaned against the side of the brick pit. He could still feel the warm air radiating off the charcoal. "Yeah. I just wish we could grow with more of the decent people instead of some of the weirdos we got running in the streets."

Yarnell hollered from the back. "I'm going to unplug the coffee. Want the last cup?"

Molosky nodded and Yarnell poured the coffee. "You're right about who's attracted to this place." He handed Molosky a full styrofoam cup. "But it's the same everywhere, except maybe in Nebraska or one of those midwestern states. People there still believe there's a difference between right and wrong. Good people. Nancy's cousin comes from there."

Yarnell walked back, closed the door, locked it with a padlock, then picked up a squeegee and started to wipe the counter near the sink. "I think all the weirdos and perverts migrate west to California, or east to New York. We sure got our share. No doubt about that. This place is like one big outpatient clinic."

When he had finished, he rinsed his hands and plucked

a hanging dish towel to dry them. "I've been meaning to ask you about The Hood. You got any leads on him?"

Molosky's expression became tense, more serious. He breathed deeply and emitted a long, sighing breath. Bert wouldn't know about Evelyn. Molosky's face became drawn, he fidgeted with the cup nervously. "Evelyn was one of his victims. She was attacked after she got off work."

Yarnell had known Evelyn for a long time. She was a good babysitter for his two small children. "Oh, my God!" His eyes opened wide, searching Molosky's face. "You're kidding." He swallowed hard. "Not Evelyn. No. Oh, my God!" He took two steps and stood in front of Molosky. Stretching his giant arms he gave Molosky a sorrowful bear hug. "I'm sorry, Ray. I didn't know. Holy God. Jesus Christ Almighty. Why Evelyn?"

The two men clung to each other for a long minute. Tears came to Yarnell's eyes. Molosky patted him on the back. "It's okay, Bert. Everything's going to be just fine. Phyllis has everything under control. I don't want you worrying yourself. She's going to be all right."

When the emotion had subsided, Yarnell released his grip and stepped back. "Anything me and Nancy can do..." His voice sounded more normal.

"Thanks, Bert. I'll let you know. Maybe later."

"We've got to do something about the guy. We just can't stand around and let him rampage in our area like this."

Molosky gulped the last of his coffee, crushed the styrofoam cup, and tossed it in a trash can. "I'm not sure what to do on this one. I've checked each case. So far there is no M.O. to speak of. The guy hits all over the district. Day and night. Doesn't seem to have a pattern. I just heard he struck a nine-year-old this afternoon. If that's true, it's the first time he's hit on a Saturday. I don't exactly know how to go about catching the guy."

Yarnell thought for a second. "What about a decoy operation? They've worked out pretty good in the past."

"I mentioned something like that to Harkness more than a week ago. Decoy operations work in small geographical areas. Maybe a square mile or so. That way, we could saturate a small area with a lot of manpower and chances of success are better. But, hell, District Five has almost twenty-five square miles. We don't have the resources to handle something that big. It would be pure luck to catch the guy in an operation that size. Spread ourselves too thin."

Yarnell shook his head. A disgusted look came over his face. "What good are the police anyway, if we can't do the job?"

Molosky tried to act confident, although he felt the same way. He patted him on the shoulder. "Easy, Bert. We'll catch him. Grab your jacket, will ya? I'm kind of tired tonight. Think I'll turn in early."

Yarnell took his Levi vest jacket from a hook on the wall. Both men started walking to the parking lot.

"I'll have another talk with Harkness. Maybe we can work something out. We'll see."

They stopped alongside Yarnell's car. Yarnell fumbled with the keys briefly, found the right one, and unlocked the door. He stopped and looked Molosky in the eye before stepping in. He drew in a deep breath. "Look, Ray, I'm glad you told me. I'll say a prayer that she'll be all right."

Molosky nodded. "Thanks, Bert. I didn't think of that. But that might be just what's needed."

Chapter Eleven

Tom and Julie Morrow left the airport in their rented Ford. The pavement shimmered in the heat.

Tom's thick glasses slid onto his nose as he turned right onto Airport Boulevard. "It sure is nice here. Not so much pollution. This might be the place to retire."

Julie snapped open her purse, took out a handkerchief, and wiped rivulets of perspiration from her brow. "I don't know if it's such a nice day. Does this thing have an air-conditioner?"

Tom fumbled with the switches. He flicked the fan on high and a stream of hot air shot through the vents.

"My God! What did you turn on? The heater? Turn it off! You want me to die of heat exhaustion?"

Tom reached and turned off the air conditioner.

"You know, you didn't have to come. This is strictly a business trip."

She smiled wryly. "Come on, dear. I'm not dumb. I know what goes on on your little business trips."

Tom let the car roll to a stop at Coleman Avenue. A

silver sedan swung in behind them. Tom checked for traffic and made a left turn.

"Sweetie, I have a lot of things on my mind. I don't need you nagging me about my business trips. Did you bring the map?"

Her expression changed to motherly concern. "I'm sorry. I'll try not to upset you. Did you take your medicine yet? Remember, the doctor said flying was hard on your heart. You should take another pill..."

He dug in his pants pocket, opened his pillbox. "Of course I remembered. Think I can't do anything myself?" He slipped the pill in his mouth and swallowed it dry, wishing he had a cold beer to wash it down.

She patted him on the shoulder, then took out a small piece of paper with directions printed on it. "Stay on Coleman till you get to Taylor Street, then make a right."

Tom looked for Taylor Street. "Bob sure is a good old boy. He didn't have to set us up like this."

"You've told me ten times. It was awful nice of Bob to let us use his place. How many times are you going to tell me? Boy, it sure is hot in this town."

Tom scratched his leg. "There's Taylor." He clicked on the turn signal and swung around the corner.

The silver car followed.

"There's the high school," Julie said. "We're supposed to pass the high school, then make another right one block down. There's supposed to be a redwood tree growing in the middle of the road. There it is."

Tom turned right. "The house is a white two-story with a blue tile roof."

"That's it, there," Julie said.

Tom glanced at the house and pulled the car to the curb. The silver car passed slowly, unnoticed. Tom shut off the engine and patted Julie on the leg. "Looks like an old fraternity house. Too bad we can't stay there."

Julie turned her eyes toward him. She seemed calm. She rested her hand on his. "The garage looks cute, though. Come on, let's go see."

They got out of the car and walked up the cement driveway to the converted garage. Tom carried their overnight bags.

"You have the key, dear?"

Tom jiggled in his pocket. "You bet I do. Right here." He unlocked the door, pushed it wide and waved her through.

She walked past the double bed to the back. "Oh, Tom, I like it. It's small, but look... it's got a little stove and a refrigerator."

Tom watched her and smiled warmly. He let the door shut. "I'm glad you like it. I kind of like it myself."

Julie walked over to the small bathroom. "And a tub and shower over here. I really like this."

There was a knock at the door.

"Get that, will you, honey?"

Tom was still smiling as he reached for the door. "Maybe it's Bob. He said he might be in town. That would be nice." He pulled the door open. His face shifted. Bewildered.

"Who is it, Tom?"

The man at the door stood erect. He wore a hood.

Tom was taken by surprise. *A prank*, he thought. *That's what it is. A prank.* "May I help you?" He grinned and hoped the man would take off the hood and smile back.

"Get out of my way, four-eyes."

Tom's face went flush. "What do you mean—"

He was unable to complete his sentence. The hooded man swung his fist. The blow was a direct smash to Tom's left eye. His glasses shattered into his face. He fell back to the bed. Trickles of blood began to flow down his cheek.

The hooded man moved quickly, stepped inside, and closed the door.

Julie stood motionless. What was going on? She tried to move, but her body was fixed in terror. Her eyes froze in a trance.

The man moved toward her. He shoved her against the wall. His eyes roamed over her. "One word out of you, cunt, and I'll break your face. You understand?"

Her eyes bulged wide, uncomprehending.

"Did you hear what I said, cunt? Not a word."

Julie nodded, her face taut in frightened helplessness. Her hands spread flat against the wall. Her breath was coming in short, spurting gusts.

The man moved back toward Tom. "Get off the bed," he commanded and struck Tom in the face again. The blow turned Tom's face sheet-white and nearly knocked him unconscious. The hooded man flung Tom off the bed onto the floor near the kitchen table. "Get off the floor, you fucking weakling. You can watch the show firsthand." He took hold of Tom by the shirt and lifted him into a kitchen chair.

"Please don't hurt him!" Julie pleaded. "He has a bad heart."

The hooded man grabbed at her face. Julie felt his cool leather glove on her cheeks. "I told you to shut up." He pushed her head into the wall and held it stiff for a second. Then slowly his grip loosened and his hand slipped down her neck. "I like that dress. It's colorful." His hand moved to her breasts and squeezed hard. Pain shot through her body. Her mouth locked tight. Her head braced against the wall. She did not cry out.

His hand latched onto the top of her dress, and with one powerful downward thrust, he tore it from her. He used the rags to tie Tom to the chair. "You better get the rest off before I get back, lady. Hubby here is becoming impatient to watch the show." With that he patted Tom on the cheek, then quickly turned on Julie.

Julie stood naked. Shame mixed with fear. She glanced over at Tom. He remained motionless, powerless. She felt helpless.

The stranger's hand rummaged her body. "Kneel down, cunt, and suck my cock."

The hooded man grabbed the back of her head and stabbed himself into her mouth. Julie nearly gagged. "You make a fine cocksucking cunt. Now get up. I said get up." He yanked at her hair until she stood in front of him again. "Fucking cunt. When I say move, you move. You understand?"

Cold, trembling shivers raced all over Julie's body. She nodded because she could not speak.

"Get over on the bed and kneel down."

The hooded stranger turned his eyes toward Tom, who had his eyes closed tightly. "Open your eyes. I'm going to fuck your old lady like a dog."

Tom opened his eyes into a wide, transfixed stare.

The hooded man climbed on the bed and jabbed himself into Julie from the rear. Julie tried to remain calm. She could not fight the man. She blanked out what was happening to her.

Tom's eyes remained rigid on the wall across the room. His heart pounded, then fluttered in uneven beats.

"Your wife ain't a bad piece." The hooded man untied Tom. "Let's see how you do."

He forced Tom to undress and get on the bed. "One thing about fucking, when I'm in the mood, it doesn't make any difference whose hole it is. You're as good as your old lady."

"He... hel... ppp..." Tom tried to speak but his voice faded. His face turned white. He gasped for air and rolled over on the bed. His eyes rolled up and he clutched at his chest.

"Oh, my God!" Julie ran to him. "It's his heart!"

The hooded man stepped back and zipped up his jeans. "I wish I could say I was sorry, cunt, but he missed a good fucking, that's all."

He slapped Julie hard enough to knock her off the bed, and left her sobbing on the floor.

Chapter Twelve

Molosky sat behind his desk. Once a week he did his paperwork. For him that was quite enough. From his IN basket he grabbed a clump of papers, slapped it atop the desk, and began sorting. He divided the papers into two stacks.

San Jose's answer to the ten-most-wanted list was a daily pink sheet called "CRIME." The pink paper kept all the policemen up-to-date on the comings and goings, the shootings and muggings, within the city. It also listed all locally wanted criminals, their descriptions and possible whereabouts.

Molosky put the pink sheet aside. He glanced over at the remaining papers, not really wanting to read them. First came the two-page general order commanding hash marks to be worn on the sleeves instead of the current stars. He floated this order into the basket which stood alongside the wall.

Molosky scanned several other sheets. They all found their way to the round file. The bottom paper was a typewritten note from Pete Maggenti of the Sex Assault Detail. It read:

> Dear Ray:
>
> I am using this contemporary form of communication because I have been overworked and underpaid, oversexed with cases, and underprivileged at home. If you know what I mean? This is to inform you that, in case you didn't know, there is a mad rape ape running all over your district, causing the women there great consternation, and placing upon my delicate shoulders the responsibility of catching him. Up here he's known as "the hooded prick," but you may refer to him simply as "the hood" if that be your pleasure. If you're not doing anything but riding around in your new police car these days, I would appreciate a little help in apprehending this perverted sex offender.
>
> Love and kisses,
> Pete

Molosky smiled whimsically. Suddenly the phone rang. "Field Operations, Molosky."

"Ray, Doug Sanders up here in Vice."

Doug Sanders: part-time drunk, overweight, divorced three times. An emotional disaster, but an excellent cop. The police department was his first and only love. Molosky had often wondered what made Sanders tick.

"Doug, what's going on? How's life been treating you?"

"Shit man, not bad...not bad at all. Been away from this joint for two solid months on vacation, I ain't married and the whores think I'm great. Got back a couple of days ago, been kind a banging it around with the guys and heard about the hooded creep that's been patrolling your area. Not good for the stats."

"You can say that again. Not good for a whole lot of reasons besides stats. You got any ideas on how to catch him?"

"Hell, no, not right now anyways," Sanders was quick to reply. "I got a get myself reoriented first. Haven't even had a chance to talk to my old buddy Harkness yet. Maybe a decoy plan. Now there's an idea...just popped into my head. Anybody thought of that one yet?"

"I've mentioned it to Frank a couple of times. He was cool about it, but said he'd look into it. A lot of man hours involved in something like that. I don't think he'd mind, but convincing the higher-ups could be a problem. Chief might buy it, never know."

Sanders only grunted, and Molosky could hear him strike a match. When he started up again, Molosky imagined him talking with a cigarette between his lips. "Well...I didn't have a big elaborate plan in mind like Frank would. He likes to overkill sometimes. Only need a company of men, not an entire army." Sanders coughed. "Listen, Ray, tell you what. You let me handle Harkness. Him and I go back a long way. It's a selling game, that's all. I know how to move through his mind. He wants to look good like everybody else around this damned place. I'll sell him on making himself look good. He'll buy."

"Think so?"

"Know so. I'll have my boys keep an eye out for the slimebag. Don't worry about Harkness. Catch you later."

Molosky clicked the receiver down and checked his watch. Almost late. He gathered up the pink sheets and made his way to roll call.

He slipped through the back door of the briefing room and found a place in the last row. Darrell Wells had not yet begun. By the time he started, Molosky was scanning the latest pink sheets, looking for wanted people who lived or stayed near his district.

> CANCELLATION: of 211 warrant on Dwight Alfonso Gomez. Picked up in District Five by Sheriff's Office Warrant Division.

Molosky concentrated on reading as Darrell Wells continued through the watch list. He looked for a recent description of The Hood and began to notice how many rapes there actually were. He had read through thousands of pink sheets and observed probably as many descriptions of rape suspects, but he had never thought much about them, except of course that they were criminals, deviates, or perverts who should be arrested. But he never realized the sheer quantity of rapes.

"Hey, Sarge, you got anything you want to tell the troops?"

Molosky looked up toward the lectern upon hearing this question bellowed by the officer next to him. Darrell Wells eyed him. Molosky shook his head and continued reading. As he flipped to the last loose-leaf pink sheet, he found the latest information printed about The Hood.

> STOP AND INTERVIEW—The Hood. For multiple forcible rapes and kidnappings; vehicle unknown at this time. Three victims state it was a light-colored or possibly a silver mid-sized car. Two victims saw no car. One victim described it as a silver, late-model Oldsmobile Cutlass, no further information.
>
> SUSPECT: White male adult, 6-1, 190, voice is said to be young, 23-28 yrs., wears black leather-type gloves. Always wears the hood as described in previous "CRIME"—white, appears to be sheepskin. Never uses a gun or knife-type weapon. Is said to be physically strong. Has struck eight times so far. No pattern. He hits day or night and so far only in District Five. This information being printed because the Sergeant working the case believes the silver Oldsmobile described by last victim to be accurate. Forward all interview cards to Sgt. Maggenti, Sex Assault Detail.

Molosky went back to his office after roll call to finish some more bits of paperwork, then got his car and went on patrol.

* * *

Molosky picked up the microphone to put himself in service. "Control, Sixty-five hundred, clear. How's the district look?"

"Sixty-five hundred, clear. District Five units all in service except for Fifty-one. He's on a two-sixty-one report at San Jose Hospital. Rape occurred about two-and-a-half hours ago in a garage apartment off Taylor."

"Ten-four, Control, any description on the suspect?"

"Suspect on two-sixty-one: white male adult, head covered with a white hood. Victim thinks she saw a possible vehicle as it left the area. Vehicle described as a silver, late-model sedan. Nothing further."

"Ten-four," Molosky said dryly and replaced the microphone. He grew silent for a long moment. Why always in *his* district?

Molosky parked in the emergency lot and walked toward the hospital entrance. The automatic sliding glass doors separated, allowing him to enter the outer section of the Emergency Room.

"In here, Ray." Yarnell waved from the X-ray office desk. He was talking on the phone. Molosky stepped through. "Sit down, Ray. How are you doing? I'll be with you in a moment."

Shortly, Yarnell hung up the phone. He scratched his head, then rubbed the back of his neck. "This is an ugly one. I just got the okay from Nancy to bring the victim home. She can spend the night at our house. She has a son. He's not home right now. Lives somewhere in San Francisco. I'll try him a little later. It'll probably be better if she stays with us, anyway. That way she can kind of get herself together." He let out a long breath through his mustache. His forehead wrinkled in distraught furrows.

"Her husband's up in I.C.U. Apparently the entire thing took place in front of him. I think he was about to be raped when his heart gave out. Doctors don't know if he'll make it or not. Ray, we've got to do something about this perverted bastard. We can't let him get away with this. This son-of-a-bitch is beginning to piss me off. If *I* catch him, I'll beat the bastard to a pulp."

Chapter Thirteen

"I'm sorry I'm late. I ran into some unexpected problems."

Colleen sat at the table and gave a pleasant smile. She wore a modest short-sleeved black cotton dress trimmed with red lace. "I was beginning to get worried. I ordered just a short time ago. I wanted to eat before we went. You did say nine, didn't you?"

"Yeah, Professor Evans said that his last class ended at nine. He wanted us to meet him in his classroom. Said it would give us a better picture of what he does and that sort of thing. We still have a little time."

The waiter approached the table. "Ray, you're running behind tonight. Several hours as a matter of fact. What happened? Crime on the increase again?"

Molosky grinned as he looked up at the waiter. "Webster. Colleen Brennan. Colleen, Webster, the best waiter in the city."

"Flattery and big tips will get you everywhere. Colleen, it's a pleasure to learn your name. Your dinner will be ready in just a minute. Can I get something for you tonight, Sergeant?"

"I don't think I'm going to have time to eat a hot meal. How about a small salad with Thousand Island and a cup of coffee?"

"Coming right up."

Colleen slid the white cloth napkin off the table and placed it on her lap. "How are Evelyn and the family?"

"They were all right, until tonight. Phyllis told me that Evelyn's boyfriend George called to say that he didn't want to see Evelyn anymore.... Doesn't feel right about her since the rape, or something like that."

"What did he say? Did he give any reasons?"

"Just that he didn't feel right about what happened, and that his feelings toward Evelyn had changed. He didn't have any good reason. Just feelings."

"Pardon me if I don't seem surprised. I didn't know Evelyn had a boyfriend. But... well, it fits."

"Yeah. I think I've heard of it before. But that was back when I was in high school. I thought times had changed."

"You're talking about the soiled rag theory. Evelyn's been soiled; therefore she should be cast aside."

Webster served them both.

"It just kind of shocked me, that's all. You always hear about it, but you never think it could happen in your family. I don't know. It just doesn't make any sense."

"I don't have any answers for it either. I only know that it happens. And it happens frequently. Probably goes back millions of years to our animal past." Molosky pondered that for a while.

"It makes you wonder, doesn't it? We've come so far, and yet we've hardly moved. You about ready? Sorry to rush you. But Evans... maybe he'll have some answers for us."

Room 505 was on the top story of the Engineering Building. Their steps echoed as they climbed the empty exterior staircase. When they stepped onto the second-floor platform, Molosky glanced over the railing and briefly surveyed the landscape below. Not a half a block away he spotted the figure of Marvin Ashwood lumbering across the street toward a well-lighted student restaurant. Before walking in, he cupped his hands around his face and pressed them against the window. Molosky shook his head. Seemed like Ashwood was always around, always had been, always would be: the eternal man of District Five.

Reaching the fifth floor, he pulled open the door and held it, allowing Colleen to enter first. They were a couple of minutes early so they slowly meandered down the empty hallway holding hands. As they strolled, they browsed the bulletin boards on each side of the hallway.

"A lot of job openings for civil engineers and architects. I wonder why he teaches in this building."

"Probably the only space available," Molosky answered without thinking.

Across from Room 505 they stopped and scanned another bulletin board. Molosky took only casual notice of the name and description of the class listed under the name Professor Hugo Evans: "Sociology 150—Social Engineering (Sexuality and Society)."

Colleen's expression was more concerned. "When I get the chance, I'll call one of the deans I know over at Santa Clara. See what she knows about this type of class. Maybe she's heard of Evans."

Suddenly, the classroom door opened with a slam. Noisy students poured from the room. Molosky and Colleen stood close to the opposite wall.

"Sergeant Molosky, I presume." The voice was clear and precise.

Molosky looked up.

"Please come in. Welcome. I'm Hugo Evans." He held out his hand politely. He was a tall, diplomatic-looking man. His brown hair was edged with gray at the temples. His face was thin and his jaw severe. He wore a neat, sober business suit. His eyes were penetrating, confident.

"This is Colleen Brennan, a friend of mine. I hope you don't mind..."

"Not at all. Come in, please."

Molosky walked into the now-vacant classroom, followed by Colleen.

"Let me start off by telling you that what I teach is an elective course only. The funds do not come from the university. The university only provides the space in which to conduct the lectures. Otherwise, there is no connection between us. It is a five-year project. We are in our second year. Funding comes from a federal grant."

Molosky seemed impressed. "Must be an important project, then, for the government to invest so much money."

Colleen listened, but did not add to the conversation.

"Well, I don't know about that," Evans said. His tone was casual, but his face was serious. "It's only two million dollars in five years. That's a drop in the bucket for Uncle Sam." He gestured for them to look toward the back of the classroom. "Let me show you what we do here."

Evans walked behind his desk, opened the center drawer, and started flicking switches. The back wall of the classroom separated in the middle and opened into a larger space which was dark. "Let me shed some light on our main arena," Evans quipped, turning on a few more control knobs.

When the lights came up, Molosky and Colleen didn't know exactly what they were seeing. It was a suite of smaller chambers contained within an extensive room which looked like a cross between a warehouse and a museum.

"Please. Follow me." Evans led them along the left side of the classroom. "Some people are shocked at what I teach," he said, "but that usually passes after the first class. Once they realize the truth about themselves and the world they live in, most people reach the same conclusion which I so grudgingly came to many years ago."

They entered the large room. Evans pointed to a magazine rack against the wall. Molosky's eyes narrowed as he recognized some of the magazines—*Penthouse, Playboy, Oui*—but there were dozens of different titles, all featuring color photographs of naked young men and women. Some of the covers depicted couples engaged in sexual acts.

Colleen showed no outward sign of her thoughts. Her eyes briefly scanned the covers of the magazines.

"The magazines serve as a form of stimulus—like an appetizer," Evans explained. "They also serve to point out that—"

Molosky blushed. His face showed a deep concern. His eyes shot to Evans.

Evans picked up a *Playboy,* leafed through it, then put it back. "Before I go any further, perhaps I should explain what the class is all about, so you won't be so apprehensive." He smiled reassuringly.

"What I teach are the theory and the elements of eroticism. We encourage cooperation, but, of course, we don't encourage practice in the classroom. The grant would hardly permit that." His eyes moved from Molosky and met Colleen's. "Perhaps I can sum it up for you in two words—reality and fantasy. That is essentially what it's all about. We attempt to take the run-of-the-mill average student, arouse his or her erotic imagination, then take those fantasies and transform them into reality." Molosky started to interrupt. Evans quickly raised a hand to silence him.

"It is for the betterment of the student as well as society. It helps them rid themselves of doubts and fears and insecurities. They become better able to function and compete in the outside world."

Molosky's questions were swept away and he didn't know what to say. Evans eyed him cautiously. "Let me explain further as I show you around. After we're finished here, we can talk." Evans walked ahead. "You see, the students are encouraged to browse through the magazines. This gives them the basic contents of what society preaches. It gives them a cosmetic picture certainly. A fantasy. But fantasies are part of the real world."

Evans gestured toward a small lecture hall area with cushioned seats. There was a large movie screen at the front. "This is our movie theatre. Most of the films we show are commercially made. Although we do get some special documentaries, and occasionally there is an educational film made." Evans flicked on the projector. The screen came alive with a couple vigorously engaged in intercourse.

He turned it off and turned toward the side wall. "Over here we have our informational charts. These serve as a ready reference and basically show enlarged diagrams of the human form." He stepped close to the charts and pointed. "Erogenous zones, reproductive organs, and over here several different sexual positions."

Molosky shook his head and chuckled softly. This wasn't for real. Must be some kind of joke.

Colleen's eyes were crystal clear and fixed directly on Evans.

Evans's voice remained steady, his posture erect. "When the students have completed their assignments at the magazine table, and have watched one or two films, then I start grading them. They are required from this point on to transform their fantasies into live objects. From this point on, the class becomes a workshop."

He led the couple across the room to a walnut-finished door marked Dressing Room. He opened the door and ushered them through. It was an expensively decorated room with lights and mirrors and makeup tables.

"We have a full-time seamstress, and she in turn has two assistants. She gets the movies two weeks in advance. Her job is essentially to prepare duplicates of the costumes the players wear in the films. It's quite an exacting art. The students are required to come in here and disguise themselves like their favorite character in the movie. Some of them are quite good at it. They completely transform their physical beings and become exact duplicates."

Molosky scratched the back of his neck. Was this all for real? "I don't understand. This doesn't make any sense."

Evans unbuttoned his coat, took a watch from his vest pocket, looked at it, and put it back. "Have you ever heard of idols, Sergeant? All people throughout recorded history have had their idols. Even in biblical times there were idols. It's the same in our time. All these kids have are sex idols. That is all they are offered. They have nothing else. So they want to comb their hair and dress and act like their sex idols. What's wrong with that? It's perfectly natural. I supply the makeup, the wigs, and the costumes. They read all the same magazines and watch the same movies, then they copy them. It takes imagination."

Evans smiled wolfishly and let his eyes stray to Colleen. "Couple of years ago, we couldn't get enough Farrah Fawcett wigs. All of a sudden, everybody wanted to look like Farrah Fawcett. People are sheep. I'm sorry to have to say that, but it's the truth."

Colleen did not respond, but held her gaze on him.

Evans lowered his eyes and slowly shook his head. Molosky wondered what he was thinking.

They stepped out of the room. The professor's voice remained steady though more sober. "In an effort to determine what sort of settings are most conducive to eroticism, the students are required to design different sets to fit their fantasies."

He led them around a broad circular path past three bedroom sets. "Under the conditions of the grant, we supply all the needed props and furniture—beds, haystacks, cars, phone booths, even quadraphonic sound systems. The students design a set that matches their erotic fantasy."

Suddenly, Molosky had the urge to leave. His mind felt tight and stretched at the same time. What did all this have to do with rape? What did it have to do with anything? He let his eyes wander over the room. This is not what America is all about. He looked at Colleen, hoping to get the same reaction from her. Colleen moved her eyes to him, gave him a quick solemn glance, then shifted back to Evans.

The professor continued. "In this room over here"—he gestured to a fancy, secluded area nearer the corner—"we will try a new experiment next fall to determine how to simulate the experience of sexual relations with a person of higher status than oneself. The experiment will be an ongoing one. Several people have agreed to be the status object and bring with them their status symbols."

Evans chuckled. "One man wanted to bring his Cadillac

El Dorado." He pointed at Molosky's uniform. "Your uniform would be a good status symbol."

Evans rubbed his chin thoughtfully, his expression turning more serious. "From my observation, modern men and women cannot accept themselves as mere human beings, with problems and sorrows and joys. Somehow they need to objectify their personalities and transform themselves into nonpersons in order to survive. I don't quite understand it all yet. Maybe this new experiment will help clarify things."

He paused briefly. "Have you seen enough?" He escorted them back into the smaller classroom and walked over to his desk. "I encourage questions, you know. Please sit down. The name of this particular class is Erotic Theory. I teach the fantasies of sex. I leave the sex education terminology to high school instructors. To me, sex is just that—sex. The more you can get out of it, the better off you are. I believe that everybody is entitled to the most energetic orgasms he or she is capable of."

Evans thought for a moment, then directed his words at Molosky. "You see, Sergeant, you have to understand the times. Our industrial society has grown and blossomed. We now need more conformity, more efficiency, and more productivity."

"Regimentation?" Molosky offered.

His comment was ignored. "The traditional family has been replaced by institutions. Men and women are trapped in and by these institutions. They realize this but can do nothing."

Molosky sat dumbly silent. He could only listen and hope that Evans was wrong. Colleen remained calm, her attention unwavering.

"So they simply admit defeat and turn to sex. Sex becomes an end instead of a beginning. A catchall, a form of mutual masturbation. Not an expression of warmth and tenderness, but merely an urge with no strings attached. It is one of the few areas where people are able to act with complete abandon. It is out-of-control pleasure. It becomes an end unto itself. You can see it in the way people dress, the way they move, all their little mannerisms. In what they buy. It's all they have left."

He leaned against the desk. "In this class, I try merely to keep the lid on. If I can keep people from being crippled by frustration and keep them from raping one another, then I figure I have succeeded."

Molosky squirmed in the chair. He wished he had never come here. He glanced at Colleen, but her strong eyes did not move.

Evans smiled patiently, as if he knew what was going through Molosky's mind. Then he turned to Colleen, and the smile on his face slowly withered.

Molosky could hardly control himself. The pent-up pressure poured out in laughter. Maybe he's right. Life is just one big fuck.

Gradually and with considerable effort he regained his composure. He wondered what Colleen was thinking. His face grew staid, his mood turned more serious, questioning. "May I ask just one thing, Professor?"

"By all means."

Molosky rubbed his forehead. "I understand what you teach here. Your students learn the art of sex and of all the sensual pleasures. You are a most interesting man, and your pupils probably study your subject with great devotion, granting many hours of their day and night to homework."

Molosky leaned forward, drew a breath. "But you do not teach love. I see your sex, your gadgets, and your fancy layout, but you have not mentioned a word about love. Isn't love included in your instruction?"

"I'm surprised at you, Sergeant Molosky," Evans answered quickly. "A man of your age. Of your experience. In your profession." He shook his head. "Have you not heard? Love is dead. It passed away long ago. Where have you been? These kids I teach, they have never asked that question. Not once. They may sing about it, and dance to its music, but they know in their souls that they are incapable of love."

"I feel I must interject here, before Mr. Evans leads us

astray." Colleen's voice was steady, the words were firmly planted within the sentence. "First of all, what you are saying is nothing new. It has become quite fashionable in the last several years to talk about the death of God or the death of love and so on. But even if you were correct, which I do not believe you are, you have carried your premise too far. The college kids I know are seeking meaningful, enduring relationships. Society offers them many temptations and distractions, but the spirit is not easily put aside. The kids today are seeking an honest and decent kind of love. I think you're misleading them."

Molosky's eyes stayed on Colleen for a second, then moved to Evans. The professor stood with his mouth half-opened, his eyes screwed up in concentration. "Well, I don't intend to belabor the point, because the project does not deal with love. That word is so vague. Out-of-date. The project deals with the mind. It deals with an art form...."

"You mean the mechanics of making love?" Colleen interrupted. "Well, you know people have been doing that for millions of years. What exactly are you trying to get at, Mr. Evans? It seems to me you are living on a one-way street. All pleasure, no responsibility. You are teaching an obsession."

Molosky regarded her with a curious eye. That was the second time she had called Evans "Mister."

"Who do you think I'm teaching here? They are the obsessed generation. They want pleasure. They are obsessed with having it and owning it. So I give it to them, as much as they can stand. And I measure the results, scientifically."

"What results?"

"Ahh..." Evans walked behind his desk and stood, feet planted firmly, shoulders back, in defiance that such a question should be asked. "The results are not all in yet. We are compiling them as we go. It will take several more years."

"Interesting way of not answering the question. Tell me, do your results measure the spirituality of sex or the responsibility for the other person's feelings?"

Evans appeared to be caught between indecision and anger. "The whole idea is to avoid responsibility," he blurted out. "That way no one gets hurt."

"Then it *is* a mechanics class, after all."

Evans looked at her with rigid, piercing eyes. When he moved his hand to his vest pocket again, the gesture was clearly more stilted than before. Out came the watch and he stared at it for several seconds.

"May I ask a question?" Molosky thought he would step into the conversation and attempt to cool it down.

When Evans moved his eyes off the watch, he shot Colleen a quick measured glance, then turned and smiled pleasantly at Molosky.

Molosky stared back with a discreet eye. "Perhaps you have misunderstood why we came here tonight. We came here to find out about rape and the victims of rape. What does all this have to do with rape?"

Evans's smile turned tolerant. "You don't understand, do you? Neither of you?" His eyes moved to Colleen, then back to Molosky. "Rape has everything to do with what I teach. Rape is part of our culture. It's what we stand for. We've elevated it and made it an institution. It's everywhere. It's been with us since time began. It is the social crime which every man has committed throughout time."

"It's a personal crime," Colleen interjected.

Evans pretended not to hear. "Name one person you know who hasn't been, quote, fucked over, unquote, by somebody at one time or another.

"You can't do it. Neither can I. That's because it's such a common thing. The boss fucking over the employee, the retailer fucking over the customer, man fucking over woman. It's all part of our society, of the whole of human experience. People take being fucked over, or whatever word you want to use, as a natural part of life."

Evans stayed with Molosky for a while, then slowly let his gaze move to Colleen. "Please excuse the vulgar language. However, I find it quiet accurate when speaking of a subject such as this."

Colleen nodded abruptly and was about to say something when Molosky put his finger to his lips, asking her to wait for a minute. Molosky studied Evans's expression before he spoke. The man looked older than his years. He appeared to be wearing a hairpiece. "Everyone knows that man has got this power problem. You're not telling us something new. It's just your solution. How the hell is this going to stop anything? You're taking an already powerful instinct and making it an obsession. An obsession, but without meaning. Without responsibility.

"It seems, to me anyway, that you're creating a whole new set of problems. You teach the one side of man and leave out the other." Molosky glanced at Colleen. "What about the caring part? Or the spiritual part? You can't just treat human beings like animals. There's more in them than that."

Evans sat down behind the desk and folded his arms in front of him. His expression turned uncertain, his eyes more distant than before. He took a deep breath and blew it out slowly. "Let me try, one more time, and see if I might make you understand." His voice was more strained now. "Rape is man's power play over woman. We all know that. The dominant male raping the weaker female. On that we all can agree.

"However, what you fail to understand is that that is how we define our natural condition." His words were spaced and enunciated clearly. "That is how the game is played. It has been passed down to us over millions of years. It has become the natural order of things. Can you understand that? Man fucks over his fellow man every day. Why not rape a woman? It's all part of the same thing.

"I teach fun and games here, because that's all that's left." Evans shrugged his shoulders. There was a look of self-disgust on his face. His eyelids drooped; the lines around his mouth seemed more pronounced.

Colleen turned toward Molosky and spoke softly but very distinctly, so that her words carried to the front of the room. "What do you think, Ray? Should we recommend this for Evelyn? So that she'll turn out to be a better, more sensitive, more compassionate person?"

Molosky studied her with humor in his eyes. He loved her wit. He smiled wryly and looked to the front of the class. "Sorry, Evans. But she's right. You're just producing animals here. Furthermore, I think you know that. Through all your intellectual bullshit, you know it. You know exactly what you're doing. The great American con game."

Chapter Fourteen

The radio had clicked on and the announcer had gone through a dozen or more weather reports before Molosky finally woke up. He had been in a heavy, sound sleep and it took him several minutes of rubbing his eyes and scratching his head before he was able to focus his mind. He wondered where Noah was. Sitting up, he yawned again, looked around the room, and spotted the cat stretching his front legs on the rug near the door. "Well, good morning, Sport."

Molosky showered, shaved, and dressed in casual clothes. On his way out the back door he checked for his wallet and car keys and drove to Colleen's for a real live date. Colleen needed a new car and he had promised to help her look for one.

Ernie Klosterman's dealership was a theatrical showcase for expensive American-made cars. It was an all-glass structure; its unseen steel support beams were dressed over—in the showroom by heavy ornate paneling, and in the back room by painted Sheetrock. The second-story office area was divided into two sections. Half was used by the secretaries, salesmen, and promotion people, and the other half was Klosterman's pretentiously decorated business office.

Klosterman's flamboyant advertising was what drew people to his showroom. He believed in going that extra mile when it came to catching the eye of the buying public. On one occasion he gave a new car away to a skid row alcoholic. He had his portable TV cameras follow him as he drove around the downtown Rescue Mission looking for the perfect beneficiary. When he found him, Klosterman and a buxom blond model presented the poor unfortunate with the keys to the car. Klosterman smiled humbly and gave a tearful speech about how lucky he had been in his life and how he wanted to share his prosperity with those less fortunate. That advertisement ran for the entire month of December. It catapulted Klosterman into the public eye, made him an overnight controversy and thus locally famous.

Molosky didn't like Klosterman. He didn't like his style, and he thought that his ethics were manipulated to fit the occasion.

"You know, I don't understand why we're going to that joint," Molosky said to Colleen.

Colleen sat in the passenger's seat and eyed the traffic. "I wouldn't go there either, but they've got the best prices in town and I need a car, a good used one. If I can save a couple of hundred dollars, it'll be worth it."

Molosky scratched the back of his neck and turned onto Stevens Creek Boulevard. All of a sudden, traffic slowed to a near standstill. "Well, we'll see. What's going on here? I'm glad they're open late tonight." Molosky slowly became irritated, first at the thought of buying a car from Klosterman and then at the slow traffic. "You know, maybe this is some kind of sign that we should go somewhere else."

"You can't get out of it now. We're too close. There's a spot in that driveway. Can we park there?"

"Probably not supposed to." Molosky swung the car into

the space and turned off the engine. "But who cares? It beats driving in that traffic. We can walk faster than that."

They got out and strolled along the sidewalk toward the dealership. From a distance, Molosky eyed the new car showroom and could make out what appeared to be flashing neon lights and exploding fireworks. Faintly, he could hear what sounded like a marching band.

"Sounds like a party," Colleen said.

Molosky grinned sarcastically. "If Klosterman is having a party, you'd better hold on to your wallet."

As they approached the showroom, they could see that a small crowd had gathered around a brightly lighted area. The music blared. Slowly, they worked their way around the back of the crowd to a place where they could see. Six cars stood in front of the glass-encased showroom. They were brand-new, spotlessly clean, brightly polished, ice-blue Cadillacs. Molosky didn't know what to make of it. There were six nearly nude young women dancing on top of the cars.

Molosky made a quick decision to get out of there. He took Colleen by the arm. "Colleen, let's go some place else."

As they turned around to leave, they bumped into the enormous girth of Ernie Klosterman. Suddenly the music stopped and there was instant silence. The lights went out, the band stopped playing, the crowd hushed.

"Ahh, Molosky, San Jose's finest. Long time no see. You're not on duty tonight. But I recognized you anyway. Saw you and your girl friend pull up over there. Hope our little show didn't offend your lady friend." Klosterman's long, hairy eyebrows fluttered up and down; his lips curled into a dirty smile.

Klosterman wore a dark brown suit, orange tie. His fleshy face was creamy white, his lips thick and raspberry colored. On his head he wore a red hairpiece which fell forward from time to time and had to be brushed back. He puffed on an enormous green cigar.

"I'm glad you stopped by tonight. We're having our gala celebration. The new models. As a matter of fact we're filming our new advertisement inside. Come on in. I'll get you some champagne."

Molosky eyed him with suspicion, then he turned his gaze to Colleen. "Well, what do you think?"

Colleen hesitated, studying Molosky's face. "Might as well. We've come this far."

"Now there's a sensible decision. Come. Follow me." With that, Klosterman raised his right arm in the air and snapped his fingers. The bright lights came on, and the music and dancing started up again.

They followed the huge man through the glass doors into the sleek building. There was a crowd inside, people milling about the new cars, drinks in hand, chatting lightly. Molosky scanned the big room as he walked across the carpeted floor toward the opposite end of the building. Everything seemed to sparkle—the showroom, the people, the cars, the polished wooden walls.

"We'll take the elevator to the second floor. Our promotion people have set up a small studio. They're filming now. I'll show you how it's done."

The elevator door opened and they were quickly lifted from the showroom. At the second floor, a young man in a gold blazer stood ready to greet them. "Good evening, Mr. Klosterman," he said, bowing courteously.

"Are they still filming?" Klosterman asked.

"Yes, sir."

"This way." Klosterman motioned to them with his cigar and marched toward the door marked Promotion Studio. Once inside, he gestured with his finger to his lips for them not to talk. He slid along the back wall followed by Molosky, then Colleen.

"We hired a downtown prostitute to film this commercial," Klosterman whispered in Molosky's ear. "She's a part-time model. Hustles her ass when jobs are scarce, which has been most of the time. We've been training her for two weeks. This is only her second time in front of the camera. She's not bad. A little dumb, but she's got what it takes. Listen."

Molosky held Colleen's hand as he watched. There were

cables and cameras and bright lights. The set seemed to be crowded with people, probably technicians and set designers, Molosky imagined. His eyes strained. He thought he recognized the model. It was Candy, the prostitute who had walked his district for years. He shook his head in disbelief. She looked different. The makeup, the hair, the dress. She walked around a polished black Trans-Am.

"Okay!" said a short man with a lean face. He got up from the chair marked Director. "Let's try again. Makeup, why don't we give her one last touch-up?" He walked over to Candy. She appeared nervous, her movements tight and restless. He put his arm around her. "Listen, Candy, you've come a long way in just a couple of weeks. You've got the body. You've got the gestures. We'll dub in the music and the voice later. All you have to do is what you do every day. Now, let's go through it once more. If you remember what we're trying to do here, it will be easy.

"Step one. We'll start with you lying on the hood. I want a lot of sensuous lip movements. Pretend like you're downtown...coming on to a man."

He moved to the middle of the car. "Step two. I want you to slide off gracefully and walk over to the door. Keep your head aimed toward that camera over there." He pointed to the camera in the back. "Lean on the door and move your hips around, then stick your butt out." He demonstrated the move.

"Step three. Open the door and slide in behind the wheel. Remember, show a lot of leg—all the way up, right. That's it. Then caress the steering wheel...that's it. Good. I like those lip movements. Now take hold of the gear shift and maybe move your hand up and down, like...good action. I like it.

"Now, one last thing before we shoot." The director stood in front of Candy and held her shoulders. "I know you're a little nervous. I think that's good. All the other good actresses I know are nervous when they stand in front of the camera. It's perfectly normal. So relax, you'll do just fine." He gave her a warm, fatherly smile. "Remember, acting is just pretending. If you can, I want you to think of this as a classroom. Pretend that you are the teacher and you're teaching something very important to the men. They don't have much in their lives, but together you and I can give them something. You give them sex. You teach them that they really are bold and daring. You teach them, and while they're learning, we'll sell them this car."

He lifted his hands from her and gave her another paternal smile. "I know you can do it, teacher. We'll try one more take, then we can all have a break. How do you feel? Good? Great!"

Candy nodded shyly.

"How did you like it, Molosky?" Klosterman stared at Molosky, then fluttered his eyebrows when he glanced at Colleen. "You did say your name was Colleen, didn't you? Follow me to my office. We can talk there if you like."

As they walked passed the elevator, Colleen suddenly stopped and tugged on Molosky's arm. "I don't know. Maybe you were right. We shouldn't have come here. All I wanted to do was look at cars. We can go, if you like."

Molosky reassured her with the touch of his hand. Before he could say anything to her, Klosterman had stopped and turned around. "I can't stop you from leaving. I didn't know you came here tonight to buy a car. I thought . . . well. I wish you wouldn't be mad or upset with me. You know, I'm basically an honest man. I couldn't have gotten this far if I weren't. You know, I have a certain reputation to live up to. I sell good-quality cars and I sell them at the lowest prices in town. That I can tell you is the plain truth."

Molosky could see right through Klosterman's honesty line. "Listen, fatman, your talk is cheap just like the rest of this tinsel town of yours. The lady said that she wanted to leave, and that's just what she's going to do. If you don't mind?" The elevator door opened, and he ushered Colleen inside.

The door closed without Molosky saying another word.

During the short ride down he contained his feelings of outrage by holding tightly to Colleen's hand.

When the elevator doors parted on the first floor, they were treated to a visual panorama of beautiful people. The gala celebration was now in full swing. The band had moved inside and was playing American marching music. The partygoers talked easily and moved with charming gracefulness. The women were in sleeveless dresses and painted faces; the men, in smart suits and an occasional tuxedo. The champagne flowed briskly.

As they headed for the door, Molosky noticed a familiar looking man talking with one of the dancers on the far side of the showroom. He reached back in his memory to visualize who or where he had seen the man, and remembered that he was the real estate guy he'd met behind the office building the day after Evelyn's rape.

"Who's that?" Colleen asked, noticing Molosky's expression.

"Oh, his name is Owen Sheldon. A local real estate salesman I met a little while back, that's all."

Chapter Fifteen

The party lasted till shortly after midnight. When the music had stopped and the partygoers had drifted off, Klosterman threw his own private party for himself and a few of his chosen employees. Candy was invited for sex.

And she gave willingly. She enjoyed giving pleasure to men. She uncovered for them, danced and teased and excited them. When it was time, she let them come to her. She let them play and fondle and caress. When they exploded, she took great pride.

It was nearly three o'clock when the private party broke up, leaving Candy and the general manager the last people in the building.

"I'm glad you came tonight, sweetie. You showed us a real good time. You can sure put out," the manager said as he rode down in the elevator with her.

"That's what I get paid for. I'm glad somebody appreciates it."

The elevator door opened onto the first floor. They walked across the showroom to the door on the opposite side. "You don't have to take me all the way. I'll be fine. I'm a big girl now."

The manager pushed open the door for her. "That's fine with me. I'll see you tomorrow. You guys are shooting again, aren't you?"

"Yeah, but it will be at night. See ya."

Candy marched in long, quick steps along the cement path close to the building, then out onto a wide asphalt area which led to the parking lot at the side of the building. The night air had cooled considerably, and there was a light foggy mist which hung several feet off the pavement.

When she reached the end of the wide area, she followed a dotted white line which skirted the edge of the parking lot. The lot was dimly lighted by the night lights from the showroom and a tall street lamp which stood a hundred feet away at the driveway entrance.

As she approached her car, she fluffed her hair back, then opened her purse and fished for the car keys. Her body felt tired. She needed a hot bath, then maybe some breakfast and twelve hours' sleep. Finding the key, she slipped it into the door and tripped the locking mechanism, swung the door open wide, and sat sideways on the front seat. She thought that she should buy more comfortable shoes. High heels weren't cushy enough for dancing. But...the men liked them. She slipped off her shoes and tossed them into the back, squared herself in the driver's seat, and closed the door. She wondered if someday she would have enough money to get rid of her smaller car and move up to one of Klosterman's flashy big ones.

Her purse was full of twenty-dollar bills, and it was her habit to hide her earnings before she started the car. Pulling her wallet out from her purse, she took out the cash and placed it in a plain brown bag. She then pressed the bag flat and tossed it on the floor near her feet. *Who would ever think of looking in a dirty old bag?* she thought.

Before starting the car she fluffed her hair again, then reached to turn the key. As her hand touched the coldness of the key, her eye caught the glimmer of a light coming from across the parking lot. She twisted her head to see what it was.

A set of headlights glared at her. She wondered who it was; maybe one of the men going home, but then she remembered she was the last guest to leave.

Suddenly the lights raced out from their position and sped across the parking lot toward the side of her car. Holy shit! It's going to ram me. At the last possible second, the strange car swerved to miss her. It skidded to a halt directly behind her.

Who was it? What was going on? Candy jerked her head around and peered out the back window. At first she couldn't make out who it was. Then the door of the strange car opened and she caught the silhouette of a hood as someone stepped from the car.

Candy went rigid for a moment then gasped for air and turned almost completely around in the seat. The man quickly stalked toward her door. Her eyes, unblinking, froze on him. A lightning bolt of panic shot through her. Her stomach tensed into a painful ball of muscle. Her teeth clamped, locking her jaws tightly.

A torrent of thoughts and images flooded her system. Klosterman's fat prick. The man with the large hands. Rape. The man wanted to rape her...wanted to subdue her and humiliate her. Not again. Not ever again. She would die first.

Her thoughts vanished for a split second, and she managed to suppress her fears long enough to click the door lock. She gaped at the white hood as the man neared the window. He grabbed at the outside door handle, but it would not move. He pulled and tugged at the door, but it held. Candy could feel the violence in the man even through the car door. The car began to rock from side to side.

"You'd better open the door, cunt." His voice was strong, only slightly muffled from the inside of the white hood. The man pulled and yanked at the door for several seconds. Finally he lowered his face and let the hood come within inches of the window. Candy could feel his eyes attach themselves to her body, then lock onto hers.

She went rigid again. Her mind desperately wanted her limbs to move, but she was frozen.

The hooded man stood erect and started wildly pounding on the roof and kicking savagely at the door.

Suddenly, Candy's muscles released her. She felt her hand move. The seizure had passed. But what could she do? She was trapped. How could she get away? She looked around desperately for someone to help her. First to the flashy showroom, but it was empty; then toward the light at the driveway. A police cruiser slowly drove down the street and disappeared from sight.

Her hand moved to the ignition, grabbed the keys, and turned. The engine was cold, and it groaned and sputtered as it tried to turn over. "Please start," she sobbed, pumping the throttle.

She kept her head tilted up, her eyes locked on the white hood. Suddenly, he stepped back, turned, and kicked violently at the side window with the heel of his boot. The window shattered. The heel of his boot came through and punched Candy's face. Small fragments of glass were pushed into her cheeks and cut her eyes.

"I told you to open this fucking door." He reached through the shattered window and grabbed her by the throat.

Candy knew what was going to happen, but she would not submit to it willingly. She would not let it be done to her without a fight. Her face was bloody, and she could feel the bits of glass in her eye, but she would not give up. She clutched at the man's hand gripping her throat. Grabbing his wrist, she twisted her body and tried to pull him off balance. The strong arm tensed, then violently jerked back. But her clutching hands held onto the muscular arm.

The powerful left arm of the hooded man flexed again. This time his arm whipped free, but his glove was stripped away. He stood up erect and stared at his white, naked left hand as if puzzled.

Candy did not stop her frantic movements. She scrambled across the seat and reached for the passenger door. Her hands fumbled with the door latch, then moved to the unlocking mechanism and popped it up. She pushed at the door and it started to give way. Her body was weak from fright. She had to push it with her shoulder to get it to swing out. She could feel the dampness hanging in the air as she held her bloodied eye and fell to the pavement, hoping against hope that someone would see her. The police car couldn't be more than a couple of blocks away. *Maybe he will return and see me. Please, someone help me,* she thought, and slowly struggled and managed to stand up. She had to gather enough strength to run for the light at the end of the driveway.

Suddenly she felt a pulverizing pain in her stomach. Her body lifted off the ground and buckled against the side of the small sedan.

"You shouldn't have done that, cunt." The man's voice rasped. "I'm gonna have to do more than just fuck you now."

The toe of his boot came at her like a hammer, first crushing her right breast, then cracking her ribs. She gurgled in her throat and fell to her knees, her mind fading, tears and blood rolling down her cheeks.

"Now that's better. That's how I like 'em." He grabbed her head and pulled it to his groin. "To top this little session off, I'm going to fuck you over good. And you're not only going to submit, you're going to like it. Understand, cunt?"

Candy remained motionless on her knees, her head bent down, her spirit broken. She would do anything to make the man go away.

The hooded man stepped to the side, then grabbed her under the arm, lifted her off her knees, and pushed her back against the car.

"Take off your clothes, cunt."

She sobbed and leaned against the car. Her body was numb from pain. She couldn't move.

"Did you hear what I said, cunt?" The hooded man moved close and grabbed her chin and snapped her head up. "Did you hear me, cunt? Take off your clothes and do it now!"

His eyes were glistening with violence. They fixed on her like large gripping stones.

Candy tried to move her hands, tried to will them to the top of her dress, anything to keep him from hurting her more. But her arms wouldn't budge. They only hung lifeless at her sides.

"Fucking cunt!" he roared. He grabbed her dress and ripped it from her, then yanked off her pantyhose and panties and threw her to the pavement.

Candy tried unsuccessfully to blank out what was happening to her. She remembered the first time. She was sixteen. Under the bleachers. Three animals had raped her. Horrible memories she thought she had long forgotten.

The man fingered and grabbed at her. He pinched her breasts hard—so hard that blood spurted out from one. She groaned in agony and tried to erase from her mind what was happening to her. She hated men. Hated them for what they did to her.

When he was through, the hooded man stood and stepped back.

Candy could not move. Her body lay limp. Her head moved back and forth with intermittent, convulsive groans.

"Will you shut the fuck up, slut!" The man raised his boot and kicked her in the face. The heel of the boot broke her jaw.

Chapter Sixteen

Dotted throughout the police building—on doors, on bulletin boards, and on the watch commander's desk—were drawings of the hooded rapist. The talk was everywhere. It ranged from petty jokes to serious concern. But Molosky hated all of it.

His spirit was sorely in need of uplifting. He had been frustrated by the hooded rapist for too long. Something had to be done to catch him. Inwardly, he craved a stimulant or at the very least some type of professional support to grasp on to. Something, anything which would let him know that other people were on his side, that the justice system he had served so well would not let him down. Molosky needed the strength which only action could bring. His spirit had been bogged down for too long, and it required an attempt be made, a positive series of steps taken to catch the hooded man. He had been down—down on society, down on himself for too long.

After roll call, when the other officers had left the room, Molosky sat and leafed through several pink sheets, not really paying attention to them. He wished he could take a long vacation. Santa Barbara was nice this time of year. From the corner of the room he heard the door open, but he didn't bother to look up.

"Hey, Ray. Let's go. The captain wants us."

Molosky glanced up. It was Doug Sanders. He looked as if he had lost some weight. What did Harkness want?

"Come on, will ya? We got a big meeting with the chief. We're all invited. Come on, starts in a couple."

Molosky eased out from behind the long row desk and walked toward the door. He felt the first signs of relief. He knew a top-level decision had been made. He studied Sanders's face for confirmation. "The force finally going out after that bastard, huh? Did you talk to Harkness?"

"I can't confirm anything yet. Harkness might know. I've been working on him all week. My guess is the mayor's daughter got it. But what the hell do I know?"

The two men marched down the hall toward the elevator. Molosky could see Frank Harkness walk out from his office to the elevator and push the red button on the wall. As they approached, he nodded first to Sanders, then to Molosky.

"Gentlemen."

The elevator door opened and they boarded.

"Sorry I couldn't give you guys more notice. I just got the word a short time ago myself." He shifted his glance to Sanders. "Remember all our little discussions?"

"Sure, Frank. Got a rough draft of what we finally decided on right here." Sanders opened a manila envelope he had tucked under his arm. He seemed a little nervous.

Harkness continued. "We'll go with that plan. It's more concise than the one I orginally had in mind, but we'll stick with it. At least for now. Manpower is really critical. Can't afford to drain the whole city."

The elevator door opened and they exited and walked toward the chief's office at the far end of the corridor. As they entered the outer area, Harkness spoke to Molosky. "Well, Ray, this is what you've been badgering me about. I think we're going to get down to some old-fashioned police work and put that pervert where he belongs."

"I'm ready, Frank. Best words I've heard in a long time."

The secretary led them into the inner office. The chief greeted them and had them sit in one of the straight-backed chairs placed in a circle in the middle of the room. Molosky took his place and let his eyes follow the chief as he walked back to the door. Pete Maggenti appeared with his briefcase and was duly escorted to the circle.

Molosky wondered why the chief was so spartan with his furnishings. His office had plain walls, white and clean. His desk stood diagonally in the corner near a long rectangular window. It was an ordinary-sized business desk and uncluttered.

Maggenti took his seat and that left one empty. The chief walked slowly around the outside of the circle, hands down by his sides, holding the room in silence. He was a tall, angular man. His face was large and rugged-looking, his hair a salty gray. He wore a white shirt and a dark blue business suit.

When he had completed the circle, he stopped and stood behind his chair. His deep-set eyes slowly made their way around the circle, stopping and acknowledging each man individually. Molosky sat directly across from where he stood. When the chief's glance focused on him, his eyes seemed to show a certain compassion. Molosky wondered if he knew about Evelyn.

"Gentlemen, I'm glad you could all make it. I hope my accommodations are adequate." His voice was soft, his words precise. He gently patted the back of the chair in front of him. "I prefer to spend the taxpayers' money on manpower and equipment rather than on expensive sofas that rarely get used." He smiled wryly.

The men sitting in the circle acknowledged this, nodding and returning the smile. Molosky liked the chief. He used to be an outstanding street cop. And as he worked his way up, he had never lost his feel for the ordinary officer.

"I wish I had some good news for you this afternoon, but I don't. If the man were sitting in a jail cell in San Quentin, that would be good news. But he's not. And that's what we're all here about today. We're going to see if we can put him there." He paused and took his place in the empty chair.

"We'll start with you, Pete. Why don't you give us a brief rundown on the progress of the investigation?"

Maggenti showed his college education poise. He slid his dark-framed glasses out from his inside jacket pocket and placed them on squarely. Reaching down, he flicked open his briefcase and withdrew a thick manila envelope, opened it, and placed it on his lap in front of him. He stared at it briefly, then lifted his head toward the chief. "To date there have been eighteen rapes, and one other attempted. The suspect thus far has left no physical evidence which would lead to his apprehension. We have the glove, but it's a common type brand, sold at most department stores."

Maggenti paused and flipped through his papers. "I have nothing further that you don't already know."

The chief nodded. "And the attempted? Do you have anything on that yet?"

"Not yet, Chief. I know that the victim was the mayor's personal secretary. It happened just a few hours ago, just after lunch. The victim was delivering a package for Her Honor, downtown. Apparently, the attack was foiled by a passerby. Don't have much more than that. The reports aren't in yet."

Molosky looked at Sanders with confirming eyes. Sanders was almost right. It wasn't the mayor's daughter who was attacked, just her secretary. He nodded to Sanders. Pretty good guess, he thought. Politicians. They sure move fast when it's one of their own.

"Molosky, you've been following this case rather closely, I suspect. Do you have anything to add?" The chief spoke with a quiet patience born of long experience in matters such as these.

Molosky let his eyes move from man to man, then settle on the chief. "The man hits at random, but so far only in my area. I think he lives somewhere in the district, or used to live there. Or he works or used to work there.

"Further"—he shifted in his seat—"he uses his car a lot. He doesn't run from the scene too far before he finds his vehicle. He always drives away. That could he helpful. That it's always nearby.

"One other thing Pete forgot to mention. He's trying to get a list of all the people who were at that party at Klosterman's. Our man could have been at the party." He moved his eyes to Maggenti.

"Good point." Maggenti acknowledged Molosky and turned to the chief. "It was one of those 'open to the public' affairs. We've been in contact with Klosterman's people. They're cooperating, but it'll take time. Got a lot of names to check out."

The chief nodded and turned to Harkness. "Frank, you think this pervert can be stopped? I rely on you, you know."

Harkness sat straight, hands on top of his gunbelt. "And I rely on the troopers. I think if we're diligent enough and luck is on our side, we can." He turned his head and smiled at Sanders. "Sergeant Sanders and I have been over several different plans for a large-scale decoy operation. Our main problem, as you well know, is the square miles we'd have to cover. We're not going to be able to saturate the district. We don't have the manpower. However, we've come up with a plan which is practical and can be implemented in its entirety within twenty-four hours."

He gestured for Sanders to present the plan.

Sanders returned the look with a long questioning glare. Molosky could tell that Sanders was nervous about talking in front of the group, especially the chief. Sanders leaned down and put his elbow on his knee, then sat back, straight. He wiped his chin with his palm. Before talking, he coughed in his fist to clear his throat.

"Well, ahhh..." He stammered and cleared his throat again, then drew a deep breath. "It breaks down like this. The best we can come up with is five teams; four members to each team, that includes the decoy. We can draw eight officers from my unit. The rest will have to come from Field Operations and Administration. Narco might be able to lend us two, maybe three. We'll need one more sergeant to handle the relief team." He coughed again and crossed his legs. His words seemed to flow more easily the more he talked.

"I've lined up several leased vehicles for the operation. Franklin over at the garage has been a big help on that. He said he'd have them serviced and ready to go as soon as he could. We can count on him for tomorrow."

When Sanders stopped talking, the chief acknowledged him with his eyes, then turned to Harkness. "Sounds like you guys have done your homework. What do you think, Frank? You gonna need more manpower?"

Harkness remained steady. "You know me, Chief. I'd like to put an army out there and do the job in style. It's a good plan, though. We're a little thin, especially on the west side. It's a standard enough operation. It's solid. Just a little thin, that's all. But I'll put my stamp on it. We can make it work. I've been in contact with the other watch commanders. They can give us the manpower as soon as we have the okay."

The chief sat silently for a long thoughtful moment. Then he stood and made his way to the back of his chair. "Then we have a go. Frank, keep an eye on this one for me. Let me know if you need more people."

Harkness acknowledged him with a curt nod. Molosky swelled with emotion. Finally the good guys were going to strike back.

Chapter Seventeen

It was warm that evening, the temperature hovering in the low eighties. A thick, foul cloud of smog settled around the foothills to the east and turned the sky a brassy orange color. However, the sun's rays managed to pierce through and the heat seemed to be everywhere. Molosky felt good. He knew that with Harkness in command the decoy operation would succeed and the hooded monster would soon be behind bars.

After loading the shotgun and checking his police cruiser, he slowly accelerated out of the west side parking lot onto Mission Street and placed himself in service.

"Control, Sixty-five hundred, ten-eight," the operator said, "be advised your district is clear of calls, all units are ten-eight on the board. Slow night."

"Ten-four," Molosky answered.

Four uneventful hours later Molosky found himself driving toward the Hyatt House. "Control, Sixty-five hundred, clear code-seven?" he said, requesting a break to eat.

"Sixty-five hundred clear," the operator said.

"I'll be at the Hyatt House." He swung the patrol car to the front of the coffee shop. Entering through the motel lobby, he could hear music coming from the cocktail lounge.

"Would you like a table?" asked the blond hostess in the fluffy white sweater.

"No, thanks," Molosky said. "I'll sit at the counter. Where is everyone tonight?"

"The dinner crowd hit early," she said. "You should have seen this place an hour ago. It was packed."

Molosky took a seat at the brown formica-top counter. He eyed Colleen. Her hair swished and gleamed as she glided across the floor.

"Excuse me, waitress," he said gruffly, "I'd like a little service here, if you don't mind?"

She turned around, startled, frowning at first, but when she saw who it was, a simple smile lighted up her face. Her pale blue eyes sparkled as she looked at him. "Ray!" she said, walking toward him. "Well, I'll be. I was just thinking of you."

Molosky liked the way she smiled at him, with happy eyes. It made him feel warm and good. As he returned her smile he could feel a certain tension beginning to grow inside him. "I've missed you. It's only been a week, but still, I've missed you."

"That's nice to hear. I kind of feel the same way."

Molosky leaned on the counter so he could be closer to her. "You know, I was thinking." He looked at his watch. "I was thinking of a party. Kind of a celebration. You know, just you and me."

She gently took hold of his arm and turned it so that she could see the dial on his watch. "My relief gets here in about an hour."

"I'll try to get off by then, if you're game."

"A celebration, huh!" She tilted her head down and let her eyes tease. "And a party to boot."

"Sounds like fun, don't it?" A shy grin showed on Molosky's face.

"I think I'd enjoy that." Her eyes sparkled, her smile brightened.

"Give me the keys to your place. I'll pick up the champagne, and some chips or something, and meet you there."

Quickly, she walked away and disappeared behind a door which led to the kitchen area. She returned momentarily and handed him her house key. "I'd never do this for anyone else. I want you to know that."

Molosky began to backpedal. "Need to keep the champagne cold. Didn't mean to be overly aggressive. I'll just put the bottles in the refrigerator and wait outside."

"You just stash the champagne in the fridge, and don't be late. Hate to be kept waiting outside my own place."

Getting several hours off was no problem for Molosky. That night the city had two extra sergeants who could cover for him. Molosky made a quick stop for the party necessities and drove straight to Colleen's. Opening the locked front door, he felt along the inside wall for the light switch. He flicked it up, and the lamp in the living room came on.

The room was a soothing harmony of contrasts. The chocolate-brown rug contrasted with the curtains and a brightly colorful oil painting of a bridge at sunset. Above a beige sofa hung three small landscape paintings, framed in walnut. The gentle natural scenes brought life to the blandness of the white-painted Sheetrock. A red ribbon hung from a pale green lampshade.

Molosky pushed the door shut with his elbow and stepped into the kitchen, which was directly adjacent to the living room. He put Colleen's house key on top of the wooden serving counter, then took the two bottles of champagne out of their bag and laid them in the refrigerator. He opened several of the cabinets before he found the wineglasses, took two of them down from the top shelf, and then grabbed two cereal bowls, one for a bag of almonds and the other for cheese crackers.

"Anybody home?" he heard Colleen say.

"Nope," he said. "Just the local police, lady."

Molosky stepped from behind the kitchen counter and gave her a warm smile. Walking up to her, he put his arm around her slender waist. He felt a tinge of excitement being close to her. "Just getting ready for our private party." His voice was soft.

Colleen snuggled into his arms and pressed herself against him. Reaching up, she let her arms gently flow around him. She hugged him, first letting her cheek brush up against his chest, then letting her eyes drift to his.

He held her tight and when he spoke, he whispered. "Did I ever tell you how beautiful you are? You know I like you very much." He bent his head close to hers and kissed her waiting lips.

Colleen responded, holding him close.

The warmth of their long embrace aroused them. When they parted, Colleen caressed his face with her fingertips and whispered softly, "I'm glad you came tonight." She let her hand turn over and brush lightly against his cheek. "You look tired."

Molosky moved his hand and gently stroked her soft hair. "I am. It's been a bad summer so far."

"Ah, my poor boy." Her voice was louder; a bright, playful smile spread across her lips. "Why don't you pour us a glass?" She pulled away. "I'll change into something more comfortable and be right back."

Molosky grinned as he followed her with his eyes until she left his sight. "I've got two bottles of the best," he said. "Got some cheese crackers for you and a big bag of almonds for me. But I'll share them." He walked back behind the counter, took a bottle from the refrigerator, and poured two glasses. Then, holding the glasses, he balanced his way back into the living room.

"Why, thank you," she said, stepping alongside him and taking the glass from his hand. "You are a very kind person. Do you like my dashing party dress?" She spun around, holding up the glass of pink champagne. Her evening party gown was a light blue, floor-length velour bathrobe.

"You look beautiful, Colleen," he said. "Here's to you, in your gorgeous blue gown."

She smiled and stepped close. "And here's to you. A man—a beautiful, sensitive man."

They kissed lightly, clicked their glasses and toasted.

"Let's sit on the sofa." Her voice was quiet, subdued.

Molosky sat next to her and put his arm around her shoulder. "Did I ever tell you that I'm sort of an old-fashioned guy? I mean, I've been around and all that. But deep down inside, I'm just your basic old-fashioned kind of guy." He reached and set his glass down on the coffee table in front of them. Then he gingerly lifted hers and set it down.

"Come here and let me hold you." He wrapped his arms around her.

Colleen responded, holding him tightly.

"Colleen," Molosky whispered, "I love you. I can't hold it back any longer. I've loved you for a long time."

There was a long, tense silence. Colleen squeezed him harder. "Oh, God, that feels good to hear." She clutched him tightly and held him for a long moment, then tilted her head toward him. "I love you too. You like to keep a girl waiting, don't you?"

Molosky smiled with an intense emotional glow. His heart pumped wildly, and he felt a strong surge of sexual excitement. He brushed his lips against her forehead, then kissed her more strongly on the cheek. When their lips met again, it was a hungry, desirous, passionate kiss. Their tension was electric. They wanted each other. They wanted to confirm their love.

When their bodies met, it was with an uncontrollable fervor. The power of sex combined with their love for each other was an intensely emotional experience. Their bodies craved each other. When they joined together, they surrendered themselves. They became one, and in giving up became complete.

Chapter Eighteen

The sound of a garbage truck haltingly moving down the street woke Molosky first. Colleen lay warmly next to him. In the first seconds of being awake, a nervous twinge ran through him. He wasn't sure where he was. Rolling his head to the side, he smiled serenely as he let his eyes touch her still-sleeping face. Then he lifted his head and softly kissed her cheek. She purred peacefully and Molosky could see only the hint of her radiant smile.

Presently, he slipped out of bed and got dressed. Holding his shoes, he tiptoed into the kitchen and finished dressing. He had to search the cabinets for the coffee, and when he found it he had to settle for instant. But he didn't mind. He found the kettle, filled it, and put it on a burner. He was searching for a knob to turn on the stove when he heard Colleen's voice.

"It's the one on the far left."

Molosky eyed her, then continued his search for the knob. "This one?" He tilted his head toward her.

She nodded her approval. "Is there enough water for me?"

He yawned, putting his fist to his mouth to cover it. "Yeah, filled it. Probably take a couple of minutes before it boils."

Colleen's yawn was more timid than his. "I think I'll fix a pot of tea." She walked up to him and slid her arm around him. "I'm glad you stayed."

"Come here." He leaned toward her and kissed her softly. "I'm glad that I love you. It makes me feel warm and good. I'm glad I stayed." He pressed himself against her and held her for a moment, then lightly kissed her on the tip of the nose.

She stayed close to him briefly, then pulled away, opened a cabinet over the counter, and took out an all-white porcelain teapot with a chipped spout. "You have to work tonight?"

Molosky watched her as she guided her hand to a small red apothecary jar where the tea was stored. He scratched his chin and could feel the bristles. "Tonight we start working twelve-hour shifts. Fact is, it starts midday. We're going to run a decoy operation to catch the rapist. I might not see you for a while, but I'll call." He reached into a drawer to the side of the sink and withdrew a spoon. "Need one?" Colleen nodded. He handed it to her and took out another one and placed it in his empty cup, then leaned against the refrigerator. "What I really need is a vacation. A long one."

"You can say that again. You need one. Do you some good." She let her eyes come to him. "You know, I've never told you this before, but I've never pictured you as a cop. You're too nice a guy. I don't know how you stand it sometimes. You're too mellow."

Molosky's lips compressed into a weak smile. "I wonder about that occasionally myself. But I've been doing it a long time. Somebody has to do it." He paused briefly, lifted the teapot, and absently inspected the chipped spout. "Couple of days on the coast would be nice. You have any time off coming?"

"Not really. But I could manage a few days."

Molosky puckered his lips as he thought. "I'll see what

I can do after this operation. I think I can swing it. Santa Barbara would be nice."

"You know I grew up there. Lived there till I was nine. Near the old mission. We'll have to make a visit there."

When the water was boiling, Molosky lifted the kettle and filled the teapot first, then poured hot water into his cup. "I'll check on reservations."

She gestured for him to sit at the kitchen table. "You look so tired, Ray, like you haven't slept for a month. You need to get away."

Molosky slid into the kitchen chair, stretched, and then clasped his hands behind his head. He sucked in a long, deep breath. "Had a dream the other night. Scared the hell out of me. Maybe you're right... maybe I should try some other occupation."

"See? Now you're dreaming about your job. And it's scaring you." She shook her head. "You're too nice a guy."

"Yeah, well, maybe."

"I'm sorry. Didn't mean to sound like I was scolding. I shouldn't have said that. It's just that I get scared for you. That's all. Tell me about it. I want to know."

Molosky sat for a moment, thinking. "That's quite all right. I need a scolding every now and then. Keeps me in line." He stirred, then took a sip of the hot coffee. He gritted his teeth and screwed up his cheeks. "Hot, man, melt your tonsils." He mused softly. "Anyway, back to the dream. Ever tell you that being a cop is sometimes like being a garbage man? It's the truth. The dream proves it.

"It was a weird one. There were these two buildings. Skyscrapers. They were gigantic, hundred stories high and blocks long. Two of them across the street from each other, and me on the street between them." He let his hands form imaginary buildings, then moved them back to the table and the warm cup. His voice turned more serious. "In one of the buildings there were people. All kinds. Whites and blacks, fat and sloppy, tall and skinny. They were strange people, somehow. Wide-eyed and pale-looking. Kind of void of expression... blank faces. They were all there, you know, just living, I guess. I couldn't make out what they were doing. Their gestures got twisted somehow every time I tried to focus in on them."

Molosky felt relaxed; his words flowed easily. He lifted the cup and took another sip. "That's better." He licked his lips. "The building had its own magic. It glittered. You know, colored lights all over it and whatnot, clear to the tip. It was really something. Anyway, I'm standing down there and looking up at the building." He gestured with both hands stretched out in front of him. "And suddenly I see that the building isn't made of regular cement or anything like that. It's put together with television sets, radios, Coke bottles, automobiles, stereos, and all that junk we use.

"Then the people inside start taking this stuff and playing with it and using it up. But the building just creates more stuff. It's like magic." He sat back in the chair and cracked a thin smile. His eyes remained fixed on the cup in front of him. "Incredible, isn't it?"

Colleen leaned against the wall, then lifted her feet and set them on the chair next to her. With her right hand she picked up the pot and casually poured herself some tea. "Sounds weird all right. There's more, I hope. You're not going to leave me hanging. What did you do, walk in the building and join in?" She smiled wisely.

"I wish I could have, but I was stuck outside. I was in my uniform, working. As these people were consuming all the items and the building was creating even more for them, a pile of rubbish started to stack up at my feet. I look at the pile and see that it's *people* garbage, rejects from the building. And I guess I'm supposed to do something with them. So I start dragging them across the street to where the other building is."

There was a slight tension in Molosky's voice as he continued. "But I can't keep up. You know, the people are piling up too fast. So I work faster, as fast as I can. But still the stack gets bigger.

"And the other building. It's made out of thick concrete. Tall and ugly and cold. It starts to fill up. The magic building has created too many rejects.

"Then, suddenly, I hear laughter and I turn to see what it is. Everyone in the pile is standing up. I look around and everyone in both buildings is looking down at me, laughing. But this time their faces are covered with white hoods. I stand there in the middle of the street, afraid to move. It was like everyone had turned on me. Then the laughter got so loud I had to hold my ears."

Molosky blinked to switch his concentration. He looked at Colleen and smiled boyishly. "When I have 'em, I have 'em good. Noah helped wake me up, and I guess that was the end. Your everyday classical dream."

"Yeah, everyone likes to dream he's in a madhouse now and then. Makes him feel at home."

Molosky put his hands to his breast and let his fingers tap his chest lightly. "Home sweet home. The land of television sets and the world of Oz. Great stuff." He gave a half-hearted chuckle. "I guess."

He let his hand play slowly under his chin as he concentrated more seriously. "But it really isn't so funny when you get right down to it. Society's problems are no joke, people are too aggressive. It scares me sometimes. Worst part about the dream was when I turned around and everybody was wearing those white hoods. Scary! Reminded me of the rapist that's been haunting my district. Bastard."

Colleen expelled a long breath and rested her head against the wall. Silence fell for a moment. "The taming of man. It's incredible. You think it can be done?"

Molosky studied her. He really did love her. She was so sensitive and compassionate. "I don't think so. Not from what I've seen. Too much manipulation and mind-turning going on. People are taking in too much of what the world has to offer. Sacrificing themselves to material things."

"I don't know." He leaned his elbows on the table. "Listen to me talk, as if I had all the answers. It just seems like power is the only game in town. Everybody's kind of forced to play, or they end up raped."

Colleen put her cup down and reached across the table. "I can tell you've been reading *Siddhartha*. Powerful, huh?"

Molosky ran his fingers up the back of her hand, then

gently lifted it. "Good book." He kissed her hand and smiled toward her. "Let's change the subject."

Colleen felt his mood. She wanted to be with him again. She smiled lovingly. "Why don't we go back in the bedroom? I want to be close to you some more."

Chapter Nineteen

When Molosky got home from Colleen's he quickly shaved and made two phone calls. One was to his mechanic, Hal Belcher, to confirm his appointment to have his car tuned up, and the other to Doug Sanders to pick him up at the garage. When he talked to Sanders, he got the feeling that he was interrupting something. Sanders played it down and said that he'd pick him up.

Molosky watched an ice-cream truck back into the alley at the end of the street as he waited outside the small garage. He was dressed in blue Levi's and tennis shoes, and carried his short-barrelled revolver in a shoulder holster underneath his light blue cotton shirt.

From the opposite direction a dark green '66 Volkswagen with no muffler approached and pulled to the curb. "Hey, Ray! Jump in."

Molosky eyed the driver, smiled, and reached for the door. "Right on time. I appreciate the lift." He slid in and closed the door.

"I'm lucky I made it. The woman I was with is the

possessive kind. Could hardly get away. She thought I had another date or something. Screw her, she's becoming a pain in my ass. Gonna tell her to take a hike one of these days."

Molosky chuckled smoothly and watched Sanders as he reached in his shirt pocket and dug out a long nonfiltered cigarette. "You didn't marry her, did you?"

Sanders stuck the cigarette in his mouth and turned left at the next intersection. "Hell, no. Got a light, man?"

"Sorry, don't smoke."

"Wouldn't marry a dame like that. A good lay, but I don't even like her most of the time, much less love her. Been married too many times. Man, that's a losin' proposition. Sure you ain't got a match?"

"Positive."

"Goddamn, there has to be a match in this fuckin' car someplace." He bent down and with his right hand felt along the floorboard. "Ah, here we go." He snatched up an old, torn matchbook cover with one match left in it, managed a light, then tossed it out of the window.

Molosky studied his outward appearance as he wondered what had filled Sanders with so much anxiety. He was a short man, round looking, built like a bulldog. His blond hair lay limp across the top of his head, covering up a large, oval bald spot. A thin, light-colored mustache wrapped itself around his otherwise red face. He had on dark sunglasses, big and square. His shirt was long-sleeved and colored champagne pink. A pattern of tiny yellow roses ran up the sleeve, around the collar, and back down the other sleeve. He wore a frost-grey vest, green army pants, and his shoes were basic lavender with a hint of brown in the lace.

"I see you dressed for the occasion. Everybody in Vice dress so conservative?"

"I thought you'd never notice. Nice threads, huh? Picked 'em out when I was drunk last night. Stashed 'em in a pile in the corner so I'd have 'em for today. Had trouble finding the shoes when I got up. Found 'em in the kitchen cupboard. Don't remember how they got there. But what the hell! Who cares? Got 'em on, don't I? You got any aspirin?"

"Headache?"

"You know something, Molosky?" He cleared his throat and pulled on the tip of his nose. "I've always admired guys like you. Straightforward, clean-cut types. Sober, honest, and reliable bastards, all of you. No offense, 'cause I really do admire you.

"But as for me, I just accept myself for what I am: a lowly flatfoot who drinks too much, fucks too much, and eats too much. Sure you ain't got an aspirin?"

Molosky smiled in amazement. The man was full of surprises. Right in the middle of a headache, Sanders lets out that he admired him. "Got some in my locker, if you want to swing around the back."

"That's okay. Got a bottle or two in my desk. I'll grab some when we get there. You all ready for the big operation?"

"Yeah, I'm ready. We gonna have enough troops?"

"That I can't tell you. Harkness was going to handle that. My boys will be ready. As for the rest, I'm sure Frank got what we need. We should probably meet with him first thing. See what's cookin'."

The police parking lot was full, so Sanders swung across the driveway into the public lot. He made a sharp right turn and placed the car in a slot marked Handicapped Only. "I figure if you're a cop, you're handicapped. You ready, partner?"

As Molosky approached the opened door to the watch commander's office, he observed Captain Harkness at his desk. He was writing something on a yellow pad of paper.

Harkness looked up at him. "I'll be with you in a second."

Molosky sat down in front of the desk and waited. Presently, Sanders approached the door and was about to knock. Molosky quickly put his finger to his lips and silenced him. He gestured for him to come in and sit. Sanders tiptoed into the office and took a chair.

When Harkness was finished writing, he looked up at both men. "Well, you guys look like you're ready to go."

Molosky remained steady in his chair. Sanders twisted in his, then crossed his legs.

"I've been working on this manpower situation. I think we've got it pretty well ironed out, thank God. When the word got out, we had a lot of volunteers. Got the schedule worked out for today. We'll all meet in room one-oh-six." He paused to check his watch. "In twenty minutes."

Harkness kept his eyes moving to each man. Molosky could see that there was a certain strain in his face. His eyes seemed more rigid than usual, his jaw more solemn. He lifted the yellow pad of paper, carefully tore off the first page, and handed it to Sanders. "Why don't you handle the first roll call? Teams One and Two are yours. Ray, you have the other two. All good officers, no probationers. You guys decided where you're gonna place your teams?"

Sanders looked at Molosky and nodded for him to go first.

Molosky's eyes were calm. Inside he felt a tinge of excitement that the operation was finally getting under way. However, he tempered his mood for the time being and spoke in a strong, confident manner. "I want my teams to operate in two tight-knit but separate units. One of the teams will work the two shopping centers on the west side—Valley Fair and Town & Country Village. The other can work a straight shot down San Carlos between Bascom and Lincoln.

"It's a big area. Eight officers sounds like a lot, but actually it boils down to the two decoys. When the rapist strikes, he'll have to hit one of our targets. The odds are slim."

Sanders leaned forward in his seat. "You ain't tellin' us nothin' new, Ray. Jimmy the Greek wouldn't touch an operation like this. But, I got confidence. I got a way of attracting weirdos. We'll catch the son-of-a-bitch. Matter of fact, I'm willin' to bet on it."

Molosky remained unmoved, his face expressionless. When he spoke it was in a cool and steady tone. "Fifty bucks says my team sees him first. A hundred says we catch him."

Sanders pursed his lips in hesitation. "Not bad, Molosky. Fast thinking. Okay, you got it. You're on. Captain, you want in?"

Harkness tried to remain serious and businesslike, but Molosky sensed that his professional demeanor was fast crumbling. He smiled wickedly. "You guys are too much, you know that? No thanks, I'll pass. As long as somebody gets him, I'll be happy."

"Doug, you want to tell us where you're going to place your teams?"

Sanders went on to outline to them the downtown areas where his teams were to patrol. Several minutes later, after all the equipment details had been discussed, the three men adjourned their brief meeting and walked to Room 106. Sanders called the roll and Captain Harkness gave a short pep talk.

Shortly before three, Molosky left the police building and walked toward the reserve parking lot behind the garage. The yellow cab he had been assigned was parked by itself in the corner of the fenced-in area. It was a '75 Plymouth. He walked up to it and briefly inspected the car with a disgusted eye. Slipping in behind the wheel, his eyes scanned the dashboard. Over ninety-five thousand miles, he saw. He hoped it could still run. When he started it, a puff of black smoke belched out the back end and the engine coughed and sputtered. He had to try several times before it would stay running. Once it was warm, Molosky tested it by putting his foot to the accelerator. It seemed to run smoothly enough.

The car had no air conditioning, so he rolled the window down and let his arm bake. He took Highway 17 to Stevens Creek Boulevard, then made his way through the boulevard traffic and turned right on Redwood Avenue. He slowed and eyed the bus stop where Evelyn had been attacked, then made a quick right and drove into the north side parking lot. He steered into a place directly behind the bus stop. There he stopped the car and turned off the ignition.

As he sat watching the people waiting for the bus and the cars stopping and starting in traffic, he thought back to the time when he was fourteen years old. He had often thought that fourteen was the best year in his life.

"Excuse me, are you free to take a fare?"

Molosky's thoughts were broken. *What fare? Who me? I'm a policeman.* He stared out of the window blankly. A middle-aged woman with glasses was bending down and peering at him. "Sorry, ma'am. I'm supposed to pick up a party across the street in five minutes. Don't have time."

The lady looked at him with a questioning eye. "Well, all right then. I'll take the bus." She stood up indignantly and marched away.

Caught me off guard, lady, Molosky thought. *Sorry about that.* Won't happen again. He sat for a few more minutes, browsed the people, then glanced at the business building across the street. The Platinum Realty sign stood out from the others. Owen Sheldon came to his thoughts.

He started the cab again and was about to pull away when he spotted Sheldon pulling out of the driveway across the street in a newer model silver Oldsmobile. He had a passenger in the front seat with him, a woman. The car rolled up close to the street and stopped abruptly. Molosky could see the woman's expression more clearly now. Her face seemed strained and her jaw moved with a rapid, tense motion. She appeared to be yelling at Sheldon.

Sheldon sat behind the wheel with a rigid glare in his eyes. His face appeared angry and frustrated. When he found a space in traffic, he pulled out with a squeal.

Quickly, Molosky put the car in gear and steered out into the street to follow. He was more curious than anything else. He wanted to see how the salesman, Owen Sheldon, handled his own personal life.

Molosky could not get directly behind him and had to settle for one car back. As the silver car approached the stop sign at Stevens Creek Boulevard, Molosky positioned himself so he could see through the back window of Sheldon's car. The woman was still yelling. Her head moved back and forth in fast, angry jerks.

Suddenly, Sheldon's hand moved and struck the woman on the face. The woman reacted by clasping her cheek. Quickly, the silver car sped away from the stop sign, making a right turn and temporarily disappearing from Molosky's sight.

Molosky swung the cab close to the curb and whipped around the corner, but the silver car had vanished in the traffic. He accelerated as fast as he could, but was hampered by the slower cars. His eyes darted from lane to lane, but there was no silver car to be seen.

Molosky slammed the steering wheel in frustration. "Damn, they've got to be around here somewhere." He kept his eyes moving, his head twisting from side to side. Suddenly, he spotted a silver car parked at an odd angle to the side of a gas station. The passenger door flew open and the woman bounded out. With an angry gesture, she slammed the door shut and started toward the sidewalk, where Molosky was just pulling in to park.

Molosky kept his eye on her for a moment. She was pretty: tall and slender with long, flowing dark hair. She appeared to be all right, angry but unharmed. He shifted his glance to Sheldon's car. It backed up, then pulled away, rolling behind the back of the station and disappearing.

The woman walked in short, quick steps. She walked straight toward him and stopped on the sidewalk directly at his side. Molosky reached across the seat and rolled down the window.

"Need a ride, lady?"

The woman glared at him for a second, then twisted her head in several anxious movements, as if she were looking for something but didn't know what. Without saying a word, she turned and started to walk away. Then, just as suddenly, she hesitated and marched back to the yellow cab, swung the door open, and slid in.

"Where to, ma'am?"

She slammed the door, folded her arms in front of her, and remained angrily silent.

Molosky had never worked undercover before. His thoughts touched on Doug Sanders. He'd know how to act. Being a cabby would be easy for him. Molosky studied the woman momentarily, then decided to give it his best shot.

"Listen, lady. I ain't got all day. You want to go somewhere or don't you?"

The woman sat sternly, head tilted slightly down, eyes fixed in a glare. Molosky wondered if she heard him.

Suddenly, her eyes snapped around and locked onto his. "Anywhere. Take me anywhere. Just drive. I'll tell you when to stop."

Molosky nodded and pulled away from the curb. Reaching down to the seat, he toyed with the portable radio and shut it off. He drove west on Stevens Creek Boulevard. As he passed Ernie Klosterman's dealership, he remembered seeing Sheldon at the party. Molosky could not recall the face of the dancer that he was with.

He drove for several miles without saying a word. The woman remained motionless, eyes steady, fixed in space. When he got to the Lawrence Expressway, Molosky made a left and steered into the exit lane to enter the on-ramp for Highway 280.

"I would appreciate not driving on the highway, not tonight anyway." The woman's voice sounded much calmer, her words came out in low, smooth tones, not so abrupt.

Molosky maneuvered the cab to avoid the highway entrance. "Listen, ma'am, I saw you back there fighting with that guy. I stopped because I figured I could help. I'm glad you're okay. You are all right, aren't you?"

Her silence continued. Before she spoke, she turned her head and looked at Molosky. "You mean, you saw what happened back there?"

Molosky nodded. "Yeah. It was kind of an accident. I just happened to be behind you, that's all."

"The age of chivalry hasn't passed by the twentieth century, after all. You were going to help, huh?"

"Well, I don't know about that." Molosky hesitated while he played dumb. "You and your husband having a little spat, eh?"

"Shit!" The word came out clear and punctuated. "You've got to be kidding. Married to that man? Not on your life."

Molosky found himself stuck for an answer and quickly pretended to be preoccupied with traffic. When he spoke, his words came out in the form of a question. "Where were you going? Some place special?"

The woman let out a quick breath. "Can we knock off the chatter? Head over toward Saratoga Avenue."

Chapter Twenty

Molosky had dinner at Original Joe's. Leafing through the evening paper, he glanced at several uninteresting articles before giving up and turning to the sports section. The Giants were on another losing streak—nine in a row. When he was through with the paper, he passed up his second cup of coffee and asked Webster to bring him three cups to go.

After paying his check, he found his way back to the cab. Gingerly he set the cups down on the passenger side, started the engine, and steered for Valley Fair shopping center. Using the portable radio, he called Bert Yarnell.

"Bert? You on the air?" He waited for several seconds.

"Yeah, we're here. You coming out?"

"Where are you?"

"Quigley's in the pickup in front of Macy's. Scotty and Hillman just entered the store from the north side. I'm in a van, in the parking lot."

"Ten-four. I'll see you in a couple."

On his way out to see Bert, Molosky met with the other team leader, Samuel Rodriguez. Since everything had been quiet, he told Rodriguez that his team could take an hour off to eat. When they were through, Yarnell and his men would get a break.

From there he drove to the shopping center and delivered the first cup of coffee to Stan Quigley. He chatted with him for a while before driving around to the back and parking next to Bert Yarnell.

Sliding out of the cab, he handed a cup to Bert, kept the other for himself, and climbed into the van. "You got the guy in custody yet?" Molosky peeled off the lid and took a sip.

"Not yet." Yarnell played with his mustache, then checked his watch. "But it'll be dark soon. Can you wait till then?" He smiled sarcastically.

"If you insist."

Yarnell sipped and swallowed hard. On the radio Virginia Hillman's voice could be heard as she talked to a salesman from inside the store. I've been running this air conditioner for hours, it seems like. We're lucky it's still working. The only break it gets is like now, when I'm sitting for a long time. Otherwise it's running to beat hell. How's that fancy cab of yours?"

"I could have a second income driving that thing around. Everybody wants a ride. Already got hooked into one ride. Got twenty bucks for it. I'll give it to the Rescue Mission."

"That's a good place for it. I like to give them coffee. Those guys always need coffee. Get it wholesale from my brother-in-law."

"Bert, you there?" It was Scotty's voice on the radio. "She's about done in here. You coming around?"

"Yeah, I'll move up. Stan, did you catch that?"

"Got it, Bert. Across the street and into the parking lot."

Yarnell looked at Molosky. "You want to ride with me for a while? See how the operation's run?"

"Why not?"

"Scotty, any action in there?" Yarnell asked as he started the van and swung into the exit lane which ran around the back of the parking lot. Yarnell took his time, driving slowly and carefully. Traffic in the lot was beginning to thin out.

"Nothing to speak of. Couple of looks. One guy followed her for a while. Didn't make any moves against her. I think it was store security. Other than that we drew a blank. But what the heck, it ain't even dark yet. The weirdos haven't come out."

Yarnell let the idling engine carry the van into a parking slot on the east side of the building. "From here we can see Virginia no matter which way she comes out. If she uses the mall exit, we'll pick her up right over there." Yarnell gestured with his huge right arm. Molosky followed his direction. "Or if she uses the main door, we got that covered too. There she is now."

Virginia Hillman was a volunteer officer taken from Narcotics Division, where she had worked undercover for the past three years. She was a tall woman in her early thirties. She wore simple, unprovocative clothing—tennis shoes, denim pants, a gray, loose-fitting blouse. Over her arm hung a brown leather purse. She walked slowly across the parking lot to the sidewalk where she turned right and ambled west.

"Stan is over at Town & Country now. He's got himself a spot on the far west side where he can see for a mile.

"Here comes Scotty now. He's been real good at following her. Usually stays about fifty yards behind her." Yarnell chuckled softly. "One time she sat down at the bus stop and caught him off guard. Poor guy. There was no place for him to hide.

"He walked on by her. I picked him up down the way, and we kept an eye on her from the bank parking lot. It worked out fine. Scotty would make a good undercover cop. Vice maybe."

Molosky smiled. "I thought he was already into vice."

"Yeah, but he ain't getting paid for it." Yarnell pushed on the accelerator and the van responded. He steered it up to the street and made a right turn. "She'll cross at the lights up ahead and probably meander through the shops in Town & Country. We snacked around five, but she said she would like a break around now. Maybe she'll go into the restaurant over there and sit for a spell."

"Hey, Bert. I think we got a live one." Scotty's words came in a quick burst.

Yarnell jerked the van to the curb and stopped. Scotty was a short distance ahead of them on the sidewalk.

"See the guy in the brown Mustang in front of me? The guy just coming out of the lot? That's the second time I've seen him. He's been eyeing her pretty close. We'd better watch him." Scotty quickened his pace to close the gap between him and Virginia, who was just starting to cross at the light.

She heard Scotty and turned her head to see where the car was.

"I'll pull in behind him. Can you copy down his plate?" Yarnell said as he merged into the traffic lane. Molosky kept his eye on the Mustang as it rolled to a stop in front of Hillman.

Virginia eyed the car briefly, then turned her head and continued to stroll casually across the street.

Yarnell rolled down his window and turned off the air conditioner.

The man in the brown car yelled out of his window. "Hey, honey. Need a ride?"

Virginia turned her head again and stared at the man. She shook her head and quickened her pace across the street.

When the light turned green, the Mustang squealed out and sped away.

"Let's follow him," Molosky said. "See what he does."

Yarnell accelerated through the intersection.

"Scotty, we'll tail this joker for a while. See what he's up to. You stay with Hillman. You there, Stan?"

"I got her covered, Bert. We'll handle it."

The brown Mustang was forced to slow down because of traffic. Molosky copied down the license number as Yarnell pulled in behind it. "I wonder what he's up to," Yarnell asked.

"If he doesn't turn back, we can shake him down a couple of blocks up the way. We'll find out."

At the next traffic light the brown car edged over to the left-turn lane and waited for the green arrow. Yarnell swung in behind. When the arrow clicked on, the brown car made a U-turn and started back toward Town & Country Village.

Yarnell clicked on the radio. "Scotty, the Mustang's on its way back. Should be in your area in a minute."

"We're ready here. Virginia just walked into the restaurant. I'm going in and I'll sit at the counter. Stan's across the lot."

"Let's take him." Molosky reached under the seat and grabbed the red light. He fixed it into position near the front windshield and turned it on.

Yarnell had to honk the horn several times before the Mustang pulled to a stop near a small clothing store. He stepped quickly from the van and approached the car. Molosky took up a position to the right rear of the car. He watched Yarnell and was just within hearing range.

"San Jose Police, sir." Yarnell stood near the back of the man's door and held his badge in plain view for the man to see. "I'd like to see both your hands. That's it. Good. Now step from the car carefully." Yarnell took two half steps backward and held his flashlight on the man's face. He turned his head toward Molosky. "Beer cans all over the floorboard. The guy looks like he's bombed."

Molosky had left his flashlight and portable radio in the cab. Walking to where Yarnell stood, he thought that after they were through with the drunk he should get them as soon as possible.

The drunk was a short, wiry man with a pointed goatee. "You guys both cops? What was I doing wrong? Just looking for some snatch, man, that's all."

As the man talked he lost his balance and had to use the car to steady himself. His breath caused Yarnell to step back even further. "Don't get too close, Ray. He's ninety-nine percent pure."

"Pure what, Officer? Ninety-nine percent pure, huh? That's pretty good."

"Why don't we call a beat unit, and let him handle this guy?" Molosky suggested.

When the beat unit arrived, the man was handcuffed and placed inside the marked police car.

"It's a numbers game," Yarnell said, climbing in behind the wheel and fastening his safety belt. "That's what this business boils down to sometimes."

"Yeah, a crap shoot and luck. We just didn't happen to hit the rapist on that one. Why don't you swing back to my car? I told Rodriguez that I'd ride with him after dark. I want to make sure that everybody is coordinated with each other. You guys have it down pretty good."

Yarnell switched on the lights, swung the van around the brown Mustang, and headed for the west side exit.

Molosky relaxed in the comfortable bucket seat. "It's going to be another hot one tomorrow."

"Bert, you there? Bert?" It was Scotty's voice. He was yelling in the radio. His words came fast and excited. "It's him! It's him! Corner of De Salvo. The Hood. He's got her. Hurry!"

"Holy Christ!" Molosky sat up with a jolt. "Let's go. Hurry, Bert. Get this bus moving. Give me your radio."

Yarnell peeled out into traffic and headed north on Winchester Boulevard. "Son-of-a-bitch. Caught us out of position. And this stupid traffic." He threw the radio toward Molosky.

There was a traffic jam at the Stevens Creek Boulevard intersection. Yarnell honked and swerved to the right. The van bounded over the curb and onto the sidewalk, just missing a fire hydrant.

"Easy, Bert. Don't get us killed."

Yarnell floored the accelerator and the van peeled and skidded along the sidewalk, barely missing the streetlights. When they got near the corner, Yarnell steered diagonally over a large patch of grass and shot over the curb onto Stevens Creek.

Molosky switched over to Channel Two. "Control Two, this is Sixty-one fifty-one. We have a go at Stevens Creek and De Salvo. Copy?"

"Ten-four, Fifty-one. All units in District Five..."

Molosky turned back to the tactical channel. There was a scream, then some garbled noises and a loud explosion. "Scotty, you all right?" Molosky's voice was tight, his volume rising fast. *Calm down,* he ordered himself.

Yarnell pushed the van over the center divider into the opposite lanes of traffic. Oncoming cars started flying in every direction. At the next intersection, Yarnell raced through the red light and got back on the right side of the road. Molosky sat astonished for a second. He had never seen Bert drive like that before.

Ahead of them they could see Quigley's pickup slide to a halt on the opposite side of the road. Farther down they could see a marked patrol unit with its flashing lights working its way through traffic.

"Over there, there's Scotty," Molosky said sharply.

Yarnell steered the van across the roadway and skidded to a stop near the curb. Molosky kept his eyes moving in rapid glances, looking for the hooded man. Scotty lay near the sidewalk trying to get to his feet. "Holy Christ, Scotty's hurt! Where's Hillman? I'll check him. You find her."

Molosky jumped from the van and ran toward Scotty. Quigley stood to his side and was helping him up. "Scotty, you all right? I heard a shot. You hurt? Where's Hillman?"

"He knocked my gun from me. Went off in the air. I think it's over there somewhere. She's...ahh...I don't know. Near the bushes."

Molosky quickly left Scotty and ran to where Yarnell was kneeling. When he got there, Yarnell held up his hand and spoke first. "She's all right. Bruised—the guy kicked her in the ribs. He went that way, over the fence."

"Give me your flashlight."

Yarnell lifted the light. Molosky grabbed it and was off.

When he reached the fence, Molosky leaped and hoisted himself over the top. He landed in the soft dirt, crouched, flicked the flashlight on, and drew his revolver. It was a residential backyard. Quietly, he moved the light around the yard. There was no one, only garden flowers and a lawn mower in the corner.

Molosky trotted across the yard and jumped the next fence. Again there was nothing.

He listened intently for signs of movement: bushes rustling, twigs breaking, leaves being tramped on. But there was only the sound of arriving police units—sirens blaring, voices yelling for directions.

Molosky moved again. He bounded over the next fence, but this time did not stop his forward motion. He trotted across the lawn of the next yard, keeping the light beam moving from side to side.

Still there was nothing.

The results were the same after several more houses. By the time Molosky had gone half a block, the neighborhood was beginning to come alive. Dogs were barking, and people were stirring at their windows and at back doors.

Suddenly he remembered something. The car! The rapist always had a car close by. Holy Christ!

At the next backyard Molosky found his way to the gate, swung it open, and ran down the driveway. When he got to the sidewalk, he checked back toward the scene. There were police cars gathered at the corner; an ambulance was just arriving. Quickly, he turned and looked the other way. He wished he had a portable radio.

At the end of the block, a car was pulling out from the curb.

Without hesitation, Molosky started to run after it. Holy Christ, that's him!

The car moved away without noise or lights.

Molosky ran like a sprinter. His feet pounded the pavement, his arms swung wildly, and his mouth was wide open, sucking in air.

But the car moved too fast. It came to a stop at the next lighted intersection, then proceeded through and made a hard left turn.

Molosky was still a hundred feet from the intersection. The car was a late-model, silver, four-door sedan. Looked like a Pontiac or an Oldsmobile. As he reached the corner, Molosky caught a glimpse of the hooded man as he turned his head toward him.

The license number—get the license number! But the car was too far away....

Chapter Twenty-one

They filed into the office one by one, their solemn faces showing a certain schoolboy meekness. First there was Captain Harkness, hands clasped in back of him, head tilted down. Molosky followed in a green striped shirt and Levi's, his eyes fixed on the back of Harkness's head. Maggenti walked in a more confident manner, briefcase at his side, an ever-so-thin smile across his lips. Sanders was the last. He walked with a slight stoop in his shoulders, his hands clasped in front of him, his chin to his chest, eyes focused on the rug.

Each man proceeded slowly to the center of the room and took his seat at one of the stiff-backed chairs. No one spoke. No one looked at anyone else. They sat in silence and waited.

From the corner of the office they could hear the shuffling of papers, then the sharp squeak from the chief's chair. When he approached the group, he made his customary circular inspection. Molosky sat stiff, but let his eye catch a glimpse of him as he made his tour. His arm was bent, and his hand thoughtfully stroked the point of his chin. When he had completed the circle, he stood in front of the empty chair and faced the men.

"Gentlemen." His opening word was calm and polite. His angular face showed lines of strain running from the corners of his deep-set eyes. "It's been a rough day for me. We will get to that later. First things first. Frank, how are the officers?"

Harkness cleared his throat. "There were two injured, Chief. The decoy, Officer Hillman, has two cracked ribs. She wanted to come to work today, but I advised against that at this time. She's a good officer and I'd like to put her back on the team as soon as possible. Couple of days, if the city doctor gives his okay.

"Officer Scotty Dearing has a fractured jaw. The rapist knocked his gun from him, then caught him with a blow to the face. He'll be out for a while. We had to get a replacement."

The chief nodded and turned his head to Pete Maggenti. "Sergeant, you have a status report on the investigation?"

Maggenti did not look to his briefcase. He tugged on his tweed lapels, then squared his glasses. "We managed to lift three good footprints of the rapist. He wears a size eleven cowboy boot, pointed toe. I took the castings over to the lab this afternoon. Judging from the size of the boot and the depth of the castings, we believe that the man weighs between one-eighty and one-ninety.

"There were other boot markings in the grass. They ranged from four and a half to five feet apart. Based on statistical averages, we judge the man to be between five feet nine and eleven in height.

"Nothing further. No unusual markings from the print. The lab boys said to save the boots when we catch the guy. They might be able to do something with them. They admit that a comparison would be difficult, but they would try.

"We checked out everyone who we knew was at the dealership party. So far, nothing. A couple of possibles, but nothing solid."

The chief nodded and thanked Maggenti. "Keep me informed."

"Yes, sir, I will."

"Well, Sergeants Sanders and Molosky, I've read all the reports. I don't think we need to hear from you just yet."

The chief sighed softly and tapped the back of the empty chair with the tips of his fingers. "I'm not here to chew anybody out or admonish anyone. I know what happens out in the streets. I realize how fast things can get out of control. I have a great deal of sympathy for the officers who were injured. They don't get paid to have their faces broken or their ribs cracked. But, quite frankly, I wish we could have caught the son-of-a-bitch."

There was a long measured silence.

"As chief of the Department, I sometimes get caught in a bind. This is one of those times. I've been deluged with phone calls from the mayor and the City Council all day. They had a lot of questions, legitimate questions. They wanted to know how we could let one man slip away like that."

The chief tightened his lips and heaved a long sigh. "I had no answer for them, gentlemen. I know it happened. I know how and why it happened. But still . . . the responses I gave, I'm afraid, did not satisfy them."

Molosky studied the chief's face. He could tell that the pressure from City Hall was weighing heavily on the man. The stress was noticeably affecting his health. He looked pale and haggard. His eyes showed emotional exhaustion. His lids drooped and his glance had no sparkle in it. But, somehow his voice held up. The words and phrases came in clear, audible sounds, although his control seemed less than complete. Some of his sentences would trail off in tired gusts of air.

"Their position and ours are essentially the same. I tried to assure them of that; however, I don't think some of them believed me. But that's their prerogative. We can only do our best." He paused again, more briefly this time.

"I'll work on City Hall. The other area in which I can use some assistance is the media. They got wind of what happened and jumped on the bandwagon. They want to sell papers and I don't blame them for that. But not at our expense. They've been throwing a lot of names at us today, and I don't appreciate that one bit. Especially since I consider most of what they had to say a great distortion of the facts.

"I've been interviewed by several of them during the day. What I would like is for one of you to agree to be a media person of sorts for a couple of days. I think the public would be better served if they heard from one of the men who was actually in on the operation, instead of letting the big shots and the politicians slug it out. I think there is a real need for the public to hear from the men and women who actually do all the work around here but get damned little credit for it."

Everyone in the group sat silent. Who did the chief have in mind? Molosky thought for sure it would be Maggenti. He would give a good, solid, educated image to the public. He eyed Maggenti for an instant, then let his gaze drift back.

The chief stared down at Molosky and gave him a fatherly smile. "Ray, I think I shall volunteer you. I've seen you in the news on several occasions. You have a friend, Henry Fowler I believe is his name, over at the paper. Why don't you call him? Make an appointment to see him. Tell him what it's like jumping fences in the dark not knowing if some pervert is waiting in the shadows with a knife. Tell him what it's like out there."

Molosky sat silent for several seconds. "I know Fowler, Chief, but I wouldn't—"

"You wouldn't want to take advantage of your friendship, right?"

"Something like that."

"I'm not asking you to take advantage of anything, Ray. I'm just asking for the truth. Nothing else. You tell him what it's like out there and let him print what he wants. Don't lie. Just give him the straight goods. It's scary out there. Tell him about it. That's all."

Molosky nodded. "Okay, Chief. You got me. I'll do my best."

"Good. Frank, you have enough manpower for tonight?"

"Yes, Chief. We'll be all right. Midnight units will be a little thin, but we'll hold the swing shift over if it gets too busy. Some of the day units already had to be held over. Looks like a busy night, but we'll make it."

"Good. Fine. Gentlemen, I called this meeting to let you know that the pressure is on from all sides. The politicians, the press, and most of all from the public. They all have a right to be concerned. Rape is more than a social crime. It is a very personal crime.

"The heat is on, gentlemen. They are all watching our performance. Mistakes can be very costly." He let his eyes fix on each of the men individually. "I also wanted to let you know that you haven't lost my confidence in you one shred. I know how good you are. So keep up your spirits and don't let your guard down."

Chapter Twenty-two

It was shortly before seven. After Molosky had checked on his two decoy teams, he steered his cab toward the call box at the corner of Third and San Fernando Streets, where he wanted to call Henry Fowler. On his way there he thought about The Hood. He wished he could have caught him. That would have made life easier for all concerned. He wondered who and what the man was. A white man of medium height and weight. He drove a late-model car. Maybe he was a corporate man, or perhaps a car salesman. Molosky's thoughts touched on Klosterman and his party. He wondered if he had given Sheldon's name for Maggenti to check out. It really didn't matter. He probably wouldn't find anything. He rolled up to the call box and got out of the car to use the phone.

"Hello. Is Henry Fowler there?"

"Just a minute, please."

Molosky wiped his brow and hoped for cooler weather.

"This is Fowler. Can I help you?"

"Hank, Ray Molosky. How are you?"

"Ray, I'm fine. How about you? Had a hell of a night last night. You didn't get hurt, did you?"

"No, thank God. Not me. Came close though. I thought you might like to get the firsthand story of what went on last night. If you want, I'll give you the straight scoop."

"Molosky, I've always liked you. You know that. There must be a hell of a lot of pressure on you guys over there, with all the politicians screaming their fool heads off."

"It's all part of the job, I guess. I don't know what the city fathers are saying. But I do know what went on last night and I'll tell you what it's like, if you want to listen."

"Sounds interesting. You want to meet?"

"How about Original Joe's in twenty minutes?"

"Okay. I'll see you outside the main door."

When Molosky got back in the cab, he slouched down and rested his head on the back of the cushion. He wondered what he was going to tell Fowler. That he was a hero because he jumped fences in the dark? What a joke! Maybe he should just lay it out as it really was. He had been scared. Scared of the unknown: of what might be behind the next bush, of what might be waiting around the next corner or over the next fence. Scared of the dark.

"This is Service Operator One, to all decoy units." The operator's voice seemed to blare in Molosky's ear. "Channel Two operator has no units to respond to a rape-in-progress call. Suspect wearing a hood was seen entering an apartment at 111 South Fourth Street. Witness in Apartment Five said she saw the man and then heard screams coming from number six."

Molosky bolted up in his seat, quickly started the cab, and clicked on the portable radio. "Bert, you catch that?"

"Got it."

"I'm right on top of this one. Block away. I know you're far out of position. Take Two-eighty and get off at Eleventh Street. Sanders, you got any teams in the area?"

Molosky clicked off and squealed away from the curb.

Sanders came on. "Two teams, about a mile away. Heavy traffic. Be there ASAP."

"Ten-four." Molosky steered onto San Fernando, heading the wrong way on a one-way street. "I'll be there in a couple of seconds."

Molosky slid to the corner of Fourth Street, a stream of thoughts running through his mind. Holy Christ! No one to help him. The car... find the silver car! His eyes skirted along the edge of Fourth Street. No silver cars. Then he shot a glance into the university parking lot to his immediate right. Still nothing. No cars. It was Saturday.

Suddenly, from the shadows of an apartment house on the other side of the parking lot, there appeared a man wearing a white hood.

It was him, in the flesh. A trickle of fear ran through Molosky. His muscles tightened. He sucked in a mouthful of air and ordered himself to relax.

Molosky knew he had the cover of the yellow cab, so he used it to move in closer. Slowly he steered around the corner and started toward the apartment house.

The hooded man stood for a short time in the shadows. He appeared to be searching for something. His hood moved from side to side several times. Maybe he was looking for the police.

Molosky rolled the cab closer.

When the hooded man moved, he walked to the edge of the sidewalk and stared toward the cab.

Molosky stared back. He got the impression that the man recognized him.

Suddenly the man bolted from his position and darted across Fourth Street.

Molosky reacted without hesitation. He swung the car to the left and pushed his foot to the floor. The car lurched across the street. Molosky's portable radio slid across the seat and dropped to the floor.

The hooded man ran ahead. He raced onto the sidewalk and started for the steps at the university entrance.

Molosky bounded the car over the curb and onto the university grass, where he skidded to a halt. He reached for the radio and was surprised and frustrated when he felt that it wasn't there. Quickly he glanced down at the seat. No radio. Hell with it.

He pushed open the door and started after The Hood, who was now sprinting onto the campus. Molosky ran as fast as his legs could move, first up the stairs and onto a long descending, concrete walkway, then across the lawn in the main quad area and toward the Administration Building.

The quickness of the man amazed Molosky. He did not think anyone could run with such speed. Molosky stayed with him stride for stride. One hundred feet apart, the two men pumped and churned across the grass, then through the west door of the Administration Building.

Molosky lost some time when he stumbled through the thick glass door leading to the long, narrow hallway. The rapist ran for the opposite door. Molosky quickly regained his balance and pursued. He ran with speed he never knew he had. He slammed through the door at the other end of the building and saw the hooded rapist running for the outside stairway of the Engineering Building, across Seventh Street.

Molosky raced across the street after the fleeing man. Looking up, he caught a glimpse of the rapist as he reached the second-story platform of the exterior stairway. Coming to the bottom of the steps, Molosky swung around the handrail and started his long ascent. At the third-floor platform his legs began to feel the strain. At the fourth, Molosky could feel his right leg begin to cramp. By the time he approached the fifth-floor landing, his lungs were gasping for air and his right thigh muscle was beginning to knot up. He slowed to rub his hurting leg.

"Over here, Molosky," a voice said. Molosky looked up, surprised. How did the man know his name?

The hooded man stood no more than four feet from him. Molosky saw it coming, but had no time to move. The man's fist came at his face with such swiftness that Molosky couldn't react. It smashed into his left eye and knocked him completely off his feet. Molosky let out a quick groan and his body bounced down the cement stairs.

Pain shot through him. Molosky covered his eye with the palm of his hand. For the first time, he too felt the power of the hooded man. Pictures of Evelyn ran through his mind.

He lay on the cement landing and shook his head, trying to get rid of the fuzziness. When he opened his eye, all he could see was the pointed toe of the man's brown boot coming at him. The boot smashed into his chest and sent him rolling against the railing. Molosky let out an uncontrollable cry of pain. He felt something crack in his chest. The boot came at him again. This time it caught him in the stomach. His body flexed to the fetal position and he crumpled up in pain.

Holy Christ, someone help me! Molosky rolled over and frantically attempted to reach for his revolver, which was tucked under his right arm. As his hand touched the handle, he was kicked again. This time his right eye went numb from the man's boot heel. He groaned and doubled over in agony. The pain was paralyzing. Every muscle in his body seemed to hurt. He lay on the cement, a broken man.

Then the kicking stopped. His body rolled over in convulsive flashes of pain, but the torturous kicking had ceased. He turned his head and squinted his eyes at the man in the white hood.

His assailant looked huge and terrifying, standing there with his hands on his hips. His dark eyes locked onto his. Familiar eyes.

"Who are you?" Molosky asked in a weak voice. He kept a close watch on the man's boot. The pain in his chest started to subside. He sucked in a deep, reviving breath.

"I am society's child, fuck face," the man answered in a low, muffled voice. Suddenly, his pointed boot fired toward Molosky's face.

But this time Molosky was prepared. He quickly rolled aside and reached for the boot. When he felt his hand around the leather boot, he tightened his grip and twisted, then yanked until the hooded man fell.

Molosky let go, immediately got to his feet, and reached

for his revolver again. But the man moved with incredible speed. He bounced to his feet and swung his right fist at Molosky's bruised face. Molosky felt the man's fist smash against his cheek. The force would have knocked any two men out, but Molosky did not flinch. He took the blow and stood his ground.

Instead of drawing his weapon, Molosky drew up all the strength he could muster and let go with his powerful right arm. His fist slammed at his surprised opponent. The blow sent the rapist to the cement landing.

But again, the man moved with precise agility. His foot shot through the air like a bullet, caught Molosky in the stomach, and sent him back into the railing.

Molosky struggled to regain his balance. The Hood hesitated, then eased away, and headed up the stairs.

Molosky moved his battered body up the cement stairs to the fifth-floor door. He could see The Hood running for the opposite exit. Grasping his revolver, he put one foot in front of the other, and his legs began their familiar running rhythm. As he passed Room 505, his mind flashed onto Hugo Evans.

He bounded out the door and quickly angled his body toward the stairs leading to the pavement below. He could see The Hood leaping three stairs at a time. Molosky passed the third-floor landing as the man reached the concrete sidewalk below and started to run toward Tenth Street.

He did not want to lose sight of the rapist, so he took a chance to close the distance. He lunged his tired body over the handrailing at the second level and jumped onto the rock-hard pavement. His legs gave with the landing, but he managed to keep his balance. Without waiting to see if he were hurt, he started running.

The Hood dashed eastbound on San Fernando Street and darted into an alley which ran between older residential boardinghouses.

Molosky held his ribs to quiet the pain. He entered the alleyway. His legs moved with dependable reserve strength. His mind reeled with tensions, and his entire body yearned for rest. But his legs would not stop. They would not be beaten. His conditioned running movement would endure the longest races. The Hood had to be captured.

"I'm right here." The Hood jumped out from the shrubs and blocked Molosky's path; with a perfectly aimed kick he knocked the revolver from Molosky's hand and followed quickly with a lightning blow to Molosky's swollen and bloodied face. Molosky saw swirling blue, then darkness. His body went limp and began to slump to the concrete. The man swung again. This time the blow hung on the left temple.

Molosky began to fade with only a soft groan.

As he lay there letting out low moans of pain, Molosky heard The Hood pick up his gun and heard the revolver click to the cocked position. *Oh, God, spare me. Please don't let him kill me.* He tried with all the strength left in him to open his eyes.

As they became partially opened, Molosky squinted up and saw the barrel of the gun pointed at his head. He looked for the hood, but the man had taken it off. Molosky saw a familiar-looking face.

Then the boot came at him again. It was a jolting blow to the temple and Molosky was out.

Part Two

Chapter Twenty-three

Marvin Ashwood lifted his old bones to a sitting position and rubbed his eyes with the heel of his hands. Leaning against the wooden frame inside the boxcar, he pulled his legs close to his body and pushed himself to a standing position. He waited resolutely for several moments before attempting to walk. His mind was quick to function, but his body took several more minutes before he could feel the slow, warm threads of life move into his muscles. As he stood he let his eyes flirt with the sun's rays filtering through the slats and lighting up the far corner of the car. He studied their angle for a moment before concluding that it must be nearly seven o'clock, and the train should be in the station at San Jose.

With a slight limp Ashwood hobbled across the boxcar to the sliding door on the opposite side. Before opening it he pressed his left cheek to the wood, so that his eye could catch a frame of the outside. It was a still clear outside, not like in Portland.

He stepped back from the crack and stared blankly at the dark interior wall. Without realizing it, out of habit, the old man bent down on one knee, made the sign of the cross, and began to mutter a quick prayer. He was thankful for a safe journey. When he was through, he blessed himself again, stood, and mentally prepared himself for the world that awaited him.

As he opened the sliding wooden door, he could feel the warm evening sunlight splash over his body. Climbing off the car and feeling the earth beneath his tattered shoes, Ashwood caught the slightest trace of a cooling southern breeze against his deeply tanned skin. He stretched awkwardly, then extended his arm around the edge of the door and fished out his small black leather satchel. Unlatching the top he yanked out an old-style crush hat and pulled it over his thinning white hair.

The old man walked with blustery steps and snappy arm movements one would not expect from a man of his years. He took short, choppy paces, coordinating his upper body to the rhythm created by the pounding of his heels against the cement. He had found, through many self-imposed experiments, that the only way for him to ease the pain in his right knee was to warm it up as fast as possible, then to keep it warm.

He strode through an industrial area, then turned south, and two blocks later found himself at a Don't Walk sign in the middle of the financial district. When the light flicked to green, he began his pace again and crossed the street quickly. In a characteristic gesture, upon reaching the other side he stopped suddenly and appeared to be intently glaring up the next block. He remembered, several months ago he had had a rather noisy run-in with a tall street walker. The policeman he had talked to that night seemed considerate and more experienced than most. Then, as if he had made a momentous decision, the old man nodded several times in the direction toward which he was walking, then turned abruptly and started toward Second Street. Why put up with another hassle, if she happened to be working down there? Slowly, he hobbled east toward the small restaurant across the street from the campus administration building.

* * *

Sally Connors was a beefy woman of forty-two. She stood toward the back of the coffee shop wiping off the refrigerator door with a clean sponge. When she had finished, she sidestepped to the sink, where she rinsed the sponge and twisted the water out of it. As she stepped back into the counter area, she spotted Ashwood quietly shutting the door and wandering toward his favorite table in the corner.

"So we walk right by, do we? Without a word? Not so much as a hello?" Her voice was deep, her tone friendly.

Ashwood hesitated and stared at her absently for what seemed like a long time.

"What's the matter, dearie? Cat got your tongue?"

"I was just thinking, you know, like I sometimes do." Ashwood let his words trail off quietly as he turned and meandered to his favorite table in the corner.

Sally reached under the counter and took out a thick white porcelain cup, placed it on a saucer, filled it with coffee, and brought it over to the old man. "Where have you been? Haven't seen you in weeks. You just up and leave your friends without saying a word?"

Ashwood glanced briefly out of the window at the opposite end and eyed a police car driving by. "Yeah, well, I'm sorry about that, Sal. Had to go out of town unexpectedly. Friend of mine passed away in Portland. Didn't have much time. Just threw a few things together and jumped on the first train heading north. What a place to die. Portland. You ever heard of somebody dying in Portland?" His lips pursed, then cracked into a humorous smile. "The guy lived all his life in Arizona. Goes to Portland to visit a sick relative and ends up in the ground."

"We're all going to end up there," she said. "You want a cookie?"

Ashwood nodded and let his crafty blue eyes lift to meet hers. "Oatmeal, thanks."

"You know, you need more than oatmeal cookies to nourish your old bones."

The old man rubbed the stubble around his jaw and let

his eyes drift back to the window in front. Another police cruiser crept by. "Yes, well thanks for the concern, but I'm fine."

As he finished his sentence the front door opened and a man stepped through. As Ashwood continued the conversation he studied the man and tried to capture his mood. He often did this and had gotten quite good at it, studying many hundreds of students over the years. He noticed that the man had a handsome face, but that he also had what appeared to be a slight red swelling at the top of his cheekbone, just below his left eye. He also observed a bulge underneath the front of the man's shirt and that he seemed extremely protective of it, covering it with his right hand. *A gun,* he thought. No, it wasn't that shape. It was thick and round. Maybe it was a bag full of stolen money.

Sally glanced at the man as he walked toward the counter. "Excuse me, Marvin. I got a customer."

Ashwood nodded without hearing her words. As the man walked closer to him the old man was able to give his face a better examination. It was an oval face, boyish cheeks, small nose. But it was also a scared, troubled face. There were shiny beads of perspiration dotting his brow. Some were so heavy that they burst and the liquid flowed straight down, dissecting his face into several unequal vertical sections.

As the man drew nearer, Ashwood caught only a glimpse of his eyes before he turned and sat at the counter. The eyes had panic in them, but the panic was clouded over because the man only let a steeled hardness show on the surface. The man had to be a criminal, Ashwood thought. The crime he had committed was a recent one, maybe a robbery. He scrutinized the back of the man and toyed with the idea of helping him get away. The man was wearing Levi's and cowboy boots, and carrying that strange package inside his drab red short-sleeved shirt. A certain excitement began to grow inside the old man. He would love to foil the efforts of the police for all those times they had made him feel so low and so inadequate.

Out of the corner of his eye, the old man spotted another police cruiser as it rolled to a stop at the curb in front. Behind the cruiser another car followed and also parked. The second car was a big recent-model sedan. From it stepped an odd-looking, round fellow wearing a strange mixture of clothing, and dark glasses. He walked up to the curb, where he met the two uniformed men. The three conferred on the sidewalk for a moment, then started for the front door.

Ashwood's eyes returned to the man at the counter. The young man had also seen the police officers and was just turning his head toward the back wall as the door opened. Without contemplating his actions, the old man lifted his body from the chair and strode rapidly to a position just behind the man. Before wrapping his arm around the man's broad shoulders, Ashwood whispered softly to him. "I'm a friend, young man. I know you're in some kind of trouble. I'll help. Don't worry. Just smile and pretend we're long-lost friends." The old man's face broke into a cautious smile, and he surrounded the man's shoulders in a gregarious gesture of friendship.

The young man nearly jerked off the stool in one frantic spontaneous movement. His head twisted toward the old man, his jaw dropped, his lips tightened in fright. He shot the old man a burning stare, then quickly turned his head back toward the door.

Ashwood did not loosen his grip. He could feel the fear race through the man's back muscles. "Hang on, son. Smile. I'll get you out of it. That a boy, give me a smile."

It was a mere tentative easing of the lips at first, then a slight trembling smile showed through. Ashwood could tell that the man wanted to trust him, but wasn't quite sure if he should. "Sal, you want to bring my friend here a hot pastrami sandwich and a glass of beer? Over to my table. And another cookie if you don't mind."

Sally glared at him with a wide warning stare, which she held on him for a long moment without comment.

"My table is in the corner." Ashwood spoke to the young man in a commanding yet soothing tone. "Just keep smiling and follow my lead." He could feel the tension in the man's shoulders ease as he stood and then walked with him toward the back. When they got to the table, Ashwood sat down first. He gave the young man an apprehensive glance. "Please trust me. Sit down."

The man eased a chair out and sat down across from the old man. "Okay, I'll play your game. You lead. But you had better be on the level!"

Before Ashwood could reply, the short, round plain-clothes policeman bellowed so that everyone in the place could hear. "Excuse me, everybody. May I have your attention, please? My name is Sergeant Douglas Sanders, San Jose Police Department." He lifted his badge high in the air so that everyone could see. "There has been a very serious crime which has just taken place a short distance from here. We need your patience and your cooperation. Me and one of these officers will be coming around to your table. We expect you to show us proper identification and answer our questions. It won't take long. We'll try to be brief." With that, he stuffed his badge in his trouser pocket, signaled for one of the officers to stand by the door, and for the other to come with him. The sergeant made his way to the other side of the room and approached a young couple at their table.

The young man kept his icy stare on Sanders as he spoke, then changed his position in order to view the old man and catch glimpses of the officers as they moved toward them. "Your move. You had better make it good or I'm crashing through that front door like you've never seen before."

Ashwood understood that the macho talk was only pretend. Underneath it he sensed that the man was in an alarming state of panic. Ashwood had to show him that he was in control and that he could be trusted. "Calm down. You're not going anyplace. There's no time for games. Just do as I tell you."

The man's eyes were brown and enormous. They fastened on Ashwood in a brittle, cold stare. "Like I said, your move."

Ashwood let his hand slip under the table and find his satchel. "Here, under the table. My overnight bag. Whatever you're hiding, get rid of it. Easy now, no sudden moves. Just slip it out and calmly place it in the satchel."

The man shifted his eyes to the policemen, back to Ashwood, then to the floor and the overnight case. Slowly he undid one of the buttons on his shirt and withdrew the contents. Sending another quick glance toward the policemen, he slipped his hand under the table and delivered his contraband.

"There now." Ashwood forced a confident smile. "Hang on, partner. It'll be a little while before they're here. Relax."

The stranger nodded solemnly.

"Hey, Sal, could you hurry up with the pastrami sandwich?" the old man yelled to the woman behind the counter.

Sally's face remained fixed in a clouded expression. Her eyes moved to the old man, then swept across the room to the policemen. "Just a minute, Marvin. In a minute." Her voice was only vaguely controlled, as if she were not quite sure how she was supposed to reply.

Ashwood leaned over the table and spoke softly to the stranger. "My name is Professor Marvin Ashwood. I teach a class called Culture in Perspective. You are one of my former students. You graduated three years ago and are now consulting me about doing graduate work. What's your name?"

The man dropped his hand to the table and made an uneasy clenched fist, then let it go slack before tightening it again. His eyes wandered over the old man's face, then settled in a nervous trance. "Name? John. My name is John Carver."

The old man nodded his acknowledgment. He hoped John Carver was a good actor.

"Your sandwich and your cookie." Sally placed the dishes on the table, then swung her hands to her hips, stepped back, and bullied the men with her eyes. "I'll serve you the beer after I see some I.D."

"Do you mind if I check their identification first? I'm sure *he's* over twenty-one." Doug Sanders stood beside the woman and threw her a heady smile, then shifted his sarcastic eyes to the old man, then he steadied on Carver. "I need to see some type of identification."

"Yes, sir." Carver stood part way up, reached into his back pocket for his wallet, then rested back in the chair. Nervously, he opened his billfold and several business cards fell to the table. "I have my driver's license. Will that do?"

"That'll do fine."

Ashwood leaned forward and let his eyes scan the business cards. A suspicious look came to his eyes as he followed Carver's hands as they sought out his driver's license.

"Here we are, Sergeant." The stiffness in Carver's voice had disappeared and was replaced by a congenial, friendly tone. His wide eyes sparkled and his face gave off a relaxed, easygoing style. "I live at that address in Menlo Park. Down here for the day to visit old friends and, of course, my old teacher, Professor Ashwood."

The sergeant took the license and began writing something in a small note pad. "He doesn't look like no professor I've ever seen!" Without moving his head from its crooked position, Sanders lifted his suspicious eyes to Ashwood. "Some professor. I ain't never seen one dressed like that before. I bet you don't even have a wallet. No money, no wallet."

A tinge of anger sparked in the old man's eyes. Trying hard to control his feelings, he drew in a mouthful of relaxing air and let it out in a long, even burst. "I do not have any identification on me, Sergeant. I never carry any. My wife died in a car accident many years ago. I don't drive, so I don't have a license to do so. However, I do have an office on the other side of the campus, and if you like I can take you there and show you around." His eyes remained resolutely fixed on the policeman's. "And after you see my office, you can escort me to your police station, where I may explain to someone in higher authority just how verbally abused I've been by you. Shall we go?" Ashwood stood up sharply and placed his face sternly in front of the sergeant's.

"Sit down, old man, before you burn out one of your fuses. If I had the time, I'd call your bluff. I've been around too long to fall for that. Been lied to by the best." Sanders nodded his head and raised his eyebrows. "You ain't got no office no place, but I ain't got the time right now to prove it, so relax and give your ticker a break."

Ashwood had been clearly outclassed and he knew it. The fat-faced policeman was a pro at what he was doing. The old man slumped back into the chair, eyes cast down. "So you caught us in a lie. What else is new? We're a pair of bums who blew in on the afternoon Southern Pacific from San Francisco. What are you going to do? Arrest us for that? The railroad filing charges, are they?"

"You've got a sharp tongue, old man. I'd advise you to keep it quiet until I'm through here. Is that understood?"

Ashwood rubbed his hands together and bowed meekly.

For the first few moments after the police left, Marvin Ashwood sat silent, welling up inside with pride. He and the young stranger had pulled it off. He let the good feelings trickle through to his bones, and when he was filled with emotion, he let his crafty glance work its way slowly to the young man across the table. When their eyes met, it was electric friendship. The joy of relief spread across their faces. The old man's lips cracked wide, his eyes sparkled in fiery joy. "What did you think of that? Not bad for an old man and the young kid on their first go-round."

Carver twirled in his seat, slapped the side of his Levi's, and let out a loud, happy cry. "Here, let me shake your hand." He reached across the table, grabbed hold of Ashwood's stubby, calloused hand. "I thought he had you. I mean you sure had me fooled." Carver released his grip and slapped the table with the palm of his hand. "Damn, I thought you *were* one of those wacky teachers over there. Even in your dumpy clothes. Hell, you look the part to me."

Sally Connors approached the table and cast a look of distrust upon the smiling young man. "You wanted a beer." She set the glass down hard on the table. "That will be three twenty-five. You can pay now." Her arm snapped out from her side, palm turned up.

Carver stared at her absently while he tugged his wallet out and found a five-dollar bill. "Keep the change."

"Thank you." She rolled her eyes to the old man without changing her stern expression. "You promised you'd help me with the heavier boxes in the back room. Before you leave I expect that promise to be kept."

The old man answered with a compressed smile and a half-hearted wave. He fumbled with the pack of cigarettes, pulled one out, and reached for the matches inside his pocket. "I'll help, Sal. I'll be there in a moment. Let me finish this first, will ya?" He struck the match and before lighting up, flashed her a comical gaze.

"In a minute, then," she answered without changing expression. "I'll expect you."

Ashwood propped his elbows in front of him and watched her walk away. "Don't mind her. Sometimes she acts like my mother. Tries to smother me. She means well, but you understand..."

Carver did not answer but picked up the sandwich and took a big bite. Ashwood watched the smoke rise from the end of the cigarette only to be obliterated in the currents of the air conditioner. He chuckled softly to himself. "You know, me and the cops have never gotten along. Not that I'm a criminal, understand. As a matter of fact, I've never been behind bars. But they've threatened to send me there many a time. I can see you don't exactly get along with them either."

The young man took another bite and swallowed hard. "To tell you the truth, Mr. Ashwood, I've always gotten along with the police. Never had any trouble with them...that is, until today." Carver's voice resonated in rich tones. His eyes gave off a complex mixture of signals. The happy face of a young boy was broken only by a deeper, quiet intensity which seemed to smolder underneath. He bent over his plate, holding the sandwich in both his hands. Occasionally his eyes would flicker to the old man's as he talked. "You come here often? You seem to know the old lady pretty well."

"She's been a friend for a lot of years." Ashwood inhaled and blew toward the ceiling. "She owns the place, treats me kindly." He shifted his position in the chair and looked over the young man's shoulder toward the window. There were more police cars now, moving slowly up and down the street.

"You don't mind me asking—do you—if you're clean. You didn't leave anything behind, did you? They're swarming all over out there. Never seen so many in one location at the same time."

Before answering, Carver twisted around anxiously to see what was outside. "They're all over. I thought they were gone."

Bringing the glass ashtray closer to him, the old man breathed in a last mouthful of smoke and crushed the remains. "That would be nice if they would simply just disappear from our lives, but I think not. Not in this case anyway. They're hunting for someone or something." He fiddled with the ashtray while he contemplated his next words. "We both know the someone they're looking for, don't we? That's why I asked if you're clean."

Carver reached for a paper napkin and brought it to his mouth in a gesture of thought. "I don't know how I look to you, sitting here eating this sandwich and trying to act cool, while the vultures are just outside." He set the napkin down and gripped the glass of beer and took a long quenching gulp. "I needed that." He wiped his lips with the side of his arm. "But underneath I'm a bowl of jelly. I'm scared. I've done something really bad, and I'm petrified." His face showed an exaggerated shift in intensity. The boyish smile had disappeared and was replaced by a rigid jutting of the jaw and a hitherto unseen network of harsh wrinkles running from the corners of his eyes to the outreaches of his temples. "I mean, I was being chased because I beat up a cop. Might have killed him. I don't know what to do. I've never been in a situation like this before."

The old man tried to calm Carver by showing that he himself was relaxed and poised. He pretended to yawn, lifted both his arms straight up, and let them come down to the back of his head. Before he spoke he eyed the darkening bruise under the man's eye. The policeman must have given it to him, he concluded, wondering why the stranger was being chased in the first place. "Calm down," he said, using his best fatherly voice. "Apparently, you are not out of the woods yet. Can anyone identify you or your car or anything having to do with you?"

Carver's worried look eased only slightly. He took several short breaths, then downed the remainder of the beer. "I don't think so. No one knows who I am or what I look like. But..." He broke the sentence off at midpoint and stiffened in the chair as if ready to explode. "The car!" Suddenly, he jerked from his position and bolted for the door.

Ashwood did not move. He could do nothing. The young man was much too fast for him. He kept a watchful eye on him, hoping that he would not open the door.

Carver halted abruptly at the side of the door. He peered out of the window in the direction of Fourth Street. For several seconds he stayed near the window, his head moving back and forth, eyes straining to see some distant object. Just as suddenly as he left the table, he marched back with lightning-quick steps.

The old man let his eyes play over the other patrons. None of them seemed particularly concerned over Carver's abrupt movements. One or two of them gave him a casual turn of the head, but none appeared overly alarmed. Except, that is, for Sally. She stood tight-lipped behind the counter, arms folded across her chest, eyes fixed on him in a piercing glare. Ashwood did not look at her long before he was interrupted.

"Listen, old man." Carver slid into the chair and pushed aside his dishes. "I hate to bother you again, but I think I know what they're looking for. My car. No one knows who *I* am, but someone might have spotted my car. Shit! How the fuck did I get myself into this mess?" He started to slam his fist on the table, but midway through the gesture he stopped, opened his hand, and gently let it slap the surface. "Control. You've got to control yourself," he muttered.

Ashwood narrowed his eyes and scanned the young man's face, searching for something, but not knowing exactly what. With great effort he remained silent, waiting for Carver to continue.

The young man shot another fleeting glance toward the window, then with a hopeless expression returned to the old man. He swallowed hard before he could talk. "My car. It's parked in the seven-eleven parking lot at the corner of Fourth and San Carlos. I hate to ask you this, but...I don't think I should go near the car for a while. Might bring me bad luck. I can feel it. Maybe...you could..."

"You want me to get it?" Ashwood interrupted. "I will, if I can." Carver breathed a long sigh of relief. "You mean, it's that easy? If I ask, you'll do it?"

"I didn't say it would be easy. But...well...what kind is it?"

Chapter Twenty-four

The room at the top of the back stairs was long and narrow, with two large curtainless windows at either end. The open kitchen situated on the east end was clean, with only a sprinkling of clutter on top of the small refrigerator. Towels, dishes, and a small amount of canned goods were tucked neatly away in a rectangular cupboard to the right of the sink. A red votive candle sat on top of the square wooden table. The floor was covered with a cheap, grey linoleum, the drab color broken only by a well-traveled narrow strip of green rug which ran the entire length of the flat.

At the center of the room along the wall stood an unmade, steel-framed single bed with a box-spring mattress which squeaked from age. The doors, one to the closet, another to the toilet and bath, and a third which led outside, were set side by side along the wall at the head of the bed. Across from the bed was a built-in bookcase full of cheap paperbacks as well as several hardbound works, which were mainly philosophical and religious in nature.

A setting of chairs, lamps, and tables surrounded an

old Victorian sofa at the opposite end of the room. None of the pieces of furniture were matched in color or texture, but all were clean and relatively comfortable.

It was dark by the time the old man made his way up the back steps and unlocked the door. Before going inside, he let his eyes move back to the garage to make sure, for the third time, that the stranger's car was secured behind closed doors. Once inside he hoisted the satchel over the steel frame and let it drop to the top of the bed. Extending his right arm, he found two light switches and turned them. The outside forty-watt bulb blinked on and gave only minimal light for the stairway. The other switch controlled the lamp closest to the sofa. Closing the door behind him, Ashwood felt the hot stuffy air inside the room and thought that he should immediately open the windows. On his way to the kitchen he stopped at the closet, where he hung his hat on an inside hook, then stripped off his rank-smelling short-sleeved shirt and donned a fresh one. Reaching the sink, he let the cold water run while he turned the window handle and cranked it open. "Not much of a breeze after all," he muttered to himself as he plucked a glass from the cupboard and filled it with cold water.

He gulped down the water, made his way to the bathroom, then found himself hobbling toward the lighted sofa area before he realized that the pain in his knee had returned. As he passed the bed he eyed the satchel and wondered if he should open it to find out what the young man was so diligently attempting to keep hidden. As he pondered the temptation he ran his hand under his chin and felt the wiry stubble. Should he let his curiosity overcome him, or should he be patient and wait for Carver to explain it all to him? He sighed, picked the satchel from its place, and slid it under the bed. There was no guarantee that Carver would show it to him, or even explain his circumstances, but the old man figured that there was an element of trust in their blossoming relationship which should not be tampered with. "Be patient," he told himself.

Ambling into the living area, his intention was to open the window behind the sofa, but he found the comfort of its pillows much too enticing. Relaxing in their softness, he soon found it difficult to fight his drowsiness and concentrate on what had happened in the last few hours. The young man with his boyish face and troubled eyes ...Perhaps Carver wasn't Carver after all...his business cards were in the name of...or maybe he was a dangerous person...a murderer...and...he should be feared. Perhaps the authorities should be called. Maybe he should not let the stranger into his cozy room...without proof of his true identity. Perhaps he was dreaming and the entire incident never took place.

The first crisp knock on the door hardly moved the old man from his dreamy sleep. It was not until the pounding became thunderous and persistent that the old man's eyes flickered open and his mind came back to concrete reality. It was him, the murderer, the robber, the man to be feared.

"Let me in, old man," came the cry at the door.

Ashwood's mind reeled, trying to decide what he should do. He stumbled to his feet and with the heel of his hands rubbed his eyes heavily. "Calm down," he muttered to himself. It was just a young man crying for help. No need to fear him.

The pounding came again, followed by the cry, "Old man, old man, it's me, John Carver. Let me in."

"Hold on, sonny boy. I'll be there in a minute," came the old man's reply. Tapping his cheeks with his hands to assure himself that he was really awake, Ashwood started for the door. Taking hold of the knob with his left hand, he blessed himself with the right and lifted his eyes toward heaven.

When he swung the door open, he was greeted pleasantly by John Carver's fresh, handsome smile. The old man tried to put on his best welcoming face, but he thought that he did a poor job of it. His searching eyes studied the man's intent, then mechanically he let his vision swoop over Carver's appearance. The cowboy boots and Levi's were gone. Carver had changed into a conservative dress suit: modern, vested, and spotlessly clean. Ashwood wondered if it were the same man.

"Well, aren't you going to invite me in?"

It was the same John Carver all right, the old man acknowledged to himself. There was that voice and the camouflaged eyes. "I'm sorry, I didn't mean to be rude. By all means, come in."

Carver was carrying a large grocery bag. "I brought you something. Kind of a token of appreciation. You got guts, old man, and I appreciate a man like that. Where can I set this?"

Ashwood gestured slightly with his arm. "You can set it on the table in the kitchen if you like."

Carver brushed past him and hesitated briefly while he ran his eyes over the room. He put the bag on the table, and reached inside. "Let's see what we've got here. How about a carton of cigarettes. Your brand, I hope."

Ashwood nodded, surprised.

"And a loaf of French bread, sourdough, best kind. A roll of salami, and two bottles of Wild Turkey." Carver set the two bottles next to the French bread, and faced Ashwood directly. "I'm glad you made it, old man. Appreciate you being there, when I needed you." He gave the old man an embarrassed smile.

The old man gazed out of the window toward the garage with a faraway look in his eyes. "No, but I was lucky. The Lord was with me. I told you, didn't I, that I haven't driven a car in years? I was quite taken aback by all those gadgets and dials and what have you. The engine kept wanting to race ahead, and I had a little trouble holding it back, but other than that, I was all right."

"I'm glad of that. I'm glad you're all right, and I'm happy you didn't put any unwarranted dents in the fenders." He gave the old man a quick, overlit smile, the kind that does not go beyond the lips.

Ashwood returned the man's gaze with an awkward smile. "Yes, well..."

The fear which Ashwood had experienced earlier subsided and changed into an almost insatiable curiosity about the young man, John Carver. Quickly, he cleared the table and for the sake of convenience put everything in the refrigerator, except for the cigarettes. He grabbed a pack and squeezed it into his pants pocket. Pouring the whiskey into water glasses, he half-smiled at himself for the wild impulses he still possessed.

"I made it," he said, giving a silly smile and handing a glass to the sitting Carver. Ashwood stood at the opposite end of the sofa laughing, and lifted his glass. He thought he would offer a toast, and while doing so, toss out a curious bit of information to see if Carver would pick it up. He extended his arms wide to each side in a gesture of friendship. "May I offer you a toast, sir? To a stranger in passing. To a man I helped along life's crowded highway. To John Carver, or whatever your name is." He shot the man a swift, cautious glance. "I salute you." Trying to act simple-minded, Ashwood smiled foolishly and bent to touch the stranger's glass. He thought that he had struck a nerve. The man's lips curled into a smart grin and his eyes narrowed from their normal roundness. Carver lifted his glass gracefully and nodded smoothly.

"Touché." He kept his eyes on the old man's as he drank. Letting the glass down he offered a sly smile. "You forget, old man. I know you are no fool. I've seen you in action. I've seen you outfox the fox, remember." Carver crossed his legs and made himself comfortable. "But I'm pretty good at fencing myself. By the way, you don't mind if I call you 'old man,' do you? I could call you Professor Ashwood if you like."

Ashwood felt the verbal jab and chuckled some more. He took his place in the cushioned armchair across from his guest. "Not bad. You duck fast and come back swinging, don't you?"

"Like I said, I'm pretty good at fencing."

"Yes, well, let's drink up and we shall see how good you are." He raised his glass as if to toast the stranger again. "Skoal."

There was silence. Ashwood realized that he knew nothing of this man, and he searched his brain for a starting place to satisfy his curiosity. In a way he admired him. At the sandwich shop, Carver had seemed nervous to the point of desperation, even while he was acting. But here, only a few hours later, he was a new man: poised, confident, ready to take on the world.

Since they had almost nothing in common, Ashwood—after thinking for a while—figured he would start by conceding the match and going from there. "I'll tell you what. I'm not good at these word games people play with each other. I'm just a simple human being. Not a stupid one, but one who is not very good at manipulating words. I'm really too tired to box or fence or what have you. It's been a busy day, and I'll concede the game before it starts, if that's all right with you?"

There was no response in the man's face, just a brief nod of acknowledgment.

Ashwood continued, "I was hoping you'd come by. I have never quite run into a situation like the one we were in. I've never seen so many uniforms. How did you manage to slip away?"

Carver finished what was in the glass and set it on the table. "Your girl friend doesn't like me too well. I can tell you that much." His friendly tone came back. "She didn't like you leaving without paying your respects either. I asked her if she needed my help in the back, but she flatly refused." Carver chuckled, making a deep grunting sound. "She was pissed at you. Asked me where you went and what was going on between us. If she only knew."

Ashwood stood and started for the kitchen. "Why don't I just bring the bottle? That way we won't have to keep going back and forth. You want me to get you some of that salami you brought?"

"Maybe later, thanks. I don't feel like eating yet."

When the old man returned, he filled Carver's glass and set the bottle down. "Sal, she's a good old girl. Takes care of me. I'll have to call her in the morning."

"Yeah, I bet she takes care of you, you old fox. You've been hammering away on her ass in the back room. You can't fool me."

Ashwood was surprised by Carver's language and his insinuation. He mulled over the remark before saying anything. "That wasn't called for. There is nothing between her and me but friendship."

"I'll let it slide then. But remember, I've been around. Don't forget that." Carver yawned loudly, then leaned forward and grabbed his glass from the table. "I noticed your limp on the right side."

The old man adjusted his position and slid his hand into his pocket. "Mind if I smoke?"

"I knew you were low, that's why I bought them. Go ahead."

Ashwood unraveled the cellophane, tore the aluminum foil covering, then pounded the package on the back of his fist. "I've tried to quit, but it has always gotten the better of me. I know it's bad for me, but I pardon myself. I enjoy them." He stuffed his hand back in his pocket and came out with the matches. He lit the cigarette, drew in a deep breath, held it for a long, pleasurable moment, then let it out gracefully. "My limp comes from a piece of shrapnel tucked inside the bones somewhere in the knee. Old injury from the war. In this heat it's not too bad. The winter is what hurts. Acts like a barometer. The metal seems to shrink and then expand. Sometimes I think a good oil change would do more good than the pills the doctors give me."

Carver swigged from the glass and cracked an arrogant grin which showed off his polished white teeth. "So you were in the big one? What, the Army?"

The old man nodded heavily. "Yeah, but only for five months. Boot camp, then Normandy. Never made it to the beach. Our landing craft got blown out of the water a hundred yards from shore. Killed most everybody. Don't know how I made it. Just lucky, I guess. I'm a good floater." He let his eyes droop to the ashtray in front of him and moved the cigarette to it. "And you, did you serve?"

"Not in the big one, that's for sure." Carver seemed to be loosening up. His words came in easy tones. His facial expressions became more relaxed, and he seemed more receptive to comfortable conversation. He held the glass in his large hands and crossed his leg over his right knee.

"And the big one couldn't have been worse than where I was."

"Vietnam?"

"I wish! Had a brother there, so the good old Army wouldn't send me. Instead they flew me to Fort Benning for some Ranger training, then to the DMZ in Korea."

"Korea? I thought that was over in the fifties."

"That's what I thought." For an instant, Carver's eyes turned humorous and he let them smile playfully on the old man. "What a joke that turned out to be! The war goes on. Probably the same today as it was back then. Shootin' and killin' and all that good stuff." His expression quickly changed to one of sentimental sadness.

The old man followed the ash of the cigarette with his eyes. "To tell you the truth, I didn't think that there was still a war going on over there. You never hear about it in the news."

"Bravo Company, Second Division, Seventy-second Infantry." Carver bent his head slightly downward; his eyes remained still. "Middle of the DMZ someplace. South Koreans on both our flanks." He lifted his eyes to meet Ashwood's. "You want to see some fierce fucking fighters, you ought to shake hands with one of those South Korean soldiers. They don't take shit from no one; they'd rather die than give up one inch. We went on a couple of missions with them into the North. Top secret." His eyes scanned the old man's face for a hint of acknowledgment.

Ashwood understood. "You always think that kind of stuff goes on, but you let it go somehow and pretend that it doesn't."

Carver unfolded his legs and leaned forward on the sofa. "Well, it did and it does. That's where little Johnny Carver learned how to be a first-class killer. Hardened me up. Taught me that life is one great big real estate deal. Nothing else counts. Just like the Russians in Afghanistan. We can yell and holler all we want, but they own the real estate, it's theirs."

Ashwood held back his comments. Reaching down to the ashtray, he snuffed the cigarette out and leaned back.

There was a lull in the conversation. Carver drank and let his gaze spread over the room. "The first guy I saw killed was a guy just like me. His older brother had been sent to 'Nam so he ended up in Korea. A dumb kid, really. I was older and more experienced than him. We were out in the trenches one night when the firing started. He was my radio man, and I had the sixty-caliber machine gun. When the bullets started flying, I told him to keep his head down." Carver gestured, holding both hands over his head. "I raised the gun over my head and let go with a couple of blasts to let them know that we had real guns too." He let his hands fall back to his lap. "I can still remember the kid. He was smiling and giggling and telling me how proud he was of his brother who must have done this a thousand times. I held the gun up some more and blasted away. A couple of minutes later I turned around and the kid had no head. Shot clean off at the neck."

Ashwood gasped. "Holy God!"

"Holy God nothing, old man." Carver was fast to react. "If I think about it now for too long, I could start to have feelings about it. But not back then. Didn't think twice. Just picked up the radio and called Headquarters; asked them to send me another radio man. Blanked that fuckin' fool kid right out of my mind and kept shootin'."

Ashwood arched the back of his head and worked the neck muscles. "Well, it's a sick world we live in, John. I wish you hadn't had to go through that." He picked up his glass and swirled the remaining whiskey. "That's good stuff. I appreciate your bringing it over. You know, I think I'm gonna cut some salami and make a sandwich. Can I get you one to help soak up the whiskey?"

Carver was grinning when he nodded his acceptance.

Ashwood hoisted himself from the chair and started for the other end of the flat.

"Tell me, old man, is your name really Ashwood, or what exactly do I call you?"

Ashwood sensed Carver's voice was close behind him as he passed the bed and made his way toward the kitchen. "Well, you've been calling me 'old man.' You can stick to that if you want. Many of the college kids call me Marvin, and occasionally some polite soul calls me Mr. Ashwood or Sir. You can take your choice. Just don't call me Marv." He stopped and pulled open the refrigerator door. "I'll probably wake up with heartburn after eating this, but I can't resist when it's so close at hand. What do you want me to call you? You went into the service as John Carver, but your business card says something else."

He placed the salami on the table and shot the young man a swift sidelong glance. He noticed that Carver had loosened his tie and undone the top button of his shirt.

"Listen, Marvin, perhaps the less you know about me the better. Underneath my spit-and-polish and fine threads, there's a ton of hidden shit. And maybe that's where it should stay—underneath."

Ashwood began cutting the French bread into thick slices. "You know something, John? I've been around this earth a long time. I've seen and listened to a thousand stories about sin and weakness as well as courage and strength. I happen to be mildly interested in you and your story because of what we went through together today, and because, quite frankly, I kind of like you." Ashwood had a genuinely honest expression on his face as he put the sandwiches on a plate and turned to hand them to his guest.

Carver remained strangely silent for a moment, as if he were debating within himself whether or not to trust the old man. When he spoke, his words came out in low, measured tones. "I don't know what it is about you, old man. Do you usually move in on people like this? I mean, over at that sandwich shop, you must have a hundred friends. What do you want from me?"

When Ashwood was finished at the table, he gestured with his head toward the other end of the room. "Shall we?" Carver briefly held his eyes on him before walking ahead.

Once back to the sitting area, the old man filled the glasses and settled back in his chair. "You're correct in saying that I have a lot of friends. Maybe not hundreds, but quite a few. However, most of them are students and have student problems. You know the kind, housing and emotional..." He tapered off and appeared to be pondering his words. "I don't mean to imply that students' problems are less important than the rest of society's. In many respects they are bigger. Society's problems are passed on to them and many of them can't seem to handle them." He picked up the sandwich and waved it in the air. "Anyway, we can talk about them later, if you like. For now let's stick to John Carver, the unknown."

Carver waited until he had swallowed a large bite and had had another swig from the glass. "The unknown? What do you think I am? A thief or a murderer? Shit, if that were the case, life would be easy. Hell, no, I'm none of those. Just because I killed in Korea, that doesn't make me a killer now. Shit, I hated it then. Did it mostly because I was scared. Killing ain't natural for me. Fucking, now that's natural." He took another bite and spoke as he chewed. "You slay me, old man. You thought I was a killer. What a joke! Is that why you thought the police were after me?"

Ashwood listened and watched with the patience that only older people seem to have. Again he was struck by Carver's crudeness about sex; it seemed to go beyond youthful frankness into something else, something deeper. "I honestly don't know what to believe. So far all I know is a little bit of your wartime history, and that you have two names, or use two names at any rate."

"Yeah, but you don't even know that. All you saw was that I was carrying business cards with someone else's name on them. You're assuming that those cards were mine and not someone else's."

"That's correct, but I think I am assuming the right thing."

A relaxed smile came over Carver's face. "This booze has made me woozy. I usually don't drink it straight. I'm kind of a beer-and-potatoes man." Carver started to laugh. "Get it, beer and potatoes, instead of meat... and..."

"You dress like a cognac-and-potatoes man," Ashwood interrupted and chuckled out loud.

Carver became more exuberant as he slapped the side of his leg. "Not bad, old man. How about Scotch or maybe vermouth?" He hoisted himself up and stood at attention in front of the sofa, holding the sandwich in one hand and the half-full whiskey glass in the other. "Tell me, Marvin, which do you want, Scotch or vermouth?" He held his arms up and slowly twirled around.

Ashwood's chuckle evolved into a spitting laugh as he got caught between bites and gulps. "How about a bottle of Red Mountain?"

"Ahh... I look better than cheap wine." Carver twirled around again. "Tell you what, if it's a gallon bottle, then you're on."

"Make it two. Two jugs," the old man said, still smiling.

Carver's bright, half-lit expression eroded from his face and turned opaque, then more rigid. "I ain't no cunt, old man. You don't see any tits on me, do you?"

Ashwood's face showed a shocked surprise. "I don't understand, did I—"

"Let's forget it, Ashwood. Let's just forget it."

The old man sat stupefied for several seconds, wondering. He waited until Carver had retaken his seat and appeared more comfortable. "Let me just put it this way. You dress like a million, but underneath the fancy outfit there is something troubling you. I'm not sure how bad it is for you, or how you handle it, or even what it is. But I know it's there. I can see it in you, John, or whoever you are or pretend to be." Ashwood let his words fall into place while he poured himself some more whiskey and quietly offered some to his guest.

Carver waved his hand and refused the offer. Giving off a hollow laugh and following it with a long, gusty breath, the young man let his gaze lower to the table and the whiskey bottle. "On second thought, another sip or two just might hit the spot." He stuck out his arm and tilted the glass toward Ashwood.

The old man hesitated, then slowly lifted the bottle and poured.

"All right, old man, you win. So John Carver isn't my real name. But it used to be—for the first twenty-five years of my life it was. John Patterson Carver was my official full name. My cunt mother gave it to me when I was born. Never did like it."

"Pardon me?"

Carver smiled frankly. "I called her a cunt. It's just a figure of speech. A more or less accurate one at that. Fits most women, if you ask me. My mother is a weak cunt, I can't help that. It's just an honest statement of fact. I can't help it if that offends you. Life offends everybody sometimes, so we just take it. That's all any of us can do. Give it back now and then, but for the most part, take it."

"I don't think I would go that far, but you have the floor. If that's what you think of her, then that's your business."

"It's my business, all right. She drove my father over the brink and into the gutter. Her, with her flashy blond hair and her big tits."

Ashwood needed to probe. "I've never heard such anger expressed toward one's mother."

"Look, when I was growing up, my father owned a small grocery store in Campbell, on Winchester Boulevard right near the San Jose border. He wasn't what you'd call an American corporate giant or anything, but he made a good living and I used to help him out a lot. You know, stocking shelves, running errands and the like. After school and on weekends mostly. My older brother and I both did it. Dear old Mom, she stayed home and pretended to take care of the house. What was really happening was that she was taking care of the next door neighbor. Seduced that bastard and screwed his cock off. Fuck, I don't even like talking about that cunt. She used to send me over to his house to cut his lawn and take care of his yard. All the while she was playing with his prick. I bet she had a snatch that big." His hands formed a large circle. "Listen, I'm sounding bitter and I really don't mean to. I thought

I had gotten over her. I've told myself a hundred times that she was forgiven. She was weak, that's all. Human and weak."

Ashwood crossed his legs while he lit another cigarette. He had heard a lot of vulgarities in his time but never with such rage behind them. A sense of uneasiness crept over him and he sucked harder, letting the smoke stay within his lungs longer than usual.

"You don't mind, old man, if I get a little drunk, since I bought the stuff? I'm feeling kind of good now." Carver extended his arm over the table and clasped his hand around the neck of the bottle. "When I was in the service, I used to drink this stuff by the quart, all night, every night. Sometimes I'd drink half the bottle while I was fucking some Korean cunt in the ass." He poured the whiskey and gave a loud, boastful laugh. "Let me tell you, old man, that's how I survived over there. Drinking and fucking worthless cunts. And it's the same here, only here in the so-called civilized world, I have to wear a suit and act the part." Carver had his elbows on his knees as he held the glass between his hands and rolled it in his palms. Clumsily he put it down without drinking and leaned back.

The old man felt the awkward silence descend. Not knowing where the conversation would turn next, he wanted somehow to gain control, or at least steer it away from the subject of women and their private parts.

The young man remained slouched for a second before snapping his head up straight. His eyes had a watery glaze to them. "Like I was saying, it started when I was fourteen. A big chain store moved in half a mile from my father's place. That's when the trouble started. The manager was a woman. You know, one of those college-educated, know-it-all types. Insensitive bitch. She called my father several times. Told him that it wasn't her fault, but she had orders from the people on top to make it as fast and as profitable as she could."

An expression of sadness came over Carver's face. He leaned forward, picked up the glass, and concentrated on its contents. "When my father was building the business, he always told me how lucky he was to own a small business and be able to help out other people when they were in need. Back then, during bad times, when people lost their jobs for one reason or another, they would come to him. He would ring up their tabs, but they would never get charged. My father was that kind of man."

Ashwood felt a sudden fatigue. His body was not used to so much happening in one day; yet he wanted to hear the rest of Carver's story. "I've met men like that. As a matter of fact, I know quite a few of them."

"Well, he was one of them. Never hurt anyone. Tried to do good. What else can I say? He was my father."

"I understand," the old man said softly.

"That cunt put him out of business. Took her less than a year to do it, but she finally got her prices so low that hardly anybody came to buy. There would be the old faithful, and some stragglers now and then, but eventually even they stopped coming around.

"We went out of business, and we couldn't sell the building for what we had paid for it. My father wanted to start over, but..." He let the words trail off. "FUCK!"

He yelled in a loud, pounding voice. "Except my mother destroyed him. Just when he needed support, that cunt started on him. Called him a worthless prick. Hurt him bad, real bad. Made him cry, I remember that. In the kitchen, tears coming down his cheeks. Sucked him dry and left with the neighbor. Cunt.

"Let me tell you, old man. When I was fourteen it was a rotten fucking year. Me and my brother were forced to live with that fucking worthless piece of ass and her new shack job. We had to listen while she went on about Pop's inadequacies and insecurities. I get nauseated just thinking about it." Carver swirled the whiskey in the glass and stared through it.

"It ruined my father. He gave up on life and everything. Became a shiftless alcoholic and vanished. Stumbled into the house one day when *she* wasn't there and gave me a giant bear hug and told me that he was leaving and probably wouldn't be back." Carver lifted his eyes to the old man and laughed rather seriously. "My mistake, back then, was not going with him. Instead I had to take my mother's bullshit till I was seventeen: then it was the Army." He shook his head in disgust. "I don't know which was worse."

Ashwood wanted desperately to offer some words of wisdom and comfort which would help Carver climb out of his temporary torment, but his mind couldn't find the right ones. "You paint a very gloomy picture. Sometimes everything seems to go wrong all at once. This can cause you to take the wrong step."

"I stepped into hell." Carver raised his eyebrows a fraction, then straightened the knot in his tie. "But I survived, and I guess that's what counts in this world."

"There are different ways of surviving. It is a struggle, I'll admit that, but it can be a joyous struggle."

"There's a quality in *your* life. There's just fucking and survival in mine."

"If you say so."

"Want some more of this stuff?" With his index finger Carver pointed toward the bottle. "Getting down there. Lucky I bought two. You have a bathroom around here?"

The old man unfolded his frame from the chair and rose slowly. "Over here, let me show you." As he walked ahead Ashwood could feel the effects of the whiskey. His balance was not up to par and his feet felt heavy even without shoes. He opened the bathroom door and turned on the inside light. "Here you are."

"I got to take a leak. Why don't you bring some more food? We can fix it at the table."

Ashwood nodded and continued to the kitchen.

Chapter Twenty-five

When Carver got back to the sofa he leaned forward again, elbows on his knees, and made a tower with his hands, resting his chin on the apex. His sad eyes stared absently at the old man. When he finally spoke, there was an apology in his tone. "You know, when I came over here tonight, I had no intention of staying. I made my appearance to gather my things and leave. I brought you the goodies because I...well...like a bribe...so you wouldn't say anything to the police. And...I figured I owed it to you. I owed you something for helping me out."

"Life is funny," Ashwood spoke softly, "funny in the sense that it has its turns, its peaks, and its valleys. Perhaps this is one of those turns in both our lives. Sometimes you never know till it's over and you have a chance to look back. But I have that feeling, that something is happening tonight that could take you in a whole new direction."

Carver gave a short, hedging grunt. "My fate has already been sealed. Pass the bread, will ya? Did you bring the knife?"

Ashwood took the knife from behind the plate, handed

it across the table, then slid the bread over to Carver's side. "Fate can always be changed, remember that. It is a very flexible thing."

Carver sliced himself a wide piece of bread, slapped some mayonnaise on it, and started cutting thin ovals of salami. "You can believe what you want. A person knows his own fate. I really wish you'd stop calling me John Carver. You know my name as well as I do."

"Yes, well. You tell me, then I'll believe you."

"I didn't change it till I was twenty-five. After the service I spent several years hanging out in college classrooms trying to keep a C average, but sometimes not succeeding at it. Mostly I was working out at the gym, taking boxing classes or running wind sprints at the track. I kept in pretty good shape, still am.

"Anyway, one day I met this tall, good-looking girl at the track." Carver leaned back and held the sandwich loosely in his right hand. "She was a math teacher, but she was the ambitious kind. We didn't talk to each other for almost a month. She was always running in the opposite direction from me. But one day I got lucky. Got there early and found her doing her warm-up exercises, so I joined her. We talked casually, about exercises and sports and whatnot. Found out her name was Jennifer—Jennifer Jane Wallace. She preferred just J.J. for short.

"She was a three-miler and I was a sprinter. I suggested that we run together and told her that I wasn't sure I could go that distance all at once. She said she'd slow up." Carver took a mouthful of sandwich, chewed hard, and swallowed deeply. Easing his body forward, he dropped the bread to the table and gripped his glass. "Whoever heard of salami with whiskey? Heartburn city." He held the glass up to his eyes and watched it swish for several seconds before taking a huge gulp.

He leaned back and continued. "Well, good old J.J. and I started out together, but before we had gone two laps I knew that she had intended to show me up. I tried my best to keep up, but I crapped out in two miles. Just wasn't used to the distance. She didn't slow down one bit, didn't even look back. Cunt.

"For some reason we started going out together, and over a period of time I really began to like her. I even loved her." Carver nodded his head several times. "I mean, I really did love her. If it wasn't for the fact that I always got the feeling that she was competing against me, we probably could have made one hell of a team." Carver scratched the tip of his nose with his index finger and gave a forced cough. "You ever get that feeling around certain people, you know, when you start to get close to them? You enter a kind of zone of love or of friendship or whatever?"

Ashwood nodded.

"Well, with her, when I entered that zone I got all these unsafe vibrations. It was like entering a boxing ring as a welterweight having to face the heavyweight champion of the world. Sometimes being around her was terrifying. Sometimes she was so nice and loving, but I never knew when she was going to throw a knockout punch. She caught me with several jabs when I wasn't expecting them. When you're in love with someone you're so exposed, I mean emotionally speaking. I just never knew when she was gonna clobber me." Carver stopped talking and let his hand swoop over the table as he plopped the glass near the sandwich. "Do you know what I'm talking about?"

"I have a faint idea. Those situations can be very sticky. You loved her, but she kept beating you at everything. Dangerous."

Carver shook his head violently. "No, no. You missed the point. She didn't beat me at anything. After a couple of weeks I could run with her. It wasn't that she beat me at anything. But she wouldn't let up. Always the pressure. If I said the wrong thing accidentally, she'd throw me a jab. Even if I said the right thing, sometimes she'd throw me a right cross just to keep me off guard.

"Typical modern cunt, I guess. Knows all the right moves when she wants your cock. But otherwise, keeps you dancing and dodging the blows. What a way to run a relationship. Fuck, ran it right into the ground."

Carver picked up the sandwich and finished it off in two bites. "You know, old man, I don't know if you've ever gone through anything like that. I mean, the women of your generation weren't the boxing kind. But for me it was a terrifying experience. Got a lot of emotional bruises from that one. When I finally told her that I couldn't fight her any longer and gave her my reasons for conceding the match, she told me that she could accept how I felt but that she wasn't going to slow down for anybody. We shook hands and I stepped out of the ring. She quit her teaching job and last I heard had joined the police force. Good old J.J. dressed in combat boots and getting even with men! I bet she even looks like a man. Underneath the tits and up the snatch, she's a man all right. A professional success, personal failure."

Carver's mood became reflective, as if he had hit on an essential truth. "I think she's a man-hater. Deep down inside, I bet she really doesn't like men. Uses them, but hates 'em. Bitch."

The old man braced himself with both hands on the armchair and pushed himself to a standing position. "Nature calls. Can we continue on about combat boots and macho policewomen when I get back?"

Carver gave a mute nod.

When Ashwood returned he was carrying his satchel. He found Carver standing facing the window, holding the whiskey glass by its brim. Putting the satchel on the floor, he quietly pushed it under the table with his foot. "Not much of a view, is there?"

Carver did not turn his head. "Fire house across the street. Ever wake you up in the middle of the night?"

"Yes, occasionally. Their sirens are not kind to the ears. One of the hazards of living here. I put up with it."

"Do you make a fuss about anything, old man?" Carver half-turned around, jaw jutting out, eyes in a glare. "You sure put up with a lot. Doesn't anything bother you? Do you mind me asking who the hell are you? You're not a professor, that I already know."

Ashwood remained calm and did not appear startled by Carver's sudden burst of loud questions. When he spoke it was in a fluid, natural tone, giving emphasis to no particular word. "If you want a summary of my life, I am an ex-everything. An ex-child, an ex-soldier, an ex-priest, an ex-lover,-businessman, and -trash collector. I have traveled many roads on my journey and have encountered many people. I did not ask to be put on this earth, but I'm here nonetheless. The best we can do, any of us, I suppose, as we pass through this earthly time frame, is to treat our fellow travelers in such a way as to bring them comfort and ease their burden."

Carver's jaw dropped. His eyes opened into a wide, gawking stare. "An ex-priest?"

"I regard that as only one of the roads which I have been on. It was not an easy road for me. It too was filled with pitfalls and outside temptations. You see, a man is only a man. He is not a saint or a superman. I thought that by becoming a spokesman for the Lord, I would rise above my common nature and rid myself of all temptation.

"Such was not the case, although I managed for a good many years. But the secular ways of the world eventually began to clog my spirituality, and down I came. I used to think of myself as a safe harbor in life's scheme, a harbor for all those lost souls to cling to. But things did not turn out that way. Life took several unyielding turns and I ended up a drifter, separated from the harbor and sometimes unable to keep my head above water.

"So here I am. Older and perhaps a little wiser, but still adrift."

Carver found the sofa and sat down heavily. "When I'm sober, I'm not usually like this."

"You mean when you're Owen Sheldon, real estate salesman, member of the Million Dollar Club, you're not usually like this. That more accurate?" The old man rubbed his chin with the tips of his fingers and let his crafty eyes settle on the man's face.

Again the younger man stalled the conversation purposely. His expression was too complex and cloudy for Ashwood to venture a guess at what was going on in his mind. "I'm processed, just like the whole fucking world. Processed and sculptured to look and act like Owen Sheldon, the nice guy. I mean, let's face it, I dress in an expensive costume and put on cosmetic smiles. I'm willing to admit that, old man. Just 'cause I am a little drunk. I know what I am, at least on the outside. But it gets me by. I act well and sell a lot of real estate. I kind of like Owen Sheldon, he's a nice guy."

The old man thought for a second, then probed some more. "I'll agree with you that much of the world we live in has no soul, and as you have so ably put it, it is processed and cosmetic. But what about you? How did you leapfrog from John Carver the woman-hater to Owen Sheldon the nice guy?"

Sheldon did not answer the question directly. He hung his head and shook it methodically. "Don't ask me, old man. Please don't ask." He lifted his gaze to Ashwood. "All I know is that I'm not a woman-hater. I like women sometimes and I dislike them sometimes."

"You certainly haven't shown me that you love them. If you could only hear yourself talk, and feel the anger behind your words."

"Don't make me laugh." Sheldon was quick to reply in an abrupt, cynical tone. "You grew up in another world. I call it like it is... a snatch, a box, a fucking cunt. Every man I know uses the same lingo. Check the magazine racks. All you see is tits and cunts staring at you. A fucking cunt is a cunt and that's just how life is. I didn't make the rules, you know. I'm just a member of this here great society."

Ashwood adjusted himself in his chair. Suddenly he felt very uncomfortable being in Sheldon's presence. There was something radically wrong inside the salesman, and the old man realized that he could not offer any quick fix or easy answers. "I'm sure you are wrong, Owen. There are—"

"I'm sure I'm right," Sheldon interrupted with a burst. "Women have made their sole function the satisfaction of man's cock. Fuck, old man, look around. The way they dress, the way they walk. That's all they want. That's what they have become . . . servants . . . objects to satisfy me."

Ashwood breathed a long sigh. "They are people, you know. It's a mistake to generalize."

Sheldon opened his mouth as if to shout out another burst of heated words, but he managed to hold back for some unknown reason. He looked at the old man with angry eyes. Before he spoke again he swallowed loudly and drew in a controlled breath. "Maybe you're right, old man. Let's drop it. Let's change the subject."

Ashwood studied Sheldon's face intently. He did not reply.

"I did it legally. Life became one big drag after me and the cunt broke up. I got fed up with life and women especially. So I decided to sell everything I owned and move on. And I do mean I got rid of everything; the house I was buying, the car, all my clothes, shaving kit, you name it . . . everything. It came on me like a brilliant light from the sky. I wanted nothing to do with my past life. So I got rid of everything, friends and all. Took the cash and hauled ass.

"When I settled, it wasn't in Menlo Park. It was right here in San Jose. Had a new job and a new name. All done through a lawyer, real legal like." Sheldon reached around to his back pocket and yanked out his wallet. "Except for this. I kept this for memory's sake and in case I ever needed it." Pulling out his old driver's license, he flashed it across the table to show the old man. "And it came in handy just when I needed it. But I don't need it anymore." With his other hand he swept the knife to the side, then slapped the license in its place. "Tonight we shall bury John Carver for good." Holding the knife in a downward thrusting position, he stabbed it through the license, driving the point into the hard wood. "There you have John Carver, dead and forgotten." With his right hand he reached down and ripped the paper from the blade and threw it to the side.

The old man grew more tense. There was a monster in the room, dressed in the disguise of a neat business suit. Ashwood clung to the arms of the chair to hide his tremor. His eyes stayed fastened to the knife, still wavering, embedded in the table. He stifled the nausea that threatened to erupt within him, and sucked in a half-dozen uneven breaths, trying to regain his composure. It took a great effort to move, and when he did, he nervously bent forward and extended his arm under the table.

Unsnapping the top of the satchel, he anxiously let his hand feel into the bag, his fingers working like spider legs across the loosely packed contents. When he felt the strange smoothness of the animal skin, a curious, frightened look came to his face. He pulled the white sheepskin hood from its secure hiding place, opened it out, and held it in front of his eyes so that the cut-out holes stared vacantly back at him. "Good God! What is this? Who are you when you put this on?"

Sheldon leaned back cockily and twisted his arms behind his head. His expression was a wide, unbending smile, eyes glassy and fixed on the old man. "John Carver is gone, but every once in a while his spirit returns. Look, padre." He became animated now, unscrewing his arms and gesturing with his hands. "They say confession is good for the soul, so I won't kid around. It's another costume I wear. Just like my suit." Sheldon drew his arms closer to his body and slowly rolled his fingers into a fist. "That hood, old man, gives me my escape. It bestows on me a certain charisma. A certain right. It gives me the power to fight back. It grants me the power which other men only dream of. The power over the cunt. And when I exercise that power, it is the greatest feeling in the world. I become transformed and made again. It's like winning the Super Bowl every time I do it. Shoving my cock into some sleazy snatch. It's man's last stand: the rape of a woman."

Ashwood sat rigid in his chair for a long, anxious moment. A crescendo had been reached in the conversation, and he wanted to let the fever cool. Without knowing where to start, he suddenly felt a compulsion to say something.

"We are all in this together," he blurted out. "You can't escape that. You're not going to wipe out an entire sex with your act of power."

"I'm not a killer!" The response came swiftly. "I don't want to wipe out anybody." Sheldon shifted his legs in irritation, then lashed out across the table and seized the sheepskin, snapping it from Ashwood's hands in one sharp, coordinated movement. "I'll take that." He draped it in front of him and an iridescent gleam came to his eyes. "When confession is over, I'll be taking this with me." Folding it carefully, he placed it at his side and returned his fierce eyes to Ashwood.

"It's a battle zone out there. That's what you don't understand. The cunts don't want to love us any more. They want our jobs, they want our souls." Sheldon's mood seemed to change again. A sad, defeated expression came to his face. Sighing heavily, he leaned back and put his head against the pillow and stared awkwardly at the ceiling. "I think they've got mine already. Inside I've felt hollow for a long time. I'm not sure, maybe the battle is over." Lifting his right hand, he closed his eyes and massaged them with the tips of his fingers. "I'm tired, old man. Tired and drunk."

The long day and the tension had made Ashwood extremely tired. He yawned openly and let his eyelids droop nearly shut for a second. "It is very late, and I'm afraid we've both had too much to drink. May we continue this conversation in the morning?"

"Now, old man," Sheldon demanded and sat up straight, eyes wide open. "I won't be here in the morning. When I leave, I won't be coming back."

The old man paused for a second. "Pardon me for rambling," he said sleepily. "You are a troubled man, Owen Sheldon. Under that suit of yours there is a lot of ugly rage. You've been avoiding it and burying it for a long time, but tonight I think you've at least acknowledged it."

Ashwood yawned again and cupped the yawn with the palm of his hand. "Maybe that's a start. What you do from here is up to you."

When Sheldon moved his arm, his gesture was slow but economical. He appeared weary as he checked the time from his wristwatch. The liquor and the long night were beginning to show their effects. The intensity in his eyes seemed somehow to have evaporated, replaced by a drowsy, listless gaze. "I'm tired, old man. My energy has been depleted, and I am still not satisfied." His words came out in slow, lethargic tones. "Nothing satisfies anymore." He stopped talking and quietly let his words dissolve.

"I will pray for you, Owen Sheldon. I can offer you no easy answers and I cannot give you what you want, but I can pray. It is the only thing I know. Perhaps it will help."

Sheldon sluggishly hoisted his body to a standing position. "I've got to be going." He took the sheepskin hood from the sofa and stuffed it partially into the waist of his pants. He stumbled to the coat, grabbed it off the hook, and squeezed it tightly in the palm of his hand. When he looked back at Ashwood, a tentative smile came to his lips. "Well, it's been nice, old man." He grunted softly and started for the door.

Ashwood unfolded himself from the chair and followed. "I wish we could have met years ago. I'm sure we could have formed a great friendship."

"Yes, probably." Reaching the door, Sheldon took hold of the handle, opened it wide, and turned back to look at Ashwood. "You said you left the keys in the ignition?"

The old man gave a nod.

"Well then, shake my hand and wish this traveler good fortune."

The two men shook hands and quietly held each other's gaze for a long moment.

"Take care, old man. Maybe I shall see you around sometime."

"Yes, that would be nice. I shall remember you in my prayers."

Part Three

Chapter Twenty-six

The room was antiseptically clean. The air inside was motionless, seventy-five degrees Fahrenheit. It was dark, except for the low luminescence cast by the fluorescent lamp attached to the wall close to the tall bed. Molosky's body lay like a warm slab underneath the fresh white sheet. Even in a coma his heartbeat pulsed at a strong fifty-five per minute.

In a chair at the side of the bed sat Phyllis—legs crossed at the ankles, back straight, hands folded on her lap. She had just come in from a slow, meandering walk around the hospital, which ended with a short cup of coffee and part of a stale donut from a vending machine in the cafeteria downstairs.

She looked up as the door opened and a man emerged from the hallway light. He walked with a swagger, and made his way to the chair next to hers.

"It's been a long night," he whispered as he lifted his sunglasses from the bridge of his nose and wiped the lens across his knee.

"Sergeant Sanders..."

"Doug. Please ma'am, just call me Doug. Please. We've known each other for almost a week now. That qualifies me, don't it?"

"Okay, Doug. Listen, you don't have to come every night. His family has that responsibility. You look like you could use some rest."

"I don't mind really. I just got off and was on my way home. A couple of minutes here or there doesn't make that much difference. I lead a wicked life anyway. Never seem to catch enough sleep. How's he doing?"

Phyllis shifted in the chair and faced Sanders more directly. She gazed at him calmly. "He's fine. At least he is still with us. We can thank God for that. Not much change. None really. We'll just have to keep praying, that's all."

Sanders pulled on his shirt pocket and stuffed the glasses next to a pack of cigarettes. "I'm not really good at that. I've gotten too used to cursing lately. But if the Almighty will forgive me, then I'll have a go at it."

Phyllis chuckled softly and gave him a speculative glance. "The chaplain comes by every morning and afternoon. You could stay and talk to him. Make it official." Her eyes stayed on him, and she could tell by the way he moved his head and cast his gaze down that her plan for his instant redemption would have to be put off until some other more appropriate time. "Let's skip it for now. But I'll keep it in mind and maybe get you some time when you have a weak moment."

Sanders pushed out his jaw and offered a toothy grin. "Now you're talkin'. Some other time."

"How was your night?" she asked.

"Well, we didn't catch him, if that's what you're getting at. I think the guy is scared. Might not come out of hiding for a couple of weeks—whenever he thinks the coast is clear, or whenever things build up inside him too much. He's around. It might be a while, but he'll be back."

"You still don't know who he is?"

"Got a thousand leads to check out. The dicks are supposed to be at it. I don't know. It doesn't look like it'll be done soon. Too many leads and not enough bodies. The guys have got other cases to handle besides this one. Swamped. The cases just keep coming. Something has to be done with each of them. Might take forever, I don't know."

Phyllis's expression turned to one of concern. Her unblinking eyes focused sternly on Sanders. "I thought there were extra men put on this case. After all, it was one of your own who was almost killed."

"That's true; there are more men on this case, at least for now, but they're on the decoy teams. Put three new teams together and started them last night." He waved his hand to show his disgust. "What a joke that is. That's a whole different story. I'll tell you about it sometime. My point was that they're out there pounding the cement trying to pick up perverts, when they should be checking out all those cards and names we got from the area where Ray was found . . . tons of 'em." He stopped talking, put his hand down, and sighed deeply. "Everyone thinks it's so easy, but it ain't. Just when the new teams get all coordinated and everything, they'll pull them off, too. And that's when the guy will hit. Two, maybe three weeks. Mark my words. I've seen it happen before."

"Isn't there anything that can be done? There must be something."

Sanders lifted his head to stare at Phyllis through tired, glassy eyes. "Luck is one answer. I've always believed in luck. Doesn't always pay off, but you have to have it to get anywhere. But I'll bet one of the officers talked to the rapist that evening. It's a gut feeling I have. His name is in that stack of cards somewhere. I'll call tomorrow and see what progress is being made. Maybe the guy has no record. That would make it harder for us to catch him. But there's something there, I just feel it. You've got to listen to your bones sometimes."

Looking over Sanders's shoulder, Phyllis spotted the night nurse coming into the room. She took short, crisp steps and came to an abrupt stop behind Phyllis.

"It's nearly three-thirty; you both know that, I suppose.

Special privileges or not, don't you think you're overdoing it? He's not going anywhere. He'll be here when you get back. Why don't you both go home and get some sleep?"

Suddenly there was a low moan coming from the head of the bed. The nurse quit talking. Phyllis and Sanders turned and stared at Molosky. The sound came again. This time they could see Molosky's chest heave and his lips move as a deep, throaty noise emerged.

"Nurse, I think he's coming around. Nurse!" Phyllis said excitedly.

Without a word, the nurse quickly made her way to the side of the bed and bent down over Molosky. His head stirred. She lifted his eyelid and shined a small pocket light into his eye. His groan became loud and irritated when she repeated the movement with the other eye. When she released her grip, she stood back. "Mr. Molosky, if you can hear me, try to move your head."

Molosky turned his head toward the voice. He opened his mouth and tried to say something, but the words only dropped out in a semi-intelligible slur. He expelled several light gusts of air, then appeared to be working his tongue around the inside of his mouth.

"Water. Give him a little water," Phyllis said in a commanding tone.

The nurse lifted a pitcher of water from the bedside table and poured into a glass. Wrapping her hand around Molosky's head, she tilted him forward and offered the water to his lips. "Here, open and take a sip."

Molosky's lips parted slightly in anticipation of the liquid. When it came he let it run across his tongue to the back of his throat. He swallowed hard and moved his head back and forth in a gesture for the nurse to release him.

Gently, she gave him back to the pillow. "There, is that better?"

Molosky took several breaths, then swallowed lightly. "Ahh..." He tried to pronounce his first word, but it only came out in an unrecognizable muffle. He made a low, clearing sound in the back of his throat before trying again. "Is that you, Phyllis?"

"Yes, Ray, I'm right here." Phyllis moved closer to the bed.

"Sis, that you? Where am I? Sanders?"

Phyllis held her hand to her lips to silence Sanders. "I'm right here, Ray." She took his hand. "You're in the hospital. You were hurt and you've been unconscious for a couple of days. You don't have to talk if you don't want to."

"The light, Sis. If I open my eyes, don't shine the light."

Phyllis shot the nurse a sharp glance. The nurse nodded submissively. "It's okay, Ray. Try to open your eyes. The room is nearly dark."

Molosky hesitated while he moved his hand slowly around her fingers. "Here goes nothing." His voice seemed stronger. "The first thing I see better not be the ugly face of Doug Sanders." His lips strained to smile. "That you, Doug?"

Sanders rubbed his index finger under his nose, then patted his mustache lightly. "Yeah, it's me. Glad to have you back."

Molosky slowly let the lids of his eyes open. It was Phyllis he saw first. He blinked several times as if he were trying to focus but was having trouble. "Don't move. Sis, you're kind of blurry. That you?"

"I'm right here, Ray."

Molosky blinked again, then held his gaze on her. "Where did you say we are?"

"The hospital. You were hurt. You've been here for nearly a week. How do you feel?"

Molosky closed his eyes and relaxed his head on the pillow. "Hurt? I don't remember being hurt. Was it...?"

"Mr. Molosky, this is Nurse Simmons talking. You have been unconscious for the past six and a half days. You need not concern yourself with all the details at this moment. I do not wish to put any undue strain on you until the doctor has a look. Do you understand?"

Molosky waited for a moment before answering. "I understand. Sis, don't leave me." His grip tightened around hers.

"I'm afraid they'll both have to leave. Doctor's orders. After you've been thoroughly checked, visitors will be allowed. I'm sorry."

"Ray?" It was Phyllis's voice again. "It's going on four in the morning. Why don't you relax and try to sleep? I'll be back later and we can talk."

Molosky was slow to answer. "Sis, will you do something for me?"

Phyllis released her hand from his and brought it to his cheek. "I'm glad you're back with us. Go ahead, name it."

"I just want you to tell Colleen that I love her. Will you do that for me?"

"You can tell her yourself later on. She's been here every day, you know. She's a very special person. You rest now, and we'll see you later."

"Ray, you take care now, hear?" Sanders's voice was mellow and restrained.

Molosky half-smiled and gave a single nod.

For three days a team of doctors monitored Molosky's bodily functions. There was no permanent brain damage, but they had predicted that a mild form of amnesia might occur, which would only relate to the most recent past and would probably only be temporary. To help him understand exactly what had happened, a staff psychiatrist visited him several times. On the morning of the third day, after a particularly fitful night, the psychiatrist called on Molosky.

"You look like you could use more sleep; and you said you were ready to go home!" The doctor wore a white smock which had two black pens sticking out from the breast pocket. He was bald, with thin gray eyes and turned-in lips.

Molosky put *Sports Illustrated* aside and gave the doctor a suspicious look. *The mind mechanic,* he thought, and wondered if he were "normal" like the rest of the human race. "You back for more? Don't you ever give up?"

"Now, now, Sergeant, I only stopped by to see how you were getting on. How do you feel?"

Molosky rolled his eyes around in their sockets, then brought his hand to his jaw. "Well, if you must know, I feel like hell. Like I've been run over by a Mack truck and left for dead. How the hell would you feel? How the hell am I supposed to feel? I sure ain't gonna feel good about it, if that's what you think." Molosky thought for a moment, then picked up the magazine and began to leaf through it. Without looking up, he continued, "I'm sorry, Doc. I shouldn't have spouted off like that. It's just that I don't particularly like my present circumstances, and you people don't seem to want to let me out of here."

"Perhaps tomorrow that will be possible. Would that be soon enough?"

Molosky closed the magazine and placed it on the table next to him. "Go ahead and ask your questions. I'll be a good boy until tomorrow. But that's it. Permission or no, tomorrow morning at ten o'clock, I'm leaving."

The doctor walked around and stood at the foot of the bed. "I make no promises, but we shall see. May we get started?"

Molosky shifted his eyes from side to side, then nodded abruptly.

"As you recall, yesterday we were able to jog your memory up to the time you made the phone call to Henry Fowler and asked him to dinner. Do you still recall up to that point?"

Molosky formed a polite smile and scratched the top of his head. "Listen, Doc, I feel like a guinea pig around here. Tell you what. I remember everything—getting the call of the rape in progress, seeing the hooded man, and chasing him down. What I don't remember is anything after I ran through the engineering building. I saw the room number for Professor Hugo Evans... but that's the last of it. I don't know what happened after that."

"Perhaps if we take it a step at a time that might help."

"I've tried that, Doc. All night long I've tried. I remember every detail, every pain, every blow up until that point.

But after that it's all a blank. Why don't we just leave it at that? Maybe it will come to me if I don't try so hard."

The doctor reached to his breast pocket and tapped the tops of both pens. "Yes, well, I'm in favor of that. By all means, let it alone for a few days or a few weeks. It will come when it's ready. Shall we get back to the question which seems to have us both baffled?"

Molosky swallowed anxiously and let his mind slide back. "We can if you want, but I still don't have the answer."

"It wasn't that serious a blow to have you out for nearly a week. What was going on inside your head to keep you unconscious for so long?"

"I don't know, Doc. I was out cold and I can't even remember what put me there, much less why I stayed there so long. Maybe it was my way of saying that the world stinks and I needed a sabbatical."

"Perhaps you did not want to come out of it. That could be true. But for what reason? You're a big, strong, healthy man. I've read about your background. You are not a quitter and a man to give in to fear so easily. So your little vacation puzzles me."

Molosky started to answer quickly, but then closed his eyes and heaved a long sigh. "Listen, Doc, in your business there must be a million things you don't understand. People are just that way sometimes. All I know is that the last feeling I had was a tremendous fear of something or someone. I don't know whether I gave in to it or not. I suppose that bothers me, but I really haven't had time to think about it."

The doctor lifted his index finger to his lower lip and kept his eyes turned down in concentration. "Interesting; fear was your last feeling?"

Molosky grunted and the sound came out more like a cynical laugh. "Well, the guy beat me to a pulp. What do you want from me, anyway?" Molosky grunted again, this time more to himself. "Look, I chased the pervert down and when I caught him, he beat the crap out of me. Now that's not too hard to understand, is it? You guys make mountains out of molehills. I don't think my problems are nearly as big to me as they are to you. Somehow they'll work themselves out, and I'll be able to handle it. You don't have to worry about me. I'll be just fine."

The doctor tugged nervously on his starched white lapels. "Yes, well... yes, I'm sure you will, Sergeant... be able to handle your problems, that is... indeed. Yes, well, then this will be our last little get-together. I'm sure you will be fine. I'm sorry if I upset you."

Molosky eyed him direclty. "You haven't upset me, Doc. This whole *place* upsets me. When can I see some of my friends? My family is getting sick of me."

"Yes, well, I'll check with Doctor Wilson. He's the only person who can authorize that." The psychiatrist's eyes fastened onto Molosky's. "Well, Sergeant, it's been nice. I think we've accomplished something. I hope the rest of your stay here will be pleasant."

"Thanks, Doc, and short, too."

Chapter Twenty-seven

Thin sheets of white light streamed diagonally through the cracks of the curtains and worked their way across the room to where Sheldon lay by himself in a semiconscious sleep. Before the light reached his eyes, the shrill sound of the phone brought him instantly awake, and he grappled to the side of the bed toward the noise. Clumsily, he lifted the receiver and placed it to his ear. Before saying anything, he rolled his head back to the pillow and cleared his throat several times. "Hello, this is Owen."

"Phil Gates here, from the office. Did I wake you?"

"Oh, yeah, Phil. Hi! No, that's all right. I've been extra-tired lately, but I was just getting up. What's up?"

"I wanted to remind you that the company luncheon is today. I didn't want you to forget. You never know, you might win a trophy again this year. Bring Charlotte if you like. She'd make a beautiful asset. You two sure look good together."

Sheldon put the receiver to his other ear and looked to his girl friend's side of the bed. It had not been slept in. He wondered where she had spent the night. "That thing is this week already? Seems like it was just yesterday. What time?"

"Eleven-thirty cocktails, twelve-thirty lunch."

"Yeah, I'll be there. You at the office?"

"No, it's just a little after eight, but I thought I'd call everyone to make sure that we're all in tune with each other. I'd like our office to have one-hundred-percent participation. It looks good, you know, when all the big bosses are there. We've got a good office. Should be fun. I'll see you then."

"Yeah, I'll be in the office by nine. Have some work to do."

After hanging up, Sheldon absently went through the motions of getting ready. He showered and shaved and dressed from habit. As he did, his mind wandered and touched on an assortment of feelings, putting some of them together in a bizarre manner. Thoughts of Charlotte and where she might have spent the night upset him; a jealous hurt started to form in the pit of his stomach.

He thought that he loved her, but he had never really trusted her. She was so confident in her power, so dominant in sex. She could get any man to fuck her. He wished that she truly loved him. Marvin Ashwood and Charlotte Hunter... the sensitive philosopher and the cunning bitch.

Sheldon stood at the mirror and straightened his tie. Maybe Marvin would do all right. They might make a good pair; opposites do attract. He slipped into his suit jacket, resolutely nodded to himself, and told himself that he was going to have a good day, even if Charlotte was out fucking some other cock.

Standing at the back door to the real estate office, he managed a smile, but his eyes remained moody, showing no sparkle to match the curve in his lips. Sheldon walked quietly to his desk, eyeing Phil Gates as he sat reading the morning paper. "Morning, Phil. How's your wife?" He squelched the smile and wondered why he had asked such a question. What did he care about Martha Gates? She was an old, worn-out cunt.

Gates turned in his chair and cleared his throat. He wore a white shirt and colorful bow tie. "Owen, I didn't hear you come in. Trying to sneak up on me, eh?" A compressed smile spread across his face, and he let his bifocals slip down the crook in his nose. "Martha? She's fine. We were talking about you just this morning at breakfast. She's worried about you, that you haven't settled down and married yet. You know how she gets. I told her that you and Charlotte were serious." He let his hand waver in front of him. "I didn't know if that were true or not, but well... it seemed to do the trick at the time. You know how Martha is. She wants you two to come over one of these nights for dinner."

Sheldon sat at his desk, opened the top drawer, and took out his calendar. *There's another match,* he thought. *Martha Gates and Charlotte. The gadfly and the temptress; the sexless busybody and the seductive cunt. Why don't we invite Marvin Ashwood to the party? Now that would make for one festive evening.* Sheldon chuckled at his own thoughts, then lifted his eyes to Gates. "Umm... well, that sounds like it could have possibilities if I can talk Charlotte into it. We'll see. I'll let you know."

Gates rocked in his chair. "Good, then I'll tell Martha that it's a definite maybe."

Sheldon lifted his briefcase to the top of his desk and unsnapped it. He took out a box of business cards and placed them to the side. "A definite maybe, good choice of words."

The front door opened and two saleswomen walked in. Sheldon put some of the business cards in his wallet and relaxed. "Good morning, ladies," he said, suddenly lifting himself into a better frame of mind. "Going to be a beautiful day out there today."

Both women greeted the men. One of them, the younger one, sat at her desk in the front. The other walked up to Sheldon and took a place at the desk next to his.

Sheldon turned in his chair and regarded her with a gentle eye. She was fifty-nine, with full, round features. She wore a pink blouse and green pants. Her face was rosy and friendly, her eyes a chestnut brown. His face widened into a bright, flattering smile. "Vivian, you sure look pretty this morning. How'd you like to keep me company next door? I didn't get breakfast before I left the house. My treat."

In a businesslike gesture Vivian opened her purse and took out her appointment book. "Let me see here." She touched her lips briefly, then proceeded to flip through several pages of the book. "I know I've got something to do this morning. Dick Tharp. I have to show him a house at ten thirty. It should only take a minute, the house is closeby. Seems like I've shown that man every house in the listing book. It's been three months he's been looking." She closed the book and put it back in her purse as she pushed herself into a standing position. "Just one cup, then I have to get back here and clear up some of my paperwork."

The restaurant was small, family owned, and, as usual, crowded in the morning. After waiting for just a minute, Sheldon spotted a table next to the back window and led Vivian to it. When they were seated, he ordered breakfast and two cups of coffee. "I'm glad you could come." He smiled considerately. Vivian Lannon was the only true woman friend he had. She acted as his confidante and counselor and expected nothing in return except respect and companionship and, every now and then, coffee or lunch.

Vivian opened her purse and took out a pack of cigarettes along with a gold-plated lighter. She set the lighter down and pounded the pack against the side of the table. A cigarette shot out and started to roll over the edge on her right side. Sheldon reacted quickly and scooped it up. "These things are bad for your health." He held it out to her.

"Everything is bad for your health. I got up this morning and looked out of my window and saw all that brown stuff. Made me sick. That junk is bad for your health.

Don't see anybody doing anything about it, do you? Living is unhealthy."

The waitress brought the food and carefully set it down. Sheldon eyed her without expression, then turned back to Vivian. He sighed and shrugged his shoulders. "You're right about that. Life is pretty unhealthy these days, in more ways than that. Sometimes I wish it would all go away."

Vivian formed an oval with her lips and blew out the smoke in short gusts. "Don't we all. I've been wishin' that for years, and look where it's gotten me. Older and heavier." She tossed her head to the side. "Maybe a little wiser, but not much.

"You look mighty handsome yourself, Owen. Except your eyes tell me a different story. I know you too well. Your eyes say you've been through the grinder again. What happened? Another blow in your love life? You seem to have this knack for running into the wrong women. What happened? Did she turn out to be another vulture instead of that nice, sweet person you thought she was?"

"Not a vulture, but... things could be better."

"What happened this time? She kick you out? I told you when you started this whole affair that you should have her move in with you, not the other way around. Now she's got the advantage."

Sheldon fingered his water glass. "She was grabbing for the advantage, but I got stubborn. We had one of our knock-down drag-out fights. She finally left; didn't come back. Trouble is I still love her. And she knows that."

After only a few puffs Vivian snuffed the cigarette out, then poured two heaping spoonsful of sugar into her coffee. "Listen, Owen, I think you're a very nice young man. You realize that, don't you?"

Sheldon nodded silently, keeping his eyes on his plate.

"I know you think you love this woman. You do all the things that couples do these days. I mean, I suppose you make love and enjoy sex with each other. However, I'm not sure if you're intimate with her or not. They are two different things, you know. Sex is free and easy these days.

But for the majority it doesn't go very far or run very deep. A lot of bodily pleasure, but no real intimacy. And without intimacy there can't be any real love. Only erotic pleasure, but no love."

Sheldon sat back in his chair and looked out over the people in the restaurant. "Hell, I don't know. Sometimes I hate her and sometimes I love her. That doesn't make any sense, does it?"

Vivian took out another cigarette, stuck it between her lips, and lit it. "You have my undivided attention until this cigarette is done. Then, I have work to do."

"I have some stuff to do, too. Phil wants us all to be ready for the big event this afternoon. We'll sit together, how's that?"

"Right by me. You're not bringing her, are you?"

"What a joke!" Sheldon grunted and let a half-smile come to his lips. "She went out somewhere last night and hasn't come back yet. After our little conversation, she decided that my attitude toward her and women in general wasn't up to her standard, so she took off. I don't know where she went. I don't care, either."

Vivian tapped the cigarette with her index finger. "Of course you do, Owen. If you didn't care you wouldn't be so upset this morning. You want my advice? Then we have to run."

Sheldon lifted the napkin to his lips. "Of course."

"Listen, if she thinks there is something wrong with your attitude about women, or toward her, maybe she should go out for a while. She'll soon find out. So I don't want you to worry your head off. She'll be back, probably today or tonight some time. When she comes back, you should sit down with her and talk. Tell her how you feel and go from there."

Chapter Twenty-eight

For Molosky, walking out of the hospital was like being reborn. The chains which had restricted him had been unshackled and he was now free again. The police department and the hooded rapist had been pushed to the far reaches of his mind and temporarily forgotten.

It was a bright, clear day as he strutted into the warm sunshine and looked up and down the block for a cab. Not finding one immediately, he walked to the busier corner of Santa Clara Street, where his chances would be better. As he strode he was elated at feeling the fresh, warm currents of air again. No one knew he had been discharged yet, and he wanted it to stay that way for a while. He thought he might go for a run later in the day, if his energy held up. When he got to the corner he had to wait only a minute before he was able to flag a taxi.

The ride home was a quiet one. The cab driver was not the stereotypical conversationalist Molosky had expected. He drove slowly and for the most part kept to himself. As they went through the downtown area, Molosky began to pick up sounds even through the window: the hum of the engine, the blast from a passing horn, the shout of a young teenager calling for a bus to stop. And with his eyes, Molosky soaked up the familiar life of the city. A lot different from the monotony and drabness of the hospital, he thought.

When the cab pulled to the curb in front of his house, Molosky paid the fare and thanked the driver. As he entered the house he could feel the cool, stale air touch his warm skin. He walked across the living room toward the kitchen, wondering where Noah was hiding. On the dining table he found two stacks of mail. There was a note attached to an envelope on the top.

Ray,

The nurse told me that you might be out today. I've been watching the house while you've been away. I collected the mail for you; divided it into two stacks, junk and bills. I don't know which you'd prefer throwing away. Also, we have Noah. He's fine and dandy. Welcome back! I'll call you tonight.

Love,
Sis

Molosky smiled to himself. Good old Phyllis, he couldn't fool her. He took the pile of junk and sorted through it. Saving the one envelope which had to do with a special sale on classical record albums, he tossed the rest into the trash. Returning to the table, he casually began flipping through the other stack. As he did, he unintentionally let his mind slip away from the bills and wander back a short distance in time.

First to the quiet walls of the hospital, where no one shouted and no horns blared in his ears, a peaceful place where no one made burdensome demands on him. A colorless, secluded sanctuary where people cared for him and where he wasn't expected to carry on the fight. Then why couldn't he just lay back and enjoy? He could have used a couple more days of being pampered.

Setting the mail down, he strode into the living room and fingered through several record albums before he found one he liked. *The Well-Tempered Clavier* by Bach seemed to fit his mood. As the melodies repeated themselves the music flowed in soothing rhythms through his unsettled soul. Feeling the need to get off his feet and relax, he eased his body into his favorite armchair and leafed through a year-old copy of *Popular Mechanics* that he had borrowed from Bert Yarnell.

As he turned the pages his thoughts drifted again. Pictures of the hooded rapist filtered to the edge of his mind. He saw the man's tightly clenched fist coming toward his face. When it struck, it was like a ball of white lead slamming against his soft, pliable skin. Maybe he wasn't cut out to be a policeman after all. Along with the pain he had felt an overwhelming fear at that moment. Suddenly bravery and courage had deserted him. After the first blow they ran for cover and left him defenseless to fight off the evil man in the sheepskin mask.

As these unhealthy feelings came over him, Molosky was besieged by a compulsion to make things right again, to set things in order. Putting the magazine aside, he stood and came to a decision. He would start with the living room; he would vacuum, then dust and polish. Every day after that he would take another room and clean it and make it right. And he would work out strenuously and gain his health and strength back. He would not let up until he felt his power return.

With that hopeful promise, Molosky stubbornly went to work. He labored slowly, because he realized the distance he had to travel was long and he did not have his full strength yet. Methodically he went about the business of rebuilding himself. He focused his mind and concentrated on what he was doing. Suddenly, nothing mattered but the chores which he had set out to do.

When he was through in the living room, he knew that his energy level was just beginning to build. Without hesitation, he went to his bedroom and changed into his running clothes.

* * *

Owen Sheldon swung his glossy silver four-door through the parking lot and had no trouble finding a space. In the rearview mirror he checked his appearance and let his lips come to a practiced smile. From his breast pocket he found a short black nylon comb, which he used with perfect coordination, gliding it through his hair, delighting in the tingling sensation it gave him. When he was through, he replaced the comb and brushed off his suit jacket with the tips of his fingers. Feeling confident, he stepped into the sunlight and started for the restaurant.

"Isn't this a beautiful location?" he heard a woman say to her companion. He eyed the woman deliberately, then let his gaze take in the surrounding natural beauty. Villa Felice Restaurant blended graciously into the lush green landscape. Giant hillside trees sheltered its roof and provided cool shade on warm days such as this. Spacious decks flanked the exterior walls and gave expansive views of the surrounding foothills, evergreen treetops, and the smooth, silent water of Lake Vasona.

Sheldon strode through the lobby and stepped into the large private banquet room. The company secretary looked up at him and smiled happily. He walked to where she was standing behind a small, decorated card table. "Hi, Julie. Looks like a good turnout." His voice was steady and somewhat subdued. Julie was a nice person, friendly and often helpful from her desk at the head office.

She leaned across the table and pinned on a name tag. "There now, everybody will know you with that on, Mr. Sheldon. You're almost late. We'll be sitting down to eat in a couple of minutes. The bar is still open. You might have time for a quick one, if you hurry."

"Now that sounds like a good idea." Sheldon put on his best salesman's smile and politely nodded to her. Casually, he mingled through the crowd and ordered a drink at the bar. He kept his eyes moving through the room, looking for Vivian or Phil Gates.

As he stood observing the people in the room, a woman

in a low-cut dress took the back of his arm. "Owen, I've been looking all over for you. Where have you been?"

Sheldon knew the voice and hesitated before turning around. He tried to keep his smile, but felt it begin to sag from his face. He let his eyes roam over her, and he wondered if every company had a forty-year-old lush with big tits.

Her lips spread into a flashy red grin. "You like my new dress?"

"You like flaunting those things, don't you?" Sheldon's eyes grew serious. "A woman could get herself raped hanging out like that."

The woman laughed loudly. "You'd sure like to try, wouldn't you?" She moved in closer to him. "I don't know if you could handle it. Why don't you give me a call sometime, and I'll show you what it's all about." She stepped back and let her hand move down between her breasts.

Sheldon pictured himself in the white hood, fucking her in the mouth. He smiled inwardly; that would sure teach her a lesson."Why don't you tuck those things away? Everybody knows you've got them, and nobody cares."

"You do," she said as she spun around curtly and walked away.

Currents of warm air heated Molosky's skin as he stepped from the asphalt parking lot onto the grassy turf. Beautiful afternoon, he thought, and so few to enjoy it. He glanced across the lake to his familiar rest stop. There was no one walking on the path. The hills above the park were dotted with evergreens. He let his eyes scan the hillside. Villa Felice entered his thoughts as he began his jumping jacks. He should take Colleen there sometime for dinner. They had a small band and they could dance.

Sheldon had lunch in the pleasant company of Phil Gates, Vivian, and the rest of the office staff, most of whom he had no real feelings for one way or the other. The announcements and speeches were scheduled for the finish. Sheldon had worked hard all year and had made several large transactions. He felt confident that he would capture a trophy.

When he was finished eating, he leaned back in his chair and belched softly. He let his eyes play over the room, stopping occasionally on one of the people he either knew or had met casually in the short time he had been with the company. When his gaze rested on Donna Catterton, he felt a nervous pain shoot through his stomach. She was a top saleswoman and had beaten him out last year by several thousand dollars. Maybe he should have fucked her cunt off. Might have taught her a lesson, slowed her down.

After eyeing Catterton for a second, Sheldon moved his gaze to the front of the room to the main table. He focused on the thin-looking man in a dark blue formal suit. He was known to his employees as Mr. President. He appeared to be engaged in friendly conversation with his private secretary, a pretty girl in her mid-twenties. Probably getting his share of her, Sheldon mused. When the president had finished whatever he was saying to the secretary, he brought his white napkin to his lips, then pushed his chair out and stood. Briskly, he stepped to the lectern and tapped the microphone with the palm of his hand. A loud echoing sound burst through the room. Surprised, he stepped back, smiling enthusiastically. Handling the microphone more gently, he eased his sturdy head closer to it, then spoke. "This thing really booms, doesn't she? I guess everybody can hear me. Raise your hand if you can't." He stepped back and smiled broadly, then ran his thick hand through his short, lint-white hair.

When he was ready to continue, he stretched out both his arms and nodded his head several times. "Ladies and gentlemen. May I have your attention, please?" His voice was low and gusty; his rhythm was crisp. "I would like to get the awards handed out so that we can get back to work and sell more property." He stepped back and held up his arms again. A beaming smile filled the cracks in his face.

The salespeople applauded.

* * *

You're not a superman, Molosky thought. *Don't go killing yourself the first day back.* With some exertion he ground out the last set of push-ups. He could already tell that it would take time to rebuild his body. Climbing off the grass, he breathed deeply and ambled toward the starting line. He told himself that he would have to endure, at least for three miles, and trotted across the parking lot into the shade of the eucalyptus.

From the table behind him and to the side, the president took the last two trophies and held them up for all to see. "It gives me great pleasure to present this last award. Actually, there are two awards for salesperson of the year. The numbers were so close that we decided that it would be unfair not to have two first prizes."

Sheldon's glance strayed from the speaker's rostrum and settled on Donna Catterton. He should have raped her six months ago, stabbed his cock in her ass. Would have served her right. He anxiously moved in his seat and brought his attention back to the president. A pleasant smile blanketed the president's face.

"I must tell you," he continued, "that these awards are being given to two of our most aggressive, our most outgoing salespeople. I think they are outstanding examples of what America is all about. These people have shown themselves to be fair, honest, and extremely hardworking. They are intelligent when it comes to the real estate business. Our company appreciates their efforts and would like them to stand and be recognized."

Sheldon swelled with pride. Even if he had to share it with a cunt, it would still be worth it. He looked at Donna Catterton and promised himself that she would get hers before the next awards ceremony.

The president spoke again. "First, from our Saratoga office. She has once again set a record by selling $3,256,760 worth of real property this past year. She is very well known to all of you. She's our own Donna Catterton."

The room burst into applause. Donna Catterton stood up and bowed graciously. The cheers grew louder.

Sheldon's hands came together as if he were clapping. A meaningless smile stayed bolted on his face. Underneath he felt a burning nausea. She'll get hers one of these days, he thought. The Hood will fuck her snatch off. Cunt.

When the ovation had subsided, the president turned toward the table at which Sheldon was seated. "And from our West San Jose office, a man who started with our organization only three years ago. A real man's man. A hardworking, diligent, decent young man. Selling just under a hundred dollars less than Donna, I would like to present this distinguished award to Owen Sheldon."

The room came alive again with sounds of happy applause. Sheldon eased his chair back and stood. The burning sensation in his stomach quickly dissipated and he smiled warmly in response to the bracing applause. He bowed to the president in appreciation, then stretched his arm and gave several courtesy waves to people he recognized. When he spotted Donna Catterton she was smiling broadly and clapping hard. He waved toward her, his fixed smile never letting him down.

He stood for longer than he should have, but somehow he wanted and needed the love and adulation of his peers. A man's man, the president had called him. An overwhelming feeling came over him. He was a real man after all. The applause and the trophy proved it. His doubts and insecurities were dissolving.

Exhaustion set in at one-and-a-half miles. Molosky's body had been knocked out of condition, and his normally durable stride began to falter. His lungs screamed for mercy and his legs grew heavier with each step. His heart pumped wildly—a hundred and seventy-five beats per minute. The perspiration flowed profusely, draining needed fluids. His pace slowed to a crawl, even after he had taken a shortcut to the rest stop still a hundred yards away.

Sheldon clung to his trophy. Pictures were taken of him shaking hands with the president. Sheldon was able to endure even those where he posed with Donna Catterton with a minimum of inner tension. People he had never met were patting him on the back and congratulating him. He felt more than good; he was exuberant.

When the handshaking and picture-taking were over, he glowed from within. He felt like a king as he strode onto the spacious deck overlooking the lake. *All the glory is yours,* he silently exulted. After placing the gold-plated trophy on top of the railing, he stepped back to admire it and swelled with pride.

Over the edge of the railing, in the far distance, he could see the figure of a lonely runner whose stride had faltered. *Poor man,* he thought*...poor common man.*

Molosky's legs gave out only twenty-five yards short of the rest stop. He staggered to a halt. His hands fell limply to his knees. Sweat gushed onto his brow and streamed down to the point of his nose. His mouth stayed wide open, sucking in quick gasps of badly needed air. He held his eyes closed for several seconds, then began silently to issue himself explicit commands. Off your knees was the first; he opened his eyes and lifted his upper torso. His legs felt like jelly, but Molosky's mind was locked on three miles, and his legs would simply have to get with it. He walked around the rest stop very unsteadily, but with growing determination.

When he was through with his extended break and felt ready, he started up again. With considerable effort his legs slowly found their rhythm. To finish the last half, it took all the tenacity Molosky could muster.

After completing the run, he felt as though he had been carried through the desert on legs made of toothpicks. The cruel sun beamed its hot rays directly at him, cooking the sweat as it poured from his skin. He collapsed on the soft, warm grass and covered his eyes in the crook of his arm, his heart hammering in unrelenting beats, not wanting to slow.

Chapter Twenty-nine

From inside the silver sedan Owen Sheldon tapped the side of his right leg to the beat of loud rock music. He had parked in the busy little lot across the street from a long line of small offices and shops. Midway up the block the rays of the evening sun danced brilliantly off the Platinum Realty sign, which hung smartly over the door perpendicular to the rustic-looking building. He knew that Donna Catterton was inside that office and would soon be leaving for her evening real estate class at the university. Sheldon remembered how hard it had been to talk with her over the phone earlier that day but he managed to find out what he needed to know.

That morning his eyes had ached by the time he got to the office. It seemed as though he had not had a decent night's sleep since he was almost caught in the alley by that policeman—Molosky. That night he had beaten the policeman more out of fear than anything else. Sheldon ran the tips of his fingers around the outer edge of the steering wheel and broke into a confident smile. But he did beat him. The Hood prevailed, as he always would, over paper men enforcing paper laws.

From under the realty sign, he saw Donna Catterton step briskly into the sunlight and march toward him. She wore fashionable sunglasses, a modest pantsuit. Still more than a hundred yards away, she turned squarely and made her way between two parked cars, crossing the street at a long break in traffic. He lost sight of her momentarily when she strode behind a brown milk truck. Coming back into view, she turned toward him again without easing her choppy pace.

Sheldon eyed her like a hunter stalking his prey. *The bait walks like a squeaky cunt,* he mused, and shifted his vision to the large yellow two-door parked several spaces in front of the milk truck. It was a new Cadillac, polished bright yellow, with paper license plates. He angled his vision back to the woman. When she got to the rear of the car, she made another square turn and walked to the driver's door. Without hesitation she opened it and slid in behind the wheel. She started the car and let it warm for no more than a couple of seconds before swinging into traffic and speeding past Sheldon's position.

Clicking on the engine, he quickly followed. He knew where she was going; all he had to find out was where she parked once she got there.

He tailed the yellow two-door past the university campus on the San Carlos Street side, then south on Seventh Street a half block to a multitiered cement garage. There he saw the woman steer into the entrance. Silently, he watched her as he drove by, knowing where she would park. The garage; he would make his first move toward her in the garage. Maybe he would complete the job there. *The concrete cunt;* he chuckled loudly to himself.

Chapter Thirty

It was just past eight on Sunday morning. Molosky was contenting himself with a shave and a shower, then getting dressed in casual clothes. As he opened the closet door Noah sauntered out and hopped onto the bed. "Well, ol' buddy, what happened to you? Found yourself a comfy spot in the dark and slept in, huh?" Molosky sat on the bed and wrapped the cat in his arms. Noah purred happily. "There's a good cat. Hungry? I'll fix some of that crunchy stuff you like." The cat rubbed its head underneath Molosky's chin as if he understood the meaning of "crunchy stuff." "Well, let me comb my hair, then I'll fix your breakfast." He put the cat down and watched him strut across the top of the bed, then hop to the rug.

As he poured the food into the cat's bowl, the doorbell rang. Sunday morning—who could that be? After folding the top of the cat food bag and putting it back in its place under the sink, he marched to the front door.

"Well, I'll-be. Where are you coming from? Church?"

Doug Sanders was dressed in his normally elegant fashion: green army pants, bright yellow shirt, and dark sunglasses a half-inch in diameter, which gave his eyes a pinpoint look. A toothpick moved up and down between his teeth. He shrugged his shoulders for no apparent reason before he spoke. "Now don't go trying to embarrass me. The good Lord wouldn't know what to do if a guy like me entered his hallowed grounds. I was out last night and I was just on my way home. Thought I'd stop by and see how the invalid is doing."

Molosky twisted his lips into a coarse smile. "You want to step inside before the neighbors spot you? Might think you're some kind of classy salesman or something."

"Who, me?" Sanders made a looping gesture with his hands, which he ended by pointing his index finger against his chest. "A salesman?" He plucked the toothpick from his mouth and stuffed it into his shirt pocket.

"Get in here, will ya?" Molosky took him by the shoulder and physically escorted him through the door. Both men laughed. Molosky had somehow grown attached to the strange-looking vice officer. It was his loyalty that had won Molosky over. Every night, Phyllis had told him, Sanders would stop by the hospital and gain entrance by telling all the nurses that he was Molosky's hippie brother. Without fail, even if he were exhausted from the night's work, Sanders would check on Molosky's condition. Molosky appreciated that consideration.

"Doug, you look a wreck. Where did you spend the night?"

"Hell, I don't know. I think it was here in town someplace. West side; yeah, that's it, on the west side somewhere. Worked our butts off last night, then went out partying. I don't know where we finally ended up. I think we had a good time, but I couldn't swear by it. You got any coffee?"

"Yeah, there's a couple of cups left. How do you do it? You're going to die early if you keep it up."

"You sound like your sister. You're not going to preach at me, are you? We're all going to die. So what if I go early? As long as I got a bottle in one hand and a broad in the other, I'll die a happy man."

Molosky poured the coffee. "Sis has been preaching at you, eh? She's good at that. Likes to let you know when you're off base. Acts like an umpire in a lot of ways. Got me straightened out a couple of times. You should listen to her." He walked into the living room and found Sanders lying on his back on the floor, scratching the tip of his nose. A smirk came to Molosky's face. "Make yourself comfortable," he quipped.

"Thanks, I will. Just set it over there, will ya?" Sanders pointed to the coffee table next to Molosky's favorite chair. "Your sister is one for the record books. I really dug her. She worked on me for almost a week, but I held on. She couldn't break the old iron man. I tried to explain to her that sinning was so much more fun than prayin'." He paused to lick his lips. "But she wouldn't buy it. I tell you, Ray, I really like her. Solid type. We need more like her in this crummy world. Sure would be a better place to live."

Molosky shook his head in amazement. "I'll probably wander over to her house later in the day for dinner. You want me to give her a call and say that you'll be with me? You can meet the whole family."

Sanders bolted to a sitting position. "What the hell you trying to do to me, Molosky, give me heart failure? The whole family! Me against all of you at once? That's not playing fair. Jump my bones, will ya? Hell, I might end up a saint by the end of the day! I'd probably have to give up all my friends. Beside, I got a date with a big titted blonde with big green eyes. You'd love her. Why don't you get your girl friend and we'll double?"

"Thanks, but no thanks. I'll pass." Molosky hesitated and smiled in jest. "On second thought, I could give Phyllis a call and see if she'd like to go out for the evening. I owe her after all she's done for me."

Sanders twisted his body to a standing position. "Where's that coffee? This conversation is going nowhere. If you don't want to have a little fun and excitement, then the hell with you. I'll just have to get drunk and get laid without you, if that's the way you want to be about it."

Picking up the hot cup, he smiled gingerly at Molosky. "You mind if I sit on the floor? In case I fall asleep, I won't have that far to fall."

Molosky shook his head in disgust. "Sure. Make yourself at home. As if you already haven't!"

"Now let's not get picky. Remember, we're only down on this earth for a short time. We have to be nice to each other along the way. At least that's what your sister told me." Sanders grunted loudly, slapped the side of his leg, and sipped from the cup.

Molosky stretched his frame onto the sofa directly across from where Sanders was sitting. Relaxing, he crooked his arm and rested his head in the palm of his hand. "So you had a rough night both working and playing?"

"Hell, don't talk to me about work. It's the fuckin' pits. Since you were hurt, they put a bunch of extra teams into the operation, including three more sergeants. We got so many cops out there they're tripping over each other. It's like an army of cops invading the citizens. Disgraceful."

"With so many guys out, you ought to be able to pick somebody up."

"Guys are falling over each other. Nothing's getting done. Most of them are rookies, taken straight out of the academy specially for this action. They don't know which side the badge is worn on. It's a fuckin' mess."

"I bet Harkness loves it," Molosky said sarcastically.

"Yeah, he loves it about as much as I do. We're both recommending that the whole operation be scrapped before someone gets killed. It's been a long time since I've worked around rookies. They are dangerous. See a crook behind every tree. Weird, man." He shook his head disgustedly. "Weird people. They want to arrest half the folks for nothing. Had one the other night who wanted to nab a guy for walking on the sidewalk. Stopped the poor slob and asked him for identification. The guy didn't have any; told the officer that he lived just around the corner. The jerk wouldn't let well enough alone!

"So he placed the man under arrest for taking a walk

around his own block without identification. What a joke. Lucky I got there when I did. Took a lot of smooooth talkin' to get the city out of a false arrest suit. Would have been a righteous one, too."

Molosky chuckled easily and let his hand run over the worn fabric of the sofa pillow. "They wanted me to be a training sergeant three or four years back. Turned them down for that very reason. It's not that they won't be good cops someday; it's just that you get used to working with the senior guys who know their way around."

"Man, you can say that again. I feel like a baby-sitter, holding hands and changing diapers. It's driving me bananas. Frank even yelled at me the other day. He ain't *never* done that before. The whole thing is crazy."

"Must be, if it's upsetting Harkness. What's he going to do about it?"

"He's playing footsie with the chief. It's a balancing act; Frank realizes that. Public pressure can sure screw up a good police operation. Maybe by the end of next week we can whittle it down to a manageable size again." Sanders rubbed his eyes with the back of his index finger, then pulled on his nose. "I don't know what we're gonna do. It's a mess out there. Even got Darrell Wells working undercover. Old four eyes, sneaking around the backs of buildings and reading the *Wall Street Journal*. I'll tell ya, Ray, it don't look too good for the good guys, if you get my meaning."

Molosky laughed out loud. "You crack me up, Doug, you know that? Things can't be that bad out there. Somehow it's still functioning, isn't it?"

"Just barely." A hollow frown of irritation crept across his drooping face. "Got any more coffee? Then I have to get home and sleep; big night tonight."

"You got whatever's left." Molosky slid off the sofa, took the cup from Sanders, and made his way to the kitchen. Upon returning he noticed that Sanders had moved again, this time to the chair next to the coffee table. "Here you go."

"Thanks." Sanders heaved a tired sigh. "I needed this.

I'm getting old, Ray. I used to be able to do this stuff for weeks on end. Hardly ever slept. Now I'm nearly dead after only forty-eight hours. I wish I could be like you—the clean-cut, honest type." Without moving the cup he tilted his head down and slurped awkwardly at the hot coffee. "Good stuff. Appreciate this, Ray."

"Any time. I'm glad I could help." Molosky returned to his place on the sofa.

"Word has it that you're coming back tomorrow."

"Yeah, I'm feeling pretty good. Thought I'd give it a try."

"I think Frank plans on keeping you in uniform. Probably doesn't want to ruin your morale with the disaster he's got on his hands."

"That's okay with me. I didn't particularly like driving a cab around, anyway. And if it's like you say, I'll probably be better off."

"I checked that professor guy Evans out like you asked me. Man, is he weird! He's got more screws loose than I have. You know what that so-called professor teaches over there at our fine university, at taxpayers' expense?"

"Yeah, I've done a background check on him. What I want to know is, is he our man? The last thing I can remember is running past his classroom. When I did, I was sure it was him."

"Well, it ain't. Had him tailed for a couple of days while I did a little snoopin' on my own." Sanders belched openly. "Excuse me. Last night's party working its way through the system. With all the women he's got over at the campus, I found out that our Professor Evans is a closet queer. Likes little boys, or men who look like little boys. The night you were beaten, he was up in San Francisco at a gay party—an exclusive club he belongs to. Got two sources that put him there. He ain't our man. Just another one of the crazies we gotta put up with."

Molosky did not like what he had heard. Uncertain of what to say next, he remained strangely silent for a long while. When he spoke it was as if a tiny but significant bit of hope had been taken from him. "I didn't really think it was him. It's just that I thought...maybe. It was the best recollection I could come up with. I can't remember anything after that."

"You don't look too bad. Even when you were in the hospital, I've seen worse. He sure must have scrambled your brains though."

Molosky sucked in a long breath and aimed his thoughtful eyes directly at Sanders. "Well, where do we go from here? Rely on luck as usual."

"Situations dictate that sometimes. Kind of looks that way."

"What about all the interview cards you guys made out?"

"After you were decked and we found you, we tried to seal off the area for half a mile around. Must have talked to a thousand people. We got a bunch of cards and names, but what the hell do we do with them? Pete's been working on them, but hell, that could take forever. What are you going to do? A background check on more than a thousand people? It's too late now anyway. Even if we talked to the guy and got his name on paper, he's had time to put together an alibi. Doesn't take much to come up with a good story."

"What about having one of the secretaries run all the names for criminal records? That would free Maggenti."

"That's in the works on a suggestion from the chief. But I know what we're gonna find. Half of 'em are going to be college kids with no records. Out of the half with records, half of those are going to be sex-related crimes. You know, peepers and flashers, maybe a couple of rapists in there somewhere. Tracing down two hundred and fifty weirdos and doing backgrounds could take a month, and the problem might still not be solved. It could be any one of the thousand, or it could be none of them. I'll place my bet on lady luck. Banging on doors just ain't my style."

"Mine either. But somehow, in the back of my mind, I think I know the rapist from somewhere, like I've seen him before or talked to him. Nothing concrete, but a strong suspicion. Maybe if I glanced over the names, I would see one that I recognized. Could help, you never know."

Sanders played with his mustache tentatively, then yawned loudly. "That's what I've been waiting to hear. It's a long shot, but I've had this gut feeling, you know, since the incident. We got there fast enough; we just might have his name on one of those cards. But there are too many of them and not enough of us. If you got the feeling, man, we'll have a go at it. Never know!" He yawned again, this time trying to control it. "I have to go before I pass out. Your idea is a good one. But in our business all ideas are good if they work. It's worth a try." He stood and played with his mustache again. "I'll see you tomorrow. Thanks for the coffee."

Molosky walked him to the door. "You're not going to fall asleep behind the wheel, are you?"

"Never have before." Sanders reached in his shirt pocket, and with two fingers took out a toothpick and popped it between his teeth. "Tomorrow, man."

Chapter Thirty-one

When Sheldon got to the office, he exchanged pleasantries with Phil Gates, then gathered up his briefcase and his current listing book and left for an open house. The short drive from the office enabled him to reassemble his salesman's personality. America's business is selling, he told himself as he stopped for a red light. The sound of the turn signal was the only noise inside his leased car. He thought about the pleasantness of selling, the challenge of proper visual and verbal communication, the use of inflections, tones, symbols.

The light changed and he turned into Vasona Park. Sheldon thought about how he could take people here, so they could see what a beautiful park was within minutes of their newly purchased home.

He eased the car out of the park on the Lark Avenue side and was soon setting up his Open House sign in front of a contemporary two-story. He put his papers and pamphlets inside at the kitchen table, leaving the front door open for prospective buyers. On the coffeepot he found a note from the owners telling him to make himself comfortable.

Sheldon smiled and thought that there were decent people in the world after all.

"Excuse me, sir." A woman was peeking through the door. Sheldon turned to see who it was. "I saw you put the sign out. I live right across the street. Thought I'd kind of look around, if you don't mind."

Sheldon detested nosy people who checked out their neighbor's houses when they were away. Women were the worst, always sticking their heads into other peoples' closets.

"How much are they asking?" the woman questioned.

"A little over two-hundred thousand." Sheldon was purposely vague.

The woman walked into the living room without commenting. Sheldon stood erect in the kitchen. The smile on his face simmered to hostility. He plugged in the coffeepot and glanced again at the friendly note. It helped relieve the tension.

He stepped into the hallway. The easygoing sales smile returned. "That's quite all right," he said. "Go up the stairs if you like. There are three bedrooms up there and one big bathroom off the hallway."

The woman put her hand on the railing and looked up the stairway. Then she glanced back at Sheldon. He sensed that she was afraid of him; her expression was no longer curious, but was grave. "No, thanks," she said suddenly. "I've seen enough. It's a lovely house. I hope you find a buyer." She moved past him and quickly walked out of the front door.

Sheldon followed her to the doorway while he burned inside. He managed a tight smile. "Nice talking with you. Be sure to tell your friends about it."

What's wrong with me? he asked himself. *Why get so angry? She's just another cunt.* He walked back to the kitchen and poured himself a fresh cup of coffee. The pleasant aroma filled the kitchen. He sat at the table and began to finger through leftover office mail. The first letter was a brochure explaining the maximization of investment capital through real estate. As he scanned the investment guide, he wondered again if there might be something wrong with him. Was it normal to want a woman out of anger? In Korea, when his life was on the line, he did it. He was encouraged to fuck over the slant-eyed whores. Officers even did it.

He flipped through the letter, but was not paying any attention to its contents. *If it was all right then, it's all right now,* he reasoned. *The world hasn't changed. Once a cunt, always a cunt.* There was nothing wrong with him. It was nature that made his desire so strong. All men are made the same way. They all contain the same ingredients, only in different proportions. He happened to possess more machismo than the rest. He was a super stud, *the man.*

He got up from the table and walked to the bathroom. "You are in complete control," he said, admiring himself in the mirror and gently patting his hair. His hand moved slowly down to his muscular arms, he rubbed his chest, and finally he gently felt his penis underneath his slacks.

The doorbell rang. "Is anyone home?" a woman shouted.

Sheldon stepped from the bathroom and hurried down the hallway to see a man and his wife standing just inside the doorway. "Good afternoon, folks," he said as he came into the living room. "My name is Owen Sheldon. I sell real estate with Platinum Realty. If I can be of service to you, by all means let me know. Look around, take your time. There are three bedrooms upstairs."

Sheldon showed them around the house. He got two new customers with his genial manner and thorough knowledge of the local real estate market. This house was too expensive, but they liked the area and would appreciate his assistance in finding a house.

By the end of the day, Sheldon had started to feel good about himself. He had met some nice people and had an excellent prospective buyer. The phone rang as he was packing his briefcase. "Hello, this is the Kern residence, may I help you?"

"Owen, this is Charlotte. Are you busy?"

The first words he had heard from his girl friend in several days and her voice sounded like tempered steel. Sheldon did not know how to respond. "Hi, Charlotte," he blurted out. "How have you been?"

"Listen, darling, you'd better sit down. I have something to tell you. It's gonna hurt."

Sheldon grabbed hold of a kitchen chair, twisted it around, and sat down. "If it's about you and me, I think we should talk face to face."

"I think not, darling." Her response was quick and precise. "If we could talk in person that would be fine. But you've got this sexual hang-up or something. You don't communicate unless it's with your organ. To get to the point. It's time to break off our little arrangement. I'm tired of having you around. I'm tired of your vulgarities. I think it's time you packed up and left."

"But Charlotte—"

"But nothing, darling. I've already made up my mind. I've decided for both of us, so I don't want to hear any sniffling. You can handle it. You're a big boy now." She hesitated for a second, gave a short cough, then continued. "Tell you how we'll take care of this mess. I'll take a short vacation. Maybe take a trip down south to see some friends. I'll plan on a week's stay. That should give you enough time to get your stuff together and find another place. Whatever you do, I'll expect you out by mid-week—Thursday at the latest."

Sheldon's stomach knotted up. His hurt eyes stared through the coffeepot in front of him. "Ah... I don't know what to say. Ah... I don't understand. What went wrong? I thought..."

"What went wrong? Come off it, Owen. Everything went wrong. Let's just leave it at that. It was fun while it lasted. Now you can get someone else to fuck. Just be out by the time I get back."

"But Charlotte, can't we—"

"But nothing, darling. You heard me. You just get your stuff out of my house."

The phone went dead. "Charlotte, wait, will ya?" The dial tone was his only answer. He stared in a numb daze for several seconds. The end had come too fast, without warning. It couldn't have been her. She needed him. That cunt.

The longer he sat, the more he seethed. *Fucking cunts. They're all the same. Fucking hustle your balls and leave you dry. I'll take care of her. I'll rape her fucking cunt off.*

Quickly, he replaced the receiver, then picked it up again and dialed. "Come on, cunt, answer the phone. Pick it up, will ya?"

But the phone only rang. Charlotte had gone. He sucked in an angry breath and put back the phone. "Fucking cunt!"

Chapter Thirty-two

After roll call Molosky marched straight to the Sergeant's office. The wheels of the paper mill had not slowed. For two hours Molosky sat at his desk sorting through a hefty pile. Toward the bottom he read a note from Pete Maggenti:

Dear Ray,

I'll be on vacation when you get back; couldn't get out of it. Had reservations for six months; couldn't let Janet down. I just wanted to say that it's good to have you back on the first string again. Being on the injured list ain't fun.

Nothing new on our hooded friend. He's alive and well and still on the loose out there somewhere. I guess you've heard by now that our famous decoy operation failed to pick him up. They picked everybody else up, but our hero managed to elude the troopers.

I guess that leaves you and Sanders. Think you guys can handle it? Remember that evil strikes fast, and usually when man is at his weakest. Be careful out there!

Best,
Pete

Molosky cupped his jaw between his thumb and index finger and pondered the note. That would be nice, an extended vacation. The phone on his desk rang. "Sergeant's office, Molosky here."

"Ray, Sanders here. I'm glad you made it. I'm up in Sex Detail. Got stacks of names and criminal records for you to look at. You still game?"

"Yeah, I'll be up in a sec."

After clearing the paper from his desk, Molosky made his way to the Sex Assault office on the third floor. Pushing the door open, he saw only the back of Sanders's head. He was sitting at a corner desk with his feet propped up on the window ledge.

"You know something, Molosky?" he said, without looking to see who had come through the door. "This city is sinking to the pits and the perverts. Used to be a nice place to live when I was a kid. Now look at it. Smog and weirdos. A decent person doesn't know where the fuck to turn these days. People just wandering around out there trying to convince themselves that they're happy." He lifted his feet and turned to face Molosky. "What the fuck is the world coming to, Ray? I just don't know sometimes."

Mr. Middle Class himself, Molosky thought as he looked at the Vice Squad officer. "I saw Wells over at the locker room. Says you've been teaching him about your side of town."

"And he don't like it a bit. Introduced him to a couple of whores last night over dinner. All the guy could talk about was the ups and downs on Wall Street, and all the girls wanted to talk about were other things that go up and down. I'll tell you, Ray, it was hilarious. I don't think he caught onto their little innuendoes once. He just kept plugging the American way of investing." When Sanders stopped talking, his lips formed a snappy smile. "Anyway, I guess you want to look at some interview cards?"

Molosky gave a quiet nod.

"They're over here in the interrogation room. I guess they ran out of room in this dump. I found them in a box. You get a note from Pete? What the hell's with him? Taking off like that!"

"Everyone needs a vacation. He said he had made reservations a long time ago. Probably couldn't get out of them; they'd steal his deposit."

"I'm the one who needs a vacation, and I just got back from one. Between the rookies and guys like Wells, I'm going crazy. In here." He opened the door to the interview room and gestured for Molosky to enter. "The secretary, whoever she was, sure did a good job. The box on the table is full of the cards of those who have criminal records."

Molosky walked into the small room and saw a large cardboard box on top of the table. Opening the flaps, he briefly studied its contents. There were two neat stacks of paper. Lifting out the top sheet, he let his eye scan it. "Whoever it was did a neat job. Took a lot of work."

"Nice, huh? And every one of them is the same. The field interview cards are stapled to the top of the criminal record. Can't do better than that. Now all we gotta do is find one of these for the guy who slammed your lights out. The pervert is in here someplace. You make like a bloodhound and we'll find him. I got that feeling."

For the next hour Molosky diligently scoured the remaining cards. However, luck was not with him. The names, even the ones he knew, meant nothing. Only a few created a mild interest, but none struck that emotional chord of recognition.

By the time he got to the last card in the first stack, he was filled with frustration. The rapist couldn't have gotten away. Someone had to have talked to him. After placing the sheets of paper back in the box, Molosky sat for a moment, massaging his forehead with the tips of his fingers. Maybe Sanders was right. They would have to rely on luck to catch him. Whatever, he had to get out in the field.

Molosky's mood seemed to mellow as he slipped behind the wheel of the blue and white. The bucket seats, the radio equipment, the mounted shotgun were familiar to him. The police cruiser had its own aroma. It felt safe and gave him a base from which to operate. It offered him an emotional and psychological haven which enabled him not only to survive but to function in what seemed to be a world full of battle zones.

It was ten o'clock when he rolled out of the north side parking lot and gradually increased his speed. As he passed the jail, he eyed the vertical steel bars at the windows.

Wishing that the world would somehow go away, he picked up the microphone and reluctantly placed himself in service. "Sixty-five hundred, ten-eight," he announced, pushing the words from his throat.

After the operator had acknowledged him, he heard his call numbers again, but this time it was Bert Yarnell trying to raise him. Bert wanted him to name a place where they could have a late dinner. Molosky suggested Original Joe's in ten minutes, and Yarnell agreed.

Taking a detour before heading to the restaurant, Molosky steered in the direction of the university. As he cruised past the Engineering Building, he tried desperately to remember what had happened to him after he jumped from the landing. He saw himself as he landed on the hard pavement, knees buckling but somehow managing to keep his balance. As he started across the street, the hooded rapist had not been in sight.

Molosky circled the block and rolled by again. This time he pointed the spotlight down the alley as he eased on the brake. It was a long, wide alley with a cement sidewalk running its full length. The sidewalk was lined with foliage on both sides. At the end of the alley was a small one-way street which led to wider roads. He recalled gasping for air and running along the sidewalk with the hooded rapist nowhere in sight.

He scratched his chin, struggling to remember what

had happened next. Where did he see the rapist again? It had to be in the alley someplace, but Molosky's memory would not produce a clear picture. He switched off the spotlight and pressed gently on the accelerator. As he steered, his headlights caught the silhouette of a man walking briskly. Molosky eyed him curiously as he drove past. It was Ashwood, the eternal man. *Doesn't he ever sleep?*

The next day, promptly at 4 P.M., Molosky called the roll, then turned the lectern over to Lieutenant Lesley, who had an important announcement. He explained that several of the east side units had been doubled up to handle the large bands of juveniles expected to gather in that part of the city. The situation was not a new one. Throughout the summer, officers who worked that area had had to cope with unruly and often hostile crowds. The problem became acute last Friday, when two officers tried to break up a fight and were severely beaten by several youths. To protect his men from further beatings, the chief had ordered a manpower shift to the east side. Lesley expected Wells's (District One) and Molosky's (District Five) to be called first if Sergeant Edwards's men needed help.

After Lesley's orders were given, the policemen scattered to their cars. Molosky remained at a seat in the back near the bulletin board. The latest pink sheet lay at a cocked angle in front of him. He picked it up and slowly scanned the front side. Nothing new. He flipped it over and found an artist's sketch of the hooded rapist and a brief description of him. Molosky pondered the drawing. It had been weeks since his last attack. *Somehow he must be stopped before he strikes again.*

Hoisting himself up, he made his way to the third floor and the Sex Assault Office. At the desk in the corner, with his feet propped up, facing the window, was Sanders, quietly smoking a cigarette. "You know something, Molosky? I have an intuitive sense about me; it's what's kept me alive so far. It's like little antennae sticking out of my brain that tell me when to do this and when not to do that. You can understand that, can't you?"

"Yeah, everybody's got it to some extent. Sure comes in handy if you're a cop. Saves your butt sometimes."

Sanders continued staring out of the window toward the Juvenile Holding Facility a short distance away. "The reason I mention it is that I have this feeling that the hooded pervert is out there someplace. He hasn't struck in a while and he's probably getting edgy. I can feel it. He's ready to attack again. I know it as sure as I'm sitting here!" Without lifting his feet he eyed Molosky by tilting his head back. "If you noticed, you guys get Wells back tonight. We finally got rid of the rooks. Harkness sent them on their way. Gave 'em a great pep talk and a three-day weekend. That takes a big load off my mind, but I only got two teams working myself. Everybody's getting exhausted from the long hours, so I gave the other two teams the night off. That might have been a mistake. We'll see."

Sanders stood up, leaned over the desk, and snuffed out the cigarette. When he looked at Molosky again it was with serious eyes. "I thought I'd let you know what my instincts are telling me. Be careful out there. I know he's around. You want to look at some more cards?"

Molosky stood, shaken for a moment at Sanders's grave attitude. "I hear what you're saying, Doug. Let's get to the cards."

Inside the interrogation room Sanders found another cardboard box. "These are the people with no criminal records. Sit down while I go through them first and eliminate all the females and hand you the males; save ourselves some time."

Molosky nodded in agreement. Sanders slid into place and started taking the cards off the top, slapping them one at a time onto the table. Females he placed to his left, the males to his right, closer to Molosky.

Molosky heaved a hopeful sigh and started his reviewing. He held each card in his hand and let his eyes scan it for the important information: name, address, age, color of hair and eyes, height, and weight. He studied each card in earnest, but still there was nothing but faceless names.

"Here's a pair," Sanders said after almost an hour of silence. "A weird combo; interviewed 'em myself. Seen the old guy around dozens of times. He tried to pull a fast one on me. Should have booked his ass, the old coot." Sanders slapped the card in front of Molosky. "His name is Marvin Ashwood; maybe you've seen him around. I put his name on the bottom of the card—no sense in wasting paper on that old fart. I knew he couldn't rape a jelly bean. That's the guy he was with, a younger fella. The odd couple."

Molosky took the card and studied the name. "John Carver; doesn't ring a bell. What was he doing with Ashwood? College student or something?"

Sanders shook his head and lifted his eyebrows. "Good guess. That's what they tried to pull on me. The old coot was telling me he was a professor at the university and that Carver was one of his students or ex-students or something. The story was full of holes. I called him on it and made him back down, the old liar."

Molosky scrutinized the card again, then tucked it neatly into his shirt pocket. "Well, we'll see. I've always been curious about that old man. He knows a lot of people. I'll check him out. He might be able to help. Maybe he's our man after all."

They both laughed. "That'll be the day," Sanders mused.

Chapter Thirty-three

Sheldon sat somberly at his desk. The calendar in front of him had every day since Sunday blacked out. He had tried to keep his cheerful smile locked onto his face all week, but with each passing day the emotional strain seemed to weigh more heavily on him. He needed Charlotte. He wanted to explain to her that he would change his attitude, and that he would be kind and love her totally for the rest of his life. Things would be different.

The phone rang and Phil Gates answered it. "Owen, line one. Sounds like Charlotte."

Sheldon's heartbeat quickened, and he was overcome by a sweeping, joyous emotion. She had come back to him. At last he could tell her how much he really loved her. Before picking up the receiver, Sheldon composed himself by twisting the knot in his tie. He did not want to sound pleading. "Hello, this is Owen Sheldon. May I help you?" He could hear his heart as it pumped wildly in anticipation.

"Darling, have you got a minute? If not, you can call me back." It was Charlotte; her voice was cool and direct.

Sheldon didn't care about her mood, her voice, or anything. It was Charlotte. His hand quivered nervously as he held the receiver. He took a deep breath and cleared his throat. "Hi, Charlotte. I didn't expect you back so soon. How was your trip? It's good to hear your voice. Can you hang on a sec? I'll change phones."

"I'll wait," came the abrupt reply.

Sheldon pushed the hold button, unfolded his frame from the chair, and walked into the small conference room in the back. When he picked up the phone, he knew that he could win her over. "There, that's better. I moved to a back room; it's more private. How have you been?"

"I just popped in to see how the move was coming." Her words cracked over the phone in a stiff cadence. "You haven't done a damn thing, and this place is a mess. Your dirty laundry is all over and you haven't washed a dish since I left. And your trashy magazines are lying all over the floor. I see you haven't changed, dearie. I thought I told you to clear out."

Sheldon sat dumbfounded for a long minute, grappling with his shattered emotions. He felt as though his whole being had been jammed into an ever-tightening vice. She couldn't have meant that, he thought, desperately forcing a good feeling between the painful ones. "Ahhh...I'm sorry...Charlotte...things will get better...ahh."

"You're damned right they will, darling. I just made them better. I took every piece of your crap and threw it out on the lawn. When you get off work, just get your fucking ass over here and clear out. Can you get that through your perverted skull, Sheldon? Out! I don't ever want to see your face again."

The phone went dead.

Sheldon sat unable to move, his eyes in a blank stare, mouth open in an astonished gape. Compressed anger mixed with a crushing hurt. Slowly, small tremors of violence etched their way across his tense brow. No cunt could talk to him that way. His right arm tightened and began to shake uncontrollably. A savage, animal instinct began to take over.

"You all right, Owen?" Gates asked, sticking his head through the door.

Sheldon's mind whirled back to the office. Clumsily he dropped the receiver into its cradle. His mind reeled for a polite answer, but he couldn't think of any. He managed a nod, but his eyes were still in a daze.

"If you're sure you're okay, I'll be leaving early. Things are kind of slow and I thought since it was Friday... You sure you're all right?"

Sheldon covered his face with both hands and drew in a deep breath. Sliding his hands to the back of his neck, he massaged his tight muscles and forced a thin smile. "I'm fine, Phil," he responded with exaggerated friendliness. "A headache, that's all. I'll take a couple of aspirin. That should fix it."

"Good enough. There's a bottle in my desk. Take a couple if you like." Gates gave a friendly wave and closed the door.

Sheldon sat frozen in his chair. A thousand thoughts pounded his brain. A rock-hard knot formed in the pit of his stomach. His fingertips dug into the top of the table. His eyes moved in their sockets like tiny electric beads. His lips cracked, but the teeth remained clamped tight. His breathing became ragged.

He sat rigid for several minutes. When he finally moved, his steps were lightning fast. When he got to his car, he quickly opened the trunk and took out the black attaché case and his pointed boots, then jumped into the front seat. He peeled out from his parking place and sped toward Charlotte's house. It took only a few minutes to get there.

She really had done it. His personal belongings were strewn all over the front lawn to the sidewalk. *I'll kill her,* he thought in a rage, *I'll kill that cunt.* He swung the car into the driveway and skidded to a halt. Frantically, his hands moved to the attaché case for the gloves. He stretched them over his hands and grabbed the sheepskin hood. Opening the door, he twisted in the seat, untied his dress shoes, and pulled on the boots. Stepping from the car he hurriedly trotted to the back door.

He hesitated before entering. He could feel the blood hammering into his organ. *I'm going to fuck that lousy cunt. She'll never say that to a man again.* He took several wild, exhilarating breaths as he aimed short, darting glances throughout the yard. There was no one in sight.

He donned the hood and silently stepped through the door into the kitchen and slithered along the wall. There was an ugly stench spewing from the garbage overflow. He listened for sounds of movement, but there was only silence.

Slowly, he made his way through the kitchen and into the living room. Still there was nothing.

He stalked down the hall toward the bedroom, taking quiet, mechanical steps. Underneath the hood his breathing came in light gushes of warm wind. The bedroom door was closed. His hand trembled as he took hold of the knob. Slowly, he turned it. Anticipation grew. His eyes were wide with violence.

Swiftly, he burst through the door.

The room was empty.

He jerked his head back and forth. His eyes moved in sharp, piercing glances. Suddenly, he saw a piece of paper taped to the mirror. He stepped to it and tore it from the glass. On it was a handwritten note.

Darling,

I knew you'd come running. After you're done pouting, why don't you go in the bathroom and jerk yourself off? That should make you feel better. And after that, you can get with the program and clear out.

Charlotte

Sheldon could not contain his emotions any longer. He began to shake uncontrollably. His arms trembled in short spasms, then his whole body began to vibrate as if in a eizure. "Fucking cunt!" he howled. When his body moved, jerked in convulsive, violent thrusts. His fist became ke a mad ball of lead. He smashed the mirror, cracking ne glass and sending large sheets crashing to the floor. ext he turned on the walls, bashing and kicking them, pping the Sheetrock from its secure position.

He went into a wild, roaring frenzy. He knocked over amps, smashed the furniture, kicked and pounded on the alls, tore at the curtains.

When he had destroyed the bedroom, he rampaged hrough the rest of the house, kicking and screaming and recking whatever was in his path. As he moved in his iolent binge, his loud cries seemed to echo throughout he house. "Fucking cunt! Fucking cunt! I'll kill her!"

Within minutes the house was a shambles: gaping holes n windows, doors flung open, furniture broken and hrown about. From inside the sheepskin hood Sheldon ould feel the trickle of perspiration down his face. In the iving room he crouched and waved his arms like a gorilla. Ie grunted loudly, then staggered for the back door. Fucking cunt!" he roared one last time before reaching he doorway.

As he yanked the door open, he stripped off the hood nd tried to find self-control again. "Calm down!" he demanded. But composing himself was not to come so easily. The anger and frustration were not to be put aside by a imple command. His raging blood churned through his eins, keeping his system at an explosive temperature. Ie leaned against the doorjamb, still sucking in strong gusts of air. *Calm down,* he told himself again. *She'll get hers.*

When he thought he had regained his composure, Sheldon slammed the back door shut and marched back to the car. He headed downtown.

Chapter Thirty-four

It was nearly seven o'clock by the time Molosky had th
patrol car checked out and was steering onto Mission Street
past City Hall. The tall glass structure reflected the bake
orange mist created by the smog which filtered the sun'
rays. With the window rolled down, Molosky could fee
the promise of a cooling trend as a gentle breeze wafte
across his arm. After stopping at the red light on Firs
Street, he swung the car right and drifted toward th
downtown area. "Control Two, Sixty-five hundred, I'll b
ten-eight. How does the district look?"

"Sixty-five hundred, ten-eight," came the rapid re
sponse. "District Five units are all clear. Quiet in you
area so far. East side units on Channel One are startin
to back up with calls."

"Ten-four," Molosky answered as he replaced the mi
crophone. Within the hour Wells and his men would b
called, and by nine o'clock District Five policemen woul
be needed. *Everything happens at once,* he thought.

Since it was quiet for the time being in his area, an
more out of curiosity than anything else, Molosky drov

ıe patrol car in the direction of the small restaurant :ross the street from the university. Maybe Ashwood knew bout the rapist and maybe he didn't. Molosky felt the eed to talk with someone other than a policeman. Easing ɔ a stop at the curb, he placed himself out of service.

As he approached the door, he noticed a short, husky ıdy working behind the counter. She did not look up when e opened the door, which creaked loudly. Tentatively, Iolosky stepped through the opening, letting his eyes scan ıe people within. To his right, against the wall, there 'as a couple engaged in serious conversation. Behind them, lady in her mid-thirties was studying from her notebook. Iext to her arm was a thick hardcover book. Molosky ɔuld make out the words "Real Estate" on the narrow ortion of the book's jacket. On his left there was a group f students gathered around a table. When they spotted Iolosky, they turned around with puzzled expressions on heir faces.

Ashwood was not there. Maybe the woman behind the ounter knew him and could help. He approached her. Excuse me, ma'am." The woman tilted her head up and yed him in a not unfriendly way. "I'm trying to locate an ld man whom I've seen in this area before. I was won-lering if you might be able to help me."

She hesitated, narrowing her eyes and holding her lips ogether. She seemed to be pondering something of great oncern. She glanced quickly at Molosky's badge, then noved back to his eyes. "You're looking for Marvin Ash-vood, aren't you?" Her words came out in a burst, as if he did not want to say anything but felt she must. "It's ıbout that incident a couple of weeks back, with that strange young man, isn't it? I don't want to get Marvin nto any trouble."

Molosky's curiosity began to perk up. She had used the vord "strange" when she referred to the man who had ɔeen with Ashwood that day. "Mr. Ashwood isn't in any rouble, but I did want to talk to him about the man he vas with. Do you know him?"

Relief swept across her face; the muscles around her

eyes relaxed and her lips parted into a subdued smile. "Never seen him before, just that once. Came in here with his wild brown eyes, huffin' and sweatin'. Cops all over. just *bet* they were after him. You can tell, you know. The way he was acting. Marvin shouldn't have taken him in. I knew he was trouble."

"Is he staying with Mr. Ashwood now?"

"Don't know. Marvin won't talk about him. Just says that the man needed help that night, and he gave it to him. Didn't press him for more, as long as the stranger doesn't show his face in here again."

From his shirt pocket Molosky pulled out the field interview card and studied it again. John Carver. The name still didn't mean anything to him, but he was the rapist. Molosky knew it. Now all he had to do was hunt him down. "John Carver was the man's name. Does that mean anything to you?"

"I told you, Sergeant, I don't know who he was or anything else. You'll have to talk to Marvin if you want more information. I've said too much as it is. Talk to him."

Molosky noted a hint of fear in the woman's eyes. She had helped him enormously and he did not want to push her. "Could you tell me where he lives? I'll go over there and talk to him. I can assure you that he is in no trouble with the police. But I do need to see him."

The woman's eyes became foggy and full of doubt. They searched Molosky's face for some sign that she should trust him. "You promise? You sure he's in no trouble?"

"I promise. He's not in any trouble, but I have to talk to him." Molosky kept his voice as calm as possible, not letting his impatience show.

She kept a measured eye on him. "Seventeenth and Santa Clara, above the donut shop. Door is at the rear, top of the stairs."

Molosky backed away from the counter. "Thank you. I appreciate the information." He opened the door quickly and marched back to the patrol car. He steadied himself behind the wheel with a deep breath, started the engine, and peeled out from the curb.

Within minutes he was steering down the driveway alongside the donut shop. Opening the door, he heard the thump of his boot as it hit the pavement at the bottom of the stairs. He reached the top platform in seconds. Wasting no time, he stood to the side of the door and knocked hard three times. There was no immediate reply, so he waited for several seconds. As he closed his fist and was about to pound again, the door opened.

It was Ashwood, in a T-shirt, baggy pants, and slippers. When he saw Molosky he smiled knowingly. "I've been expecting you. Come in."

Tensely, Molosky stepped inside and quickly searched the interior of the stuffy apartment with his eyes.

"He's not here, Sergeant. I've not seen him since that night. I can tell you nothing more than that." The old man eased the door shut. "I'm sorry."

"You know who I'm looking for, then?"

"I do, and he's not here. I don't know where he is. May I offer you some coffee? Or perhaps a glass of brandy?"

"Listen, Mr. Ashwood, this is very important. The man I'm after is very dangerous."

"I realize that, Sergeant, but I am unable to assist you."

"What do you mean you can't assist me?" Molosky felt his voice rising in anger. "You have to assist me. You helped him escape; you know something about him."

With his head down, the old man walked across the room and sat on a sofa near the window. Keeping his eyes away from Molosky's, he spoke in a quiet but determined voice. "I wish I could help, Sergeant, I really do. But it is impossible. I'm sorry."

Exasperated, but still in control of himself, Molosky sat across from Ashwood and leaned over, jutting his face directly at him. "Listen, old man, and hear me. For months your friend has been attacking women in this city. He has gotten progressively worse with his beatings. I fear that he is out of control. The animal in him has taken over and he can no longer restrain himself. He could kill his next victim. You must help me."

Ashwood remained unmoved, with eyes cast down and

hands neatly on his lap. "He trusts me, Sergeant. I cannot help you. I'm deeply sorry."

Molosky's eyes narrowed in concentration. He had to reach the old man and make him understand. "Let me put it another way. Then *you* can carry the burden. If someone gets killed, it will fall squarely on your shoulders. I'm telling you what I know as a fact. The man you call John Carver is an out-of-control animal. He must be stopped before he strikes again. I need a clue... please!"

There was a long silence. Molosky's eyes stayed directly on the old man. He noticed Ashwood's right thumb was moving up and down, tapping rapidly against the back of his left hand. After what seemed like many minutes, Ashwood lifted his head and gazed at Molosky with sorrowful eyes. "I know he is out of control, Sergeant, and perhaps you are right. He could accidentally kill someone. I cannot carry the burden for his deeds. I will tell you this much; his real name is not John Carver. You can take it from there."

Molosky's eyes shot open wide and his jaw dropped in surprise. "Who is he?" he demanded. "I have to know."

"You have your ways, I'm sure," was the flat reply.

Molosky sat stunned for a minute. There must be a way to find out. "A phone. Do you have a phone?"

In silence the old man nodded, then gestured with his hand toward the kitchen.

Molosky immediately bolted from the chair and marched to the kitchen. He took out the index card and dialed quickly, he had to wait only two rings before it was answered. "This is Sergeant Molosky," he said curtly. "I need a driving record on a party; I have the license number—XO934349."

When the woman in the police teletype room came back on the line, she explained to him that that number had been canceled and superseded by another. Molosky asked her to send for the new number. He anxiously tapped the receiver. John Carver wasn't John Carver after all.

"Sergeant, you still there?"

"Yes, yes, go ahead."

"That number comes back to a man named Owen Sheldon, with a post office box for a mailing address."

Upon hearing that unexpected name, the receiver jolted uncontrollably out of Molosky's hand. "Holy God!" he said, his mind reeling back to that evening in the alley. He saw the hooded man jump from the bushes which had concealed him, his fist slamming into his face. Molosky could still feel the warm concrete underneath the back of his head as he lay barely conscious... the click of his revolver as the cylinder was cocked into position... his eyes squinting open, pleading... seeing... the unmasked rapist... Owen Sheldon.

The receiver dangled from the phone, striking the floor. When he came to his senses, Molosky fished with the cord and brought the receiver back to his ear. "Hello, you still there?" he asked.

"Yes, what happened?"

"Never mind. The only address on there is a post office box, is that what you said? No street address?"

"No street address, just the P.O. box."

"Okay, thanks. Route a copy of that to my folder in the Sergeant's office downstairs."

Molosky hung up the phone, but left his hand glued to the receiver. What was his next move? Lifting it again, he called Information and got the phone number for the Platinum Realty office nearest his house. Swiftly, he dialed the number and was informed by an answering service that no one was in the office. From them he got the home phone number of the office manager, a man by the name of Phil Gates. He dialed his number.

"Hello?" It was a woman's voice.

"Good evening, I'd like to speak to Mr. Phil Gates, please."

"Yes, just one moment, I'll see if he's out of the shower."

As Molosky held the phone to his ear, he eyed the old man at the other end of the long room. He had not moved and seemed to be clutching rosary beads, mumbling to himself.

"This is Phil Gates, may I help you?"

"Sir, my name is Sergeant Raymond Molosky, San Jose Police Department."

"Oh..." There was a short, bewildered silence. "Yes, sir."

"This is an emergency, sir. I need your help."

"Yes, Officer, anything. How can I help the police?"

"You have a salesman named Owen Sheldon. I need his home address. I repeat, this is an emergency."

There was another short pause. Molosky could hear paper being shuffled in the background as Gates mumbled something inaudible. "Ahh, just a minute... ahh... I know I've got it here someplace. He lives with a nice lady by the name of... ahh... Charlotte Hunter. Yes, here it is."

Molosky flicked out his pen, turned the interview card over, and held it to the wall.

"They live together, but I believe the house is hers; divorce settlement or something. The address is Fifty-five South Tampico Court, and the phone number is 555-1828. Do you need anything else? He's not in any trouble, is he? When I left the office, Owen seemed to be under a lot of pressure. Is he all right?"

"Mr. Gates, Owen Sheldon is fine. I need one more favor from you."

"Of course, anything."

"It is imperative that you not try to contact Mr. Sheldon and tell him I called. And if he should happen to get hold of you, then I would appreciate your not telling him. You have to trust me; it is important."

"Yes, well... of course. I'll do whatever you say."

"Thank you. If I need any more help, I'll call. Thanks again."

Molosky strode back into the living room area and watched the old man as he prayed. "You gave me what I needed, old man. Now we'll both have to pray that it's not too late."

Ashwood lifted his head and stared at Molosky through his aged eyes. "I've been praying for him since the night he left. Now go and do your part."

Without hesitation Molosky reached for the door and

trotted down the stairs. Quickly, he backed out of the driveway and squealed away from the front of the donut shop. He picked up the microphone and clicked himself on the air. "Control Two, Sixty-five hundred."

"Sixty-five hundred," barked the radio operator, "we've been trying to reach you. Confirm your status."

"As of now I'm clear, Control."

"Ten-four. Be advised that your district has two units out of service. Sergeant Wells's team has been deployed to the area of King and Story. East side units are completely wiped out. Your district is next up."

"Ten-four," Molosky answered as he temporarily went off the air and thought for a second. "Control, can you see if you can reach Sergeant Sanders on the tactical channel and have him come up on Two?"

"Ten-four," came the reply.

When Sanders answered the call, Molosky arranged to meet him in back of Valley Fair Shopping Center near the bookstore.

Chapter Thirty-five

Sheldon tried to relax behind the wheel, with the air conditioner blowing through the vents and hard rock music stabbing at his ears. He steered his silver sedan through the Highway 17 interchange onto Interstate 280. Rust-colored smog had settled around the eastern foothills as the sun was fast disappearing. *Another half hour and it will be dark,* he thought as he slowed to avoid striking the rear of a mustard-colored '54 Chevrolet. When he attempted to pass, he found himself hemmed in by a noisy semi with two trailers.

His mind was jammed with thoughts of Charlotte. He felt as though he had been shot with a cannon and would never recover. Her sweet, seductive charm had been yanked from him, leaving him alone and desolate. She would have to pay. Some cunt would have to sacrifice her body. Suddenly, Donna Catterton edged into his mind. It was Friday. She had a class and would be out by ten. Checking his watch, he decided he had enough time to down a couple of belts of 100 proof.

He got off the freeway as soon as he could and maneuvered through city traffic toward the downtown area. As he stopped for the red light at the corner of First Street and San Salvador, he eyed three prostitutes standing near a pornographic movie theatre across the street. When the light switched to green, he drove slowly through, turning his head to see if any of them would notice him. None did. Fucking cunts.

Circling the block, he made another pass along First Street. His eyes searched the sidewalk. He thought about fucking a prostitute in the face and wondered if raping a whore was a crime. When he spotted one walking in his direction, he smiled inwardly, knowing what her next move would be. She stepped off the curb and waved toward him. He held his eye on her, slowed, and pulled to the curb. "Fucking cunt. How long is it going to take you?" He started to count off the seconds to himself.

"Hi, there," the prostitute said.

Sheldon let his lips curve into a twisted smile. "Not bad. Under ten seconds. A pretty cunt, too."

The girl bent down; her flirting smile became uneasy. She cupped her left breast lightly. "My name is Kay. Looking for a little excitement?"

"Kay Cunt," he said in a slicing tone. "You look like a cunt, too."

The prostitute's expression changed. Sheldon could see that her smile had nearly disappeared and what was left was confused and turning rigid. "Need a date, honey?" she asked. "Lonesome tonight?"

Sheldon opened the door and stepped out. "How much you gonna charge me to fuck your face off, cunt?"

The girl stepped back and straightened her dress. "Listen, buster, you want to get laid tonight it's gonna cost you thirty dollars, take it or leave it, and watch who you're calling a cunt."

"That's what you are...darling. A cunt. That's what all women are." Before she could respond, Sheldon turned and walked away toward a small bar at the end of the block. *I should have fucked her right there on the sidewalk in front of everybody. She deserved it. Would have served her right. Teach her to flaunt herself like that.*

Before entering the shopping center parking lot, Molosky checked the real estate office across the street but found nothing. He then swung the police cruiser toward the bookstore. Sanders was easy to spot. He was wearing a brown derby and a pink shirt, and was sitting on the hood of an old yellow cab that was parked in a red zone. Molosky rolled up to him and unlocked the passenger door.

Sanders pulled the door open and started to get in. "What's up, Ray? You guys short of men downtown or something?"

Molosky handed him a city map. "See if you can find Tampico Court. I know it's out here someplace. I found out who he is. Ashwood knew all along."

Sanders flipped through the pages as the car exited the parking lot and merged into traffic. "Figures he'd know. John Carver, huh?"

Molosky steered onto Stevens Creek Boulevard and listened while Sanders gave him a quick rundown on the location of Tampico Court. When Sanders finished, Molosky continued in a businesslike tone. "It was John Carver, all right, but that's an alias. His real name is Owen Sheldon. Ever heard that name?"

Sanders shook his head. "Not that I can recall. Why? You know him?"

Molosky threaded his way around slower cars. "For several months. Sells real estate. Should have known it was him after that prostitute got raped at Klosterman's. Should have put two and two together. He was there, and before that he was at the office across from where Evelyn was raped. I should have been able to link them. The guy's good, Doug; smiles a lot and has the perfect charm to be a salesman. But underneath he's an animal. He's sick and no one recognized it." He turned onto Tampico Court. "We're looking for fifty-five; should be on your side. I'm glad we got here before dark."

"Holy Toledo!" Sanders shouted.

Molosky hastily pulled to the curb in front of the house next to number 55. "Holy God, it looks like a hurricane hit the place. You take the back and I'll get the front."

With that, both policemen were out of the car and racing toward the house. Sanders drew his snub-nosed .38 from his shoulder holster and ran down the driveway to the back. Molosky reached for his revolver and snapped it from its secure position. Standing to the side of the open front door, Molosky let his eyes scan the things that had been thrown onto the front lawn: nudie magazines, shirts and pants, whole suits still on their hangers. From inside the house he heard a sharp, crashing sound of the back door slamming against the wall. He instinctively knew that Sanders had entered from the rear.

Molosky held the magnum revolver so that the muzzle was pointing up at a forty-five degree angle. Staying close to the wall, he crouched and took a deep breath. Suddenly, he burst through the opening, his arm stretching out, the gun level at the end of his locked wrists, his feet whipping to a combat stance. He shifted his eyes quickly, looking for any sign of movement. *Holy God,* he thought upon seeing the destruction inside the house. He stepped along the wall to his right and met Sanders, who was just coming from the kitchen.

Flicking the light on in the hallway, Molosky motioned for Sanders to take the low point position. Sanders crouched and began working his way along the wall. Molosky followed a short distance behind and on the opposite side. In this manner they searched the rest of the house. But they found nothing; only the broken and torn remains of what used to be a fine middle-class house.

"Holy Jesus Christ!" Sanders blurted out. "I've never seen anything like it."

Both men holstered their weapons. "He's supposed to have a girl friend. This is her house," Molosky said.

"He ain't gonna have her much longer after she sees this place."

"That's what I'm afraid of. Maybe he ransacked the place and kidnapped her."

Suddenly the doorbell rang. "I wonder who that could be?" Molosky asked.

"Let's find out." Sanders shuffled down the hallway to the living room. Molosky followed. "Yes, sir, may we help you?" Sanders asked politely.

The man was wearing a pair of dark overalls. He had a full beard and a serious look in his eyes. When he spoke, he directed his words to the man in uniform. "Sir, I live across the street and I was just curious. All this trash thrown around for the children to see. It's not good for them. Would it be all right if I cleaned it up and threw the trashy stuff away?"

Molosky thought for a moment. The magazines could be used as circumstantial evidence. "We'll take care of that, sir. I'll send for a unit and we'll clean what we can. Do you know the people who live here?"

"Not really. Just to say hello to once in a while. The lady owns the house. A lot of guys coming and going all the time. My wife says she's the one who did all this." He held his hand to the straps on the front of the overalls and nodded toward the front yard. "Guess she threw out his stuff and left before he found out about it."

"Is that what your wife says? The woman did this and left before the man arrived?"

"Yes, sir. She got out of here before he came. I saw him myself a little over an hour ago. Heard him yelling and screaming and carrying on. I almost called you fellas. I was glad when I saw your car. Well, I won't be a bother to you. I know you got important things to do. Good night, officer, and you too, sir." He nodded toward Sanders.

After several minutes of discussion, it was decided that Sanders and one of his teams would secure the house and call for a search warrant. Molosky had to get back to his district responsibilities. They would meet later in Harkness's office to talk over further strategy.

An ominous darkness had set in as Molosky left the Tampico address. With it, the heat that had burned all summer seemed to evaporate, bringing a sharp chill. Knowing that Sanders's one decoy team was operating on the district's west side, he decided to take up a roving position downtown, near the university. *Half of police work is diligence and the other half pure luck,* he thought, hoping the latter was riding with him. He picked up the microphone and placed himself in service.

"Ten-four," the operator said bluntly. "I've been trying to raise you. Lesley wanted you to come up on One. The east side is a mess. I think he needs your help."

Molosky acknowledged Control, punched the Channel One button, and called Lesley.

"Ray, where have you been? We're gonna need your help out here."

"Sanders and I found out who the rapist is. We've been trying to run him down. Sanders is trying to get a search warrant now. Might take awhile. I can give you the whole district if you need it. Why don't you leave Yarnell and me in service in case of emergencies?"

There was a long silence. "You guys positive on the rapist?"

"Check," Molosky answered. "We got him identified. Sanders is still at his house, on Tampico Court, west side."

There was another pause, this time shorter. "Good. Let's get this crowd handled first, then we can meet with the captain."

"Ten-four. Yarnell and I will handle things over here. You have a staging area?"

"Send them to King and Lido, behind the hamburger joint."

When Molosky came back to Channel Two, he ordered his men to leave the district and form at the designated area. He told Yarnell about Sheldon and had him patrol the western half of the district while he took the east. They were to take only red-lined in-progress calls.

Chapter Thirty-six

Sheldon could smell the alcohol as it oozed from his breath. He sat inside his car and angrily tapped his thigh with his fist to the beat of the music. There was only one prostitute left on the corner across the street. "I wonder where the other cunt is? Probably selling herself. Whore."

He pulled out into traffic, then steered off the main artery into the quiet neighborhoods. The streetlights formed odd-shaped shadows across the asphalt in his path. Wanting quiet to make plans, he turned the radio off and continued drifting toward the parking garage on Seventh Street. He would enjoy *this* one more than any of the others. Donna Catterton would be stalked and hunted down. By the time he sunk his cock into her, she would be a trembling hunk of meat, begging for him, wanting him.

He swung the car onto the driveway, paid a quarter at the machine, and drove in. He made his way up from the first level along the narrow lanes, keeping an eye out for the bright yellow Cadillac. Sheldon didn't find it on the first floor or the second. The third floor had fewer cars than the others. Suddenly, Sheldon spotted the expensive yellow sedan parked next to a thick concrete pillar. He drove past and positioned his car so that his front end was aimed right at the Cadillac's passenger door, twenty-five yards away. He shut the engine off and left the keys dangling in the ignition. He made a quick time check. Ten o'clock. She would be here any minute.

While he waited, Sheldon familiarized himself with the surroundings. At the opposite end of the building, diagonally to his right, was the exit ramp leading to San Salvador Street. There were no elevators. He adjusted his rearview mirror so he could see the platform from which Donna would step. The third floor was well-lighted, but it was also deserted except for a couple of cars at the far end.

He pulled the leather gloves tightly onto his hands. *You're a man,* he thought, *no matter what Charlotte says, and the time has come to prove it.* Holding his hands in front of him, he dwelled on them intensely and rolled his fingers into a fist, slowly, methodically. His eyes glowed, his cheeks flushed, his heart stirred, and a sense of power and well-being came over him as he felt the softness of the white hood. He slipped the sheepskin over his head carefully.

Letting the silence work on the fringe of his mind, he sat tensed, unmoving eyes glued to the rearview mirror.

Suddenly he spotted the silhouette of a woman in the center of the glass. He could tell it was Donna by her straightlaced walk and the shape of her hair. From the platform she started across the parking lot. Sheldon kept his glazed eyes fixed on his prey. She was wearing a green pantsuit, and he could hear her footsteps along the cement. Underneath the hood, Sheldon's breath came in short, even bursts.

As she disappeared from view, he knew that she would be walking past his car within seconds. He turned his head as she marched by the silver sedan. In the crook of one arm hung her purse, and she was carrying notepads and books in the other. Her footsteps echoed through the garage.

"Okay, cunt, it's your turn," he said in a gasping whisper. He started the car. Putting it in gear, he let it idle as he directed the front end at the woman.

Catterton twisted her head around without breaking stride. She glanced at the car as it started to move and then resumed her march.

Sheldon smiled hauntingly from inside the white hood. He steered in behind her and could see that her pace had picked up. But she did not turn around. The car came closer. Suddenly he began honking the horn in short, steady, deafening outbursts.

Catterton jumped and almost stumbled at the first nerve-shattering blast. She held her books tightly and shot a horrified look toward the driver of the car. The loud honking continued. Her eyes bulged open in disbelief at the sight of the white hood behind the wheel. She stumbled again, this time dropping one of her books. The car kept rolling toward her.

As Catterton reached the driver's side of the yellow Cadillac, Sheldon was wildly alive inside the hood. Letting the car roll slowly, he steered it directly at her passenger door. His front bumper smashed into the side of the new car. He stared at the surprised woman. Her mouth was wide open, her face etched in fright.

With incredible speed, he lurched from the car and bounded onto the trunk lid of the Cadillac. There he stood for several seconds, feet apart, rotating his hips, making muffled grunting sounds. Catterton stepped back several paces until she slammed up against the concrete pillar.

"Your clothes, cunt! I want them off and I want them off now!" He leaped onto the roof and started jumping up and down, giving out low, animal grunts. The thin sheet metal creaked and buckled into small dents under the weight of his hard boots.

Suddenly, the sound of voices came from the platform behind him. He jerked around. It was a group of three young males, talking and laughing, walking toward the far side of the lot. They glanced his way. Quickly he jumped from the roof and started his car. Before getting behind the wheel, he shot Catterton a piercing look. She was moving to her car, fumbling for the key.

Suddenly, the Cadillac was moving. It lurched from its position and was heading for the exit ramp. Sheldon was rattled—torn between chasing Catterton and being turned in by the students. Get the cunt, that was his mission. Instantly he shifted it into drive and stomped on the accelerator. The silver sedan skidded across the cement, its rear end fishtailing.

But it was too late. By the time he had descended to the bottom of the ramp, the yellow Cadillac was gone.

Molosky swung the police cruiser onto the third floor of the parking garage. He was on an in-progress, assigned call. A group of college kids thought they had witnessed a hit-and-run accident. A silver sedan was seen backing away from the smashed door of a large, yellow American car. The driver of the yellow car had sped away as if she were running from the scene. The silver car was last seen speeding after her.

As he rolled across the cement pavement, Molosky noticed a book lying in the middle of the floor. He eased to a stop, opened the door, and leaned out to pick it up. It was a real estate textbook. His mind went back to the restaurant where he had been earlier. There was a woman studying, and she had had a real estate book at her side. He opened the book and found the name, address, and phone number of Donna Catterton printed neatly on the inside of the cover. The name meant nothing to him, so he browsed through the rest of the book. A short distance into it, he found a bookmark. It was a real estate business card. She worked for Platinum Realty.

Quickly, Molosky picked up the microphone and started to call the operator when he was cut short by her blaring voice. "Units on Channel Two, hold your traffic. Sixty-five hundred, be advised. We just had a call from the information desk. They report that a female came running into the police building, stating that she was being terrorized by a man wearing a white hood and driving a silver sedan at your location. She says that the incident started after she got out of class, in the parking garage."

Molosky closed the book and threw it to the passenger seat. It was Sheldon, all right. He was on a rampage. A slight tremor of fear rippled through his blood. He had faced the hooded man before and had been beaten almost senseless. He wondered if he could summon enough courage to confront him again.

"Ten-four, control." Molosky stated. "It's the same case. Bert, you there?"

"I copied that, Ray. You want me to start drifting your way?"

"Hold your position for now. He could just as easily have jumped onto the freeway and be in your part of town by now. No telling where he'll land. Just stay alert."

Yarnell acknowledged him, and Molosky came back to the Channel Two operator. "Control, make sure that the decoy team still working is advised of the situation."

Molosky eased down the long ramp and turned left. He began a slow patrol of the outskirts of the campus, up and down the side streets, his eyes alert to movement on the sidewalks and in the parking lots. Five minutes went by before he passed the restaurant where Ashwood hung out. If the old man had only spoken up weeks ago, this whole thing could have been over by now, and he and Colleen would be on a much-needed vacation. The radio remained silent except for the single time check at ten thirty.

Molosky rolled onto Santa Clara Street and eyed two prostitutes stepping off the curb. They were flagging down a pickup truck full of young men wearing cowboy hats. When they spotted the police car, they gingerly waved and climbed back to the curb.

"Sixty-five hundred," called the operator.

Molosky picked up the microphone and brought it to his mouth. "Go ahead, Control."

"Just received another strange call which could be related to the others. Woman at 209 North Seventeenth says she was followed home by a silver gray car. No I.D. on the driver, but she has that feeling that whoever it was is still in the area. Contact the victim."

"Ten-four. You copy that, Bert?"

"I got it. I'll be en route to back you up, but be advised I'm out of position by about seven miles. I'll jump on the highway."

Molosky acknowledged him and pressed on the accelerator.

Sheldon was sweating profusely inside the sheepskin hood. He let the engine idle for a few seconds in front of the woman's house. Switching off the headlights, he rolled away and drove around the block. He found a place to park on Sixteenth Street just north of St. James. Quickly, he stepped from the car and silently closed the door, then trotted across the street, down a cement driveway, and vaulted a wooden fence into a small backyard.

He stood for a second and let his eyes get accustomed to the darkness. They pierced the night, searching, craving. When he spotted what he was looking for, he moved quickly toward the house. With several violent jerks, he tore the telephone cable from the wall.

Molosky swung onto Seventeenth. "Control, Sixty-five hundred. Give the victim a call. Tell her to stay inside and that I'll be there in a minute. I'm going to check the backyard first, then I'll contact her."

"Ten-four," came the reply.

Molosky pushed the switch on the control panel and the car's headlights flicked off. He turned off the engine and coasted to the front of the house next to the victim's. Stepping onto the sidewalk with flashlight in hand, he quietly notched the door shut and stood alongside the car for a minute to let his eyes focus in the dark. The cool night air brushed up against his warm skin, sending small chills across his shoulder blades. He approached the woman's house and took up a position behind some tall green shrubs at the foot of her driveway. He listened intently for unusual noises. All seemed quiet.

* * *

Yarnell swung the car off Highway 17 and pushed south on Highway 101, heading for the Thirteenth Street exit.

Sheldon felt secure under the hood. He knew that the victim was trapped and would soon be his. Moving in hushed silence to the back window, he peered into the small house and stared at his prey as she paced back and forth between rooms. The battle would soon be won.

Molosky made his way with caution down the driveway. He hoisted his revolver out as he came to a wooden gate which blocked his entrance to the backyard. Using his left hand, which held the flashlight, he reached over and tripped the latch. With a loud click, the latch hammer opened and fell again. Slowly, he pushed through the gate and eased toward the backyard.

Sheldon heard the sound of the latch. What was it? Who could it be? A neighbor? A friend? He stood alongside the house tensed, waiting, ready.

Yarnell came off the freeway at Thirteenth Street.

Molosky edged into the backyard and switched on his flashlight. His eyes followed the stream of light as it moved back and forth through the rose bushes and over the top of a metal garbage can. As he reached the corner of the house, he angled the light across the yard, then close to the back of the wall.

His body froze in surprised horror. The arm which held his revolver was gripped by a sudden, paralyzing seizure. His eyes shot wide open, his mind screamed for his body to move, but the seizure would not relent.

Sheldon stood motionless, poised, his eyes riveted to Molosky's, then to the long-barreled revolver. An awesome feeling of superiority came over him. With the hood on he was a mighty animal of the jungle. With a violent, thrusting motion, he stepped toward the policeman and threw his fist into Molosky's face.

Molosky stood rooted, entranced. He saw the blow coming at him as if in slow motion, but his body would not move.

Sheldon's fist bashed into Molosky's left eye, snapping his rigid arm and jolting the gun from his hand.

Molosky's stiff body shook, then toppled as if it were a statue. A sharp blast of pain spread from the base of his skull down through his chest and then to the pit of his stomach. The memories of their first encounter flashed through his mind. *Please don't hurt me,* he silently pleaded, and his body thumped to the dirt.

Then, as suddenly as it had overwhelmed him, the seizure released him. His survival instincts took over. He knew the pointed boot would be next. Rolling on the ground toward the garbage can, he scrambled for cover. When the boot came at him, he pushed the can to the front and deflected the blow. Releasing the heavy can, he quickly struggled to his feet and immediately ducked the next blow. He heard a rush of air as the hooded man's fist whisked past his left ear.

From his crouched position Molosky swung his right arm in a circular motion toward the white mask. His fist landed ineffectively on the soft sheepskin, just below the slit for Sheldon's left eye. He swung again, this time using a straight left jab. In the darkness, Molosky could see the white hood duck his blow, and weave to the right.

From out of nowhere, Sheldon's fist found Molosky's left eye again. Blood spurted from under the eye and trickled down Molosky's cheek, but the policeman stood his ground. Crouching again like a football player, Molosky charged in an attempt to knock The Hood off balance. His shoulder struck Sheldon in the stomach and doubled him over. Molosky's strong legs churned and hammered into the ground until he was able to lift Sheldon off his feet. Off balance, he carried him back toward the house and slammed him against the side, crushing a round drainpipe. Hot air blasted from inside the white hood as Sheldon groaned and slipped down the wall.

Molosky released his grip and stepped back. With his right arm he hurled another blow at the sheepskin. He connected, sending Sheldon's head crashing into the wall with a sharp, muffled sound. He swung again, this time harder.

But the white hood ducked and moved to the left. From the corner of his eye, Molosky could see the point of Sheldon's boot lash out at him. He had no time to avoid the blow. The boot caught him just below the left knee and sent a jolt of pain racing up his leg to his groin.

While he was off guard, he heard another rush of air coming toward his face. It was a solid hit just below the eye, tearing the skin. More blood spurted onto his cheek and flowed freely. He tried to back off and regain his balance, but another blow slammed at him. Blood gushed from his nose. His mind began to reel. The courage he had summoned was fast eluding him.

He knew the next jolt would put him out. He had to do something. But his body would not do what he ordered. He struggled to keep his balance. He took another blast to the jaw. He staggered back, unable to keep on his feet, and collapsed onto the cold, moist lawn.

Yarnell turned left, off Thirteenth Street onto St. James.

Sheldon breathed in rapid bursts, his eyes burning with wild violence. He raised his boot and kicked as hard as he could. The point dug into Molosky's right thigh.

Molosky's muscle knotted painfully. He jerked to the side and groaned loudly.

Sheldon smiled savagely, his teeth locked together, his lips spread thinly. He took careful aim and swung again, this time connecting with Molosky's right temple. He was going to kick again when he saw the woman standing at the back window, her face alive and terrified. She was about to scream. Quickly, he darted back two steps, keeping his eye on her. Then he turned and raced for the back fence, leaped, and disappeared.

Yarnell slowed the cruiser at Fifteenth Street. He shut off the lights and guided the car quietly over the asphalt. As he passed Sixteenth, he glanced to the north and caught a flash of a man running. Instinctively he sensed the danger. Something had happened to Molosky. As the man came to a halt near a parked car, Yarnell spotted the white hood he was wearing.

Without hesitation he stopped the police car in the middle of the street, ten feet past the intersection. He grabbed the shotgun, stepped into the street, pumped in a round, and pushed the safety button off. Standing at the rear of the police car, he took aim. The man had ducked into the parked car, and it was just starting to roll to the corner when Yarnell sighted in on the driver's door. When he fired, the shotgun jerked sharply against his shoulder. The muzzle flashed and nine pellets dotted the side of the silver car.

Yarnell racked in another round and fired. The side windows shattered, but the car kept moving. The next round blew out the back window. The fourth blast got the rear tire. The rubber exploded, then wobbled around the rim and slapped against the pavement.

The car went out of control. Its rear end swung around and collided with the front end of a parked jeep. Yarnell ran into the intersection, fumbling for another round in his gun belt to reload. The car rolled to a stop, its engine still running, its one headlight pointed into his eyes. Bert fought to get another round secured. The car began to move, picking up speed as it came directly at him. Yarnell managed to cram in only one more pellet casing; he shouldered the shotgun, took aim, and fired. The pellets shattered the front windshield, but the car did not stop its forward momentum. Bert scrambled to the side.

Sheldon had ducked and covered his eyes. Broken glass showered around him. His foot froze on the accelerator.

The car sped forward and smashed into the back of the police cruiser.

Yarnell moved to take control.

The driver's door opened and The Hood reared his frightening head. Yarnell went for his revolver. Before his hand got to the handle of the gun, Sheldon attacked.

He swung his fist ferociously at Yarnell's face, connecting with his jaw. Blood spurted from Bert's mouth. For the first time he, too, had felt the strength of the hooded rapist. He stood his ground. Sheldon swung again.

Bert blocked the blow with his left arm and threw his right fist at the sheepskin hood.

The punch slammed into the hood and broke Sheldon's nose. Streams of blood ran over his lip and gushed into his mouth. He gagged, shook his head, and spat out the oozing liquid. Red globs started to form on the outside of the sheepskin.

Yarnell swung again. The blow caught Sheldon above the right eye, stunning him and nearly knocking him out.

Sheldon grabbed his eye, staggered, and moved back. For the first time he felt himself losing control. He began to panic. In a last frantic gesture, he swung his boot. The point shot forward and connected with Bert's groin.

Bert gasped and doubled over in pain.

Sheldon quickly moved to disarm him, but Bert grabbed the gun and held it in the holster with his strong right hand.

Sheldon went into a rage. He mercilessly kicked and beat on Bert with a wild flurry of blows and kicks. Yarnell doubled over, struggling to keep his balance.

Sheldon hastily drew back, then with a high kick he flashed his pointed boot toward Yarnell's face.

Bert tried to weave out of the way, but his movement was too slow. The point of the boot caught him squarely on the jaw. The force of the blow punctured the skin and shattered five of his teeth. He grabbed his face, trying to quell the pain. The next blow was another kick, this time to the side of his head. He toppled to the pavement with a thud and rolled over, covering his face with both hands, hoping the pain would go away.

Sheldon stomped him in the ribs.

Bert cried out in agony.

Sheldon stepped back, poised for more action.

But Bert could only roll over and sprawl face down, moaning incomprehensibly to himself. He lay on the cold pavement several seconds before trying to move.

As Bert lifted his arm to hoist himself up, Sheldon swung his boot again. The blow glanced off the back of Bert's head. Sheldon swung so hard that after the smash to the policeman's head, he wobbled off balance. He stumbled sideways, knocking his bloodied hood askew.

Bert's body shook uncontrollably for several seconds, then he passed out limply.

Blindly, Sheldon found his way back to the near-dead policeman. Feeling Bert's body, he aimed his boot one more time. The point sunk deeply into the belly of the downed man. A heavy expulsion of air was accompanied by a low, ebbing groan. Sheldon bent down and groped for Bert's service revolver with one hand while he tried to straighten his hood with the other.

"Freeze!"

Molosky stood just outside the lighted area and wiped the blood from his face. His voice was strong and determined and seemed to ring out through the suddenly stilled night air.

Sheldon yanked the gun from Yarnell's holster and stepped back, still trying to adjust the hood.

"One move and I'll blow your head off." Molosky stayed out of sight. He held his revolver in one hand while he rubbed the knot in his leg muscle with the other. He crouched and moved to his right.

Sheldon turned toward the voice, the gun by his side. He saw only blackness from the inside of the hood.

Molosky moved again. The heels of his combat boots made a soft, thumping noise as he maneuvered to a position across the street. He ducked behind a parked car and wiped his face again. He could see the profile of the hooded man less than twenty yards away. He raised his revolver, held it steady, and aimed at the sheepskin hood.

Sheldon's feet remained motionless. His body swayed as if in slow motion. He heard the tapping of the policeman's boots a short distance away. He imagined the policeman taking cover behind some bush, and listened for the sound of rustling leaves. But there was only the wet half-gurgling sound of his own breath blowing inside the twisted hood. He reached to square his mask.

"Don't move!" Molosky commanded. "Don't turn. Freeze where you are!"

Sheldon's body went rigid. His head jerked toward the unseen voice. It was Molosky, interrupting his plans again.

Molosky was crouched low behind the parked car. The pain in his right thigh was almost unbearable. The muscle pulled into a large, painful knot again. He winced and struggled to keep his composure. Letting his weaker left hand hold onto the heavy revolver, he extended his leg to the side, then clamped his hand into a tight fist and extended his arm. With a quick motion, he swooped down and pounded his fist on top of the cramped muscle. The muscle at once started to unwind, but the pain became more intense. Molosky let out a muffled, agonized grunt. He raised his arm again for a second blow. The revolver seemed to flounder in his left hand. His eyes darted back toward the hooded man.

Sheldon stood methodically, listening. Waiting. He had to get the hood off in order to breathe and to see his opponent, but he mustn't panic. Suddenly, he heard Molosky's painful grunt. Sheldon felt he had a split second to take advantage. Quickly, he reached for the top of the hood, ripped it from his face, and threw it to the ground. With his forearm he wiped away the sweat and blood from his eyes, while at the same time he drew in a long breath, turned, and raised the revolver.

Molosky froze for an instant when he saw who it was. He had known for hours that it was Sheldon, but somehow seeing his distorted face in the flesh twisted the nightmare into reality. The smiling real estate man, whose charm and graceful manner seemed so out of place with the reality of the man's inner soul.

Sheldon saw Molosky's blurry expression. He smiled savagely. "That's right, Molosky. Me!" He elevated the magnum revolver with his strong right arm, leveled the sights on Molosky's forehead, and slowly began to squeeze off a round.

A hazy confusion seemed to grip Molosky's body as he watched the revolver being lifted and pointed toward his head. Just when he thought he had control, the situation had reversed itself. He had to move. He had to do something. He watched Sheldon's hand as it slowly pulled the trigger.

Molosky came to his senses not a tenth of a second before the explosion. He ducked his head behind the fender.

The roar of the gun blasted in his direction. The bullet silently whipped through the air, and with only a slight tinny sound ripped a small hole through the top of the fender two inches from his head.

A powerful fear of death came over Molosky. He began to tremble. He was pinned down. If he lifted his head, he would surely die. He must gather himself together.

There came a second blast from Sheldon's gun. This time the bullet whistled just over his head and tucked neatly into the side of a house with only a whisper of a thud.

"Come out, Molosky. It won't hurt. You only die once."

Molosky heard the voice but could not discern the words. His mind raced. He jerked his head back and forth trying to find a way out, but all he could see was a blur of shrubs and grass and cement sidewalk.

All of a sudden and for no apparent reason he started to run. His feet were racing toward a skinny telephone pole fifty feet away.

Sheldon fired again. The muzzle flashed brightly into the darkness.

Molosky immediately hit the ground and slid headlong behind the pole. He held the revolver in his right hand. Sheldon had fired three times.

He could hear another magnum blast from Sheldon's gun. The bullet splintered the soft wood six inches above his head. He looked up and could see Sheldon getting ready for another shot.

Quickly, Molosky came to a kneeling position, used the telephone pole to steady his aim, cocked the revolver, and squeezed off. His shot cracked through the darkness.

Sheldon suddenly darted from the lighted area and began to run, taking refuge in the shadows across the street.

He can't get away this time, Molosky thought. *I won't let him.* Molosky jumped to his feet and raced along the sidewalk on the side of the street opposite to where Sheldon was running. From the radio in Yarnell's car he could hear Sanders's voice stating that he would be responding to the area of Seventeenth and St. James. Molosky headed south on Seventeenth taking long, purposeful steps, letting his lungs push and pull the air freely. As he ran he listened intently for the rapid pounding of boots coming from the other side of the street.

When Molosky heard the boots slow their pace, he took cover behind whatever was at hand, this time a tree, next time a large van. As the boots resumed their choppy sound, Molosky would pick up the tempo. Every once in a while he caught a flicker of Sheldon's silhouette tromping toward Santa Clara Street.

At the intersection of St. John Street, Molosky took up a prone position behind some thorny bushes. He could hear Sheldon's footsteps. Suddenly, they stopped just short of the lighted area. There was a long, silent pause. Molosky strained to see through the blackness, but it was useless; the distance was too great and the shadows too concealing. Just as suddenly as the footsteps had halted, they began again. Swiftly they raced, pounding the cement, then out onto the asphalt and into the light.

As Sheldon darted across the street, Molosky took careful aim and pulled back on the trigger. The bullet exploded from the chamber and the muzzle flashed. But the round had missed its target. Sheldon was still on his feet and running.

Before Molosky could get off another shot, Sheldon had come to an abrupt halt, turned, crouched to a kneel, and fired a quick burst in Molosky's direction. The bullet crackled over the top of the policeman's head, expending itself in a door frame directly behind him. *That was number five,* Molosky noted.

Sheldon took his eye from the shadows where Molosky lay and briefly stared toward Santa Clara Street. Suddenly, he stood and dashed into the shadows, running straight for the lighted area at the end of the block.

Molosky scrambled to his feet and raced across the street into the darkness. He could see Sheldon's head moving up and down as he ran for the end of the block. Molosky pushed his legs faster. Suddenly, he spotted the donut shop sign at the end of the block. *Ashwood's,* he thought. *That's where he's heading.*

He was still twenty-five yards behind Sheldon as he entered the lighted area and started up the driveway toward the back stairway. Sheldon ducked around the end of the building, and Molosky could hear his feet as they pounded on the wooden steps.

"M-A-R-V-I-N, H-E-L-P M-E!" Sheldon yelled at the top of his lungs.

Molosky's legs churned down the driveway, his revolver in his right hand. When he got to the end of the building, he immediately whipped around the corner and came to a combat stance. His eyes focused on the rapist. Sheldon had halted his forward movement and was standing on the stairs, halfway to Ashwood's door.

Sheldon yelled for the old man again. It was a deep, pleading yell that seemed to echo strangely in the darkness.

"It's over, Sheldon, give it up!" Molosky stood confidently, revolver aimed at the back of Sheldon's head, index finger tightly wrapped around the trigger.

Sheldon's shoulders sagged. He held Yarnell's gun down by his side. Slowly, he turned and directed a pathetic look at Molosky.

At the top of the stairs, just under the forty-watt bulb,

the door creaked open and Ashwood stepped onto the platform. He had his bathrobe wrapped around him clumsily. He appeared surprised. His head jerked back and his eyes moved uneasily from Sheldon down to Molosky.

Sheldon turned quickly to him. "Marvin, I need your help. They want to put me away for something that I couldn't control! Help me... please!"

Ashwood stood with a sober expression. He kept his gaze on Sheldon for a long moment, then turned toward the door. "You must go with them," he said, his voice clear, determined. "I can no longer help you. I'm sorry." He stepped back into his apartment and closed the door.

Sheldon remained motionless for a long time, his head tilted up, eyes open in astonishment. "F-U-C-K!" he roared, and began jumping up and down and pounding the side of the building.

"Freeze!" Molosky commanded.

But Sheldon could not stop his frantic movements. While yelling and screaming, he suddenly turned toward Molosky and whirled the revolver in a quick, fighting motion.

As he did, Molosky steadied his revolver on Sheldon's head and squeezed off. The gun snapped back in his hand. He held his position.

Sheldon had no time to react. He was halfway through the pull of the trigger when the bullet struck. His head exploded from the inside. The gun jerked back and fired into the air at a forty-five degree angle. He staggered to the next step, trying to keep his balance. His arms dropped to his sides. The gun dangled in his hand for a moment, then fell abruptly onto the step below.

He stood for a long time, staring toward Molosky. His face showed an expression of pained wonderment. His eyes remained fastened on Molosky's. They were wide, violent eyes, beautiful in a haunting way—bulging, unrelenting dark stones.

Suddenly, his posture began to sag. His face dropped to his chest, then his whole body collapsed and tumbled

›wn the stairs. When he hit the cement slab at the bottom
' the stairway, a faint thud was heard. His head twisted
wkwardly against the hard surface, and he died, his eyes
ide open, staring into the black night.